# MAINTENANCE IS MURDER

## A DAMAGED GOODS MYSTERY

JENNIFER L. HART

ELEMENTS UNLEASHED MEDIA

# MAINTENANCE IS MURDER

## A DAMAGED GOODS MYSTERY

Maintenance is Murder
A Damaged Goods Mystery
Hart, Jennifer L./ Maintenance is Murder

1.Mystery—Fiction. 2. Women Sleuths—Fiction 3.Property
Management—Fiction 4. Miami—Fiction 5.Contemporary
Romance—Fiction 6.BBW—Fiction 7.Alpha Male—Fiction
8.Eviction Specialists—Fiction 9. Murder Mystery—Fiction
10. Mystery Romance—Fiction Title.

Miami's hottest property management team is back in action
in an all-new mystery!

Certified Process Server Jackie Parker's life is finally on the
right track. Her cozy little bungalow is finished, her business
is booming, and her relationship with the Dark Prince is
better than she ever could have imagined. So what if she's
still living with her ex and her mother who wants them to
buy matching tiny homes? Who cares if Logan is sharing his
house with a woman on the run from her abusive husband?

No big deal if an onsite manager is stealing rent or tenants are turning tricks on her client's property. It's nothing Jackie and the guys haven't dealt with before.

Until Logan is arrested for murder.

Jackie's all set to do what she does best and find the real killer. But Logan insists she should stay out of the mix and let the professionals handle it. Sure, Logan wouldn't be the Dark Prince if he didn't have some shady dealings. But Jackie knows Logan. He's a tough guy who will do anything to protect the people he loves. He isn't truly capable of cold-blooded murder.

Is he?

# FOREWORD

A note to my fabulous readers:

So much has changed since I wrote *Final Notice.* I'm a different person than I was in 2014. The world is different. We're all older, wiser and less tolerant of bullshit. (I like to get the cussing out of the way right upfront so that you know what's coming.) Social distance has chased social media into our lives and forced us all to slow down, take a look around and readjust our course.

I started this book well in advance of the Coronavirus pandemic and finished it while my husband was locked in at the Charter data center to keep the internet running here on the East Coast. It's hard not to feel frivolous when I am sitting here playing with my imaginary friends while other people are sick or risking their lives or worrying about their finances or just in shock because the world that looked so bright on January 1, 2020, feels like it is wreathed in shadows and coated in fear.

The fact that I can't fix this, can't plan around it or bully my way through, is upsetting. But I found an escape hatch. I can roll out Jackie, Luke and Logan and watch them struggle and fight and overcome. I can set them up to fail and watch them grow from it. And there is the magic of what it is I do. Because I can offer you the hatch too, and help you escape all the stress and worry, if only for a little while. And if I've done my job right, at the end you'll feel a little bit better for it if you #stayhomeandread.

Love and light,
Jennifer L. Hart

*Dedicated to:*
*All the folks who eat cold pizza while standing over the sink.*
*Because anything else is too much work.*
*You are my tribe.*

# MAINTENANCE IS MURDER

E very Wednesday was the same—get up, take care of
my immediate needs and give the bathroom scale
the finger.

Every Wednesday except for this one.

At first, the *tap tap tap* sounded like nothing more than a
tree branch dragging intimately along a windowpane. One
problem—there were no trees outside my bedroom window.

My eyes popped open and I listened, wondering if it
would come again.

*Tap tap tap.* Then a dull thump.

No, there weren't any trees outside of my craftsmen
bungalow, but there were plenty of thick bushes. Perfect
concealment for a would-be evildoer. And while Coral Gate
was one of the safest neighborhoods in Miami, that didn't
mean we didn't have our share of crime.

My heart pounded and I looked over to my sleeping
companion. "Hey, wake up, you useless pain in the butt."

Nothing.

Why hadn't I brought Sasquatch into the bedroom?
Nothing like a ninety-pound dog of undetermined breed to

scare off an intruder. She was scarier than my bunk buddy anyway.

But Sasquatch was out in the living room, curled up on the new shag rug.

"Hey," I nudged the form on the pillow again, but he rolled over with a snore. Little beast slept like he'd done something more exhausting than stuff his gob and watch television all day.

I could call out. My ex-husband, Luke Parker, was camped out on the living room sofa. He'd run in, probably with the dog hot on his heels. And my mother, Celeste Drummond, was right down the hall.

But what if it was only my overactive imagination? I'd been having panic attacks lately and both Luke and Celeste had witnessed me coming unhinged over the last six weeks. Luke would understand. He was the most understanding guy on the face of the planet, part of the reason we could still work and live together.

But I had my pride, damn it. I was used to taking care of myself.

"Think, Jackie," I said out loud. Just because I'd had people try to kill me before, didn't mean there really was a prowler in my shrubs.

My shoulder bag was on the floor between the bed and the window. In it I had a nonlethal arsenal—Taser, pepper spray, stun gun as well as a mini Maglite. My cellphone was charging on my nightstand. So, I'd dial 91 and then shine the light in the bushes. If there was a prowler, I'd dial the other 1, spritz the creep and scream my head off.

As plans went, it was decidedly half-assed, but what more could I expect from my pre-coffee brain?

*TAP TAP TAP.* That was the horror movie soundtrack if I'd ever heard it.

I slunk out of bed, trying not to make noise as my feet hit

the new bamboo flooring Luke had finished installing last week. My foot got tangled up in the strap of my shoulder bag and I stumbled, banging my shin on the nightstand. The phone charger was new and didn't want to release its intimate hold on my smartphone. I struggled and cussed until finally, I was armed and ready.

In the bed, my companion didn't so much as twitch. Jerk.

I put the flashlight in my mouth and punched in the first two digits. I shook the pepper spray to make sure it was active and then crept in my baby doll nighty over to the window.

One problem, no free hand to flick the light switch to the on position.

Was I a crime-fighting mastermind or what?

I studied the phone and then the pepper spray. Something was going to have to get put down. After a minute's indecision, I settled on the phone and laid it gently on the freshly stained windowsill. The device was too wide and overbalanced, clattering to the floor.

If there was a prowler out there and he had night-vision goggles he was probably dying of laughter at my antics.

Pissed off that I'd been so rudely awakened and had cracked yet *another* smartphone screen, I took the mini flashlight out of my mouth and flipped the switch.

Eyes stared back at me. Human eyes.

I gave a yell, and stepped back, only to tangle my foot again in the strap of my shoulder bag. I dropped the canister of pepper spray to catch myself before I went down. My backside hit the bamboo, proving that it was indeed harder than hardwood—the floor, not my ass. The commotion woke the beast in the bed who let out a startled chirp then scrambled to the windowsill where the fiend's eyes were now lit with amusement as well as with his flashlight.

"Asshole," I seethed at the Dark Prince through the glass. "You are such an asshole, Logan Parker."

The skin around those baby blue eyes crinkled with amusement.

"And you," I cast a withering glare at my spider monkey who was hopping up and down on top of the headboard. "Way to have my back, Abu."

Logan, grin still in place, tapped against the glass again and mouthed a few words.

Bruised and embarrassed, I crawled over to the window, unlocked it and slid the double-hung sucker up. "We have this newfangled thing called a door. About ten feet thatt-away. Try it next time."

"Didn't want to wake the household." Logan popped the screen out from the sill and then used his upper body strength to pull himself through the window and in beside me.

"Just me," I grumped.

"Just you." He grinned and then leaned forward to press his lips to mine and the heat from the scorching contact melted my ire.

"You're lucky you didn't get a snoot full of pepper spray." I paused and then emphasized the last word. "Again."

Logan had a particularly nasty reaction to pepper spray, a fact I had learned the last time I had accidentally dosed him. His fault getting between me and the maniac who'd gone for my throat.

"The window was still shut. Didn't you get my text?"

"What text?" I shook my head, a little dazed. Kissing the Dark Prince should come with a side effects warning label. *Caution. May cause dizziness and loss of panties.*

"That explains why you're not dressed." His look seared me as though the thin cotton nightdress had gone up in a puff of smoke.

My teeth sank into my lower lip. Even though Logan and I were together now, we hadn't gotten physical. Well, not very physical. While we'd had plenty of heated make-out sessions, his recovery from a gunshot wound through the thigh and my insecurity about dating one Parker brother while living with the other and working with both of them had kept my libido in check.

Barely.

"It's five in the morning. Why would I be dressed? Tell me it's not the Sunnyvale complex."

Logan, Luke and I ran a property management team. Property owners hired us to help deal with unruly tenants and when necessary, streamline the eviction process. We were partway through an apartment complex's yearly inspection and it had been dragging like a government job.

Logan plucked my phone up off the floor and handed it to me. "It's not the Sunnyvale complex."

I checked my messages and sure enough, Logan had sent me one the night before, sometime after I had collapsed from sheer exhaustion. I read it out loud. "Gonna take you out for a breakfast burrito."

"See," he said as if that vague text excused scaring the everlovin' crap out of me.

"Why couldn't you have just told me last night?" I'd seen him less than six hours ago, as I'd dragged my exhausted carcass from the Big Black Truck.

"Separate work and home life, right?" His grin turned wicked. "You made the rules, hot stuff."

I had, back when I'd still been married to Luke. At the time it had seemed like the best way to keep our personal drama from contaminating our professional lives but both the Parker brothers were way too literal.

Feeling like an idiot, I pushed myself up off the floor.

"Logan, there's early and then there's plumber's ass crack of dawn. Three guesses which one this is."

Leather creaked as the Dark Prince rose to his full height of six foot three. "I thought we'd catch the sunrise."

Though the tone was nonchalant, I heard the note of wariness that had crept in. Damn it, he'd been trying to do something thoughtful. And in classic Jackie style, I'd had a spaz attack and ruined it.

Logan and I were in love but our relationship was far from perfect. There had been a lot of rough years where we barely spoke, rougher months when it seemed like all we did was fight. I'd vowed that if we ever got the chance to be together, I wouldn't squander it. Easier said than done. At times it felt like the two of us were waltzing on a field of glass shards and one wrong step would see us skewered.

My teeth sank into my lower lip. Time to pull out the big guns—raw honesty. I stepped closer to him until my almost naked body pressed into his. "It sounds wonderful. I'd love to watch the sunrise with you."

His hands cupped my backside and pulled me flush against him. When he spoke his voice was ragged. "On second thought, maybe we could stay here…."

As one, we turned to face the unmade bed.

My heart rate picked up to a pace even more frantic than when I'd believed he was a burglar. One more searing kiss and the sun would be rising without us. Because what Logan Parker really wanted for breakfast was me.

And it scared me to death.

I stepped out of his hold and made my way to the bathroom. "Let me just get changed and we can go."

"Jackie?"

"Yeah?" I paused and shut my eyes, sending up a silent prayer. *Please don't ask me what's wrong.* I refused to lie to Logan but I didn't want to tell him either. We were doing okay with things the way they were, at least for now. Life was too complicated and I didn't want to rush past the courtship phase.

But all he said was, "Wear jeans. We're taking the bike."

---

"THE BIKE," was Logan's brand spanking new 2020 Indian Roadmaster. I shivered as he offered me the passenger's helmet. "I've never been on a motorcycle before."

"All you gotta do is hold on to me." he turned to look at me but with the visor down I couldn't see his eyes. "Think you can manage that?"

I eyed the cozy bungalow where my warm bed and lazy monkey awaited, then the motorcycle. I wanted to be with Logan and riding was a big part of his life. I knew that if I refused, he wouldn't force my hand, but he'd already made so many compromises for me. This didn't seem like a very big ask.

"I'm going to have helmet hair," I grumbled and took the stupid thing.

Logan helped me secure it, then slung one of his long, lean legs over the bike. He fussed with the kickstand and then it was held up only by two wheels with his feet balanced on the ground.

I took a tentative step and he pointed. "Put your foot there and then sling your leg over."

"Easy for you to say." He had me by almost a foot and the difference was all leg.

"Come on, Jackie. You know you want to." The Dark Prince beckoned and as always, I was helpless to resist. To sweeten his sinful deal, he started the bike and then did a couple of twists with his hands so the engine growled in a rising and falling *brrraaattt brrraaattt brrrraaattt.* His hand reached out for me again.

I'd already promised him my soul. What was a little bodily peril?

He pulled, I maneuvered until finally, I was seated behind him. The passenger's seat was situated a little higher so I could see the road above his helmet.

"Ready?" Logan shouted so I could hear him through the barrier of two helmets and the engine.

I put my hands on his shoulders as confirmation and then let out a squeak as he moved away from the curb. To his credit, he didn't take off at the full speed I'd seen him use as he peeled away from the curb when he was riding alone. Still, I couldn't help but clutch him tighter as we moved through the streets.

I won't lie. I'd envisioned riding with the Dark Prince before. A few dopey fantasies in which I plastered myself against his back as we sped down the highway and off into the Florida sunset. But the daydreams focused on the nearness of Logan, not the logistics of riding.

The first few miles leaving our neighborhood were traditional stop-start. A turn here, pause at the crosswalk for the lady struggling with two badly behaved dogs. Even so early in the morning, there were some cars out, people just living their lives at the ass crack of dawn.

Then we merged onto the highway.

My hands slid down to grasp his sides and I tightened my hold on his body as the speed increased right along with my pulse. It wasn't fear I was feeling though. Exhilaration coursed through me.

The sun was just coming up when we reached the MacArthur causeway. My breath caught as golden light cast the Miami beach high rises in silhouette. Palms flanked the empty highway on either side. Puffy white clouds looked ever so snackable, painted in pastel hues of pink and yellow. Cabin cruisers bobbed in the still water. The wind tugged at my clothes as we raced along. I'd driven this road more times than I could count. Comparing the ride on the back of Logan's bike to crossing the same stretch of highway in the Big Black Truck was the difference between watching something on a rabbit-eared television in black and white and experiencing it for myself. It was postcard Miami in high definition.

I squeezed Logan tighter, this time in gratitude. A smile split my face. This was living.

He took the beach turnoff and then backed the bike into a one-hour parking place. I removed my helmet and scrambled down, graceless and jelly legged and happier than I'd been in recent memory.

Logan killed the engine and flipped up his visor. "How was that?"

I whirled in place and laughed out loud, still high from the rush. "Amazing. Like flying."

"And to think, you almost missed it." He took his helmet off and then unzipped his jacket before coming to help me with mine. "Come on, let's go for a walk."

I was tempted to pepper him with questions about the bike, the ride and whatever else came to mind when I noticed he was favoring one leg. The one where he'd been shot. "Are you okay?"

He leaned down to rub the area and winced. "Just a little stiff. Riding isn't the best way to rehab a GSW to the quad."

"Then why are we here?" I swore on all the breakfast burritos in Miami that if Logan Parker had set his recovery back just to show off his new motorcycle, I would geld him with a nail file.

He looked at me then, blue eyes the color of the lightening sky. "Jackie, I've dreamed of taking you on that ride a thousand times. It's my favorite part about living in Miami. I wanted to share it with you."

And there went my heart.

Still, he was hurting. "We can take an uber back if it's too bad."

Logan shook his head. "I just need to walk a bit. Come on."

Miami Beach was infamous for its nightlife. So early in the morning, the long stretch of sand was vacant. A few joggers passed by and a guy with a metal detector futzed about, probably hunting for tourist dropsies. I removed my sneakers, stuffed my socks inside them and rolled up my jeans to midcalf. With the helmet under my arm and shoes in hand, I felt overdressed but happy. Ocean ready, I moved to the shoreline then paused and reached out a hand for the Dark Prince.

He didn't hesitate to engulf it in his own.

By unspoken agreement, we stayed silent as we picked our way over the sand. It was cool, at least compared to the burning hot agony that would greet visitors later in the day. The breeze was steady, lifting my hair off the back of my neck, the sun sitting low on the horizon, casting a shimmering reflection out on the Atlantic.

I stole a glance at my companion. The wind tossed his dark hair around but in the bright sun, I saw a few strands of gray. My throat constricted a little at the sight. Ten years. I'd known him for ten years and we had only just started to date.

"What?" he asked, moving into my path.

I pasted on a bright smile. "It's nothing,"

"Jackie." His tone was filled with irritation. "Don't do that girl thing and make me drag an answer out of you."

"Logan," I said in the exact same tone. "Don't do that guy thing and think that you are capable of dragging an answer out of me when I don't want to talk. The Pentagon has nothing on me."

He glared down at me. I narrowed my eyes and scowled back.

His lips twitched and then he did the unthinkable. He *booped* me on the nose. His index finger just reached out and *boop*. He even made the accompanying sound effect.

My jaw dropped. "You did not just *boop* me."

"You're cute when you're irritated."

"You would know." But I couldn't contain my smile. I adored playful Logan, antics and all.

He sobered. "Tell me what's wrong."

I made a sound in the back of my throat. "Like a dog with a bone."

He didn't answer. He just turned to look out at the waves. Waiting.

Fine, if he was going to sulk and ruin the mood anyway, I might as well cop to it. "Well, I was trying not to spoil the nice morning. Or what's been a nice morning since the attempted break-in. But since you insist, I was sad because of all the time we've wasted. We've known each other for over a decade and this is only our first official date."

"Is not," he turned back to face me.

"You can't count that first night at the club."

He shook his head. "I'm not."

"Well then?" I did a palm's up gesture.

One dark eyebrow went up. "How about two months ago, at Mom and Dad's place? You were all over me."

Was he serious? "Um, that wasn't exactly a date what with you having a hole in your leg and being hopped up on painkillers. And I wasn't all over you." Though I hadn't wanted to leave his side. I had slept in the chaise lounge in the sitting room just so I could be near him.

"That wasn't a date, even though you finally admitted you loved me."

I huffed out a breath. "A date involves premeditation, sharing a meal. Stuff like that."

He reached out and tucked a strand of hair behind my ear. "How about all the times I've cooked for you? Like in the Keys?"

"Okay first of all, when I say premeditation it also means *consensual*. And you kidnapped me so you were obligated to feed me." Though some of the other things he had done weren't strictly necessary.

"It was courting," he insisted.

"Courting? What the hell is this, Elizabethan England?"

"Semantics," he shrugged. "The point is this isn't a first date because I know you. I know how you take your coffee. I know all about your messed-up childhood, your mother's struggles with substance abuse and why you went into property management, so you could help protect people so they never have to live a day on the streets the way your mom did when she was pregnant with you. Or worry about a handsy landlord letting himself into a tenant's trailer."

My lips parted. I had never voiced that to anyone before. I'd barely admitted it to myself. It amazed me, the depth of his insight.

He traced my jawline with one finger. "So has time passed? Yes, it has. But it wasn't time wasted. I've been putting the Jackie puzzle together one piece at a time. And believe me when I say I'd live the last ten years over again if it meant I get to have this moment with you."

"You don't mean that." He couldn't.

One dark eyebrow went up. "Don't I?"

The man was incredible. He either said the absolute best thing or the absolute worst. There was no middle ground with Logan Parker. I sniffled but didn't trust myself to speak.

He slung an arm over my shoulders. "Come on, I promised you a breakfast burrito. Sausage, potato and pimento cheese?"

"They're my favorite," I murmured.

His grin was infectious. "I know."

The cafe was a little hole in the wall place a few streets back from Ocean Avenue. Logan ordered two breakfast burritos with everything on them and two large Cuban coffees with milk. We sat on a bench and played native or tourist while we ate.

"Tourists." I pointed my burrito towards a man and a woman rollerblading. She wore a teal string bikini and designer denim cutoffs. He had on a unitard workout suit that gleamed and left nothing to the imagination. "Tan lines, plus the clothes are off the rack new."

"And the banana hammock isn't doing him any favors. Native," Logan pointed to an elderly lady stooped over to pick up her cockapoo's morning doo-doo in a green plastic baggy.

"Too easy. Everyone knows tourists don't pick up after themselves or their dogs. What about that guy?" I gestured to a dark-skinned guy in a gray polo and khaki pants. He wore sunglasses and a Rolex and moved with purpose.

Beside me, Logan grabbed my hand. "Put your helmet on."

"What's wrong?" I turned to face him, only to see he was donning his headgear.

Dropping my burrito, I pulled my helmet on, wondering who that man was and why Logan was so intent on hiding our identities from him.

The well-accessorized man strode into a storefront nearby. Logan pulled me up and moving casually but intently, steered me back over to where the motorcycle was parked.

I climbed on and we crossed the causeway, heading back into downtown. I half expected Logan to head for home, but instead, he pulled over into a convenience store parking lot and flipped up his visor. "Do you have your phone?"

When I nodded he added, "Call Corrine."

Corrine was Logan's tenant. She lived in the bungalow next to mine. I fished the phone out of my jean's pocket. "What do you want me to tell her?"

Logan's expression turned grim. "That her husband is in Miami."

## 2

---

I let myself back into the house while Logan went next
door to check on Corrine. She had sounded badly
shaken over the phone.

"Hey," Luke said emerging from the second bathroom
looking sleep rumpled and scruffy. "I heard Abu freaking out
from the cage and was just going to knock and make sure
everything was all right. Did you go out?"

He eyed the passenger's helmet still tucked under my arm
then the sand on my cuffs.

"Logan took me for an early morning ride." No, it wasn't
at all weird talking about a date to my ex-husband. I refo-
cused on the more immediate situation. "Logan spotted
Corrine's husband a couple blocks from the beach. He sort of
freaked out and we beat feet out of there. Do you know
anything about it?"

In addition to being Logan's tenant, Corrine was also the
Dark Prince's side rescue project. All I knew was the little
Logan told me, that Corrine had needed help escaping a bad
marriage situation. For a while, she'd pretended to be

15

Logan's fiancée, part of the reason she and I had never really bonded.

Luke frowned and headed for the hall closet. "Not much, only that the guy was abusive. She doesn't like to talk about it, understandably. I'm going to shower, should I let Abu out?"

"Put on PBS first. He's less likely to throw a tantrum if Curious George is already on."

Luke grinned and shook his head. "Spoiled creature. Sasquatch is out back."

I rubbed my eyes and headed for the coffee pot. My newly renovated kitchen gleamed in the morning sun, white cabinets with glass fronts on the uppers that classed up our mismatched plates. Matching stainless steel appliances and slate gray quartz countertops. It was almost enough to make me want to risk the wrath of the kitchen curse and learn how to cook.

Speaking of wrath....Abu appeared, wagging his finger and hopping up and down on the counter. He looked like a furry, ticked off librarian.

I put my hands on my hips and stared him down. "Oh, hush. Your cage is nicer than most of the places I lived growing up. And it certainly smells better."

It was, too. Luke had constructed a little habitat, complete with a platform bed and wall to wall carpet remnants. It sat on my low dresser and though he never fought me about going in, Abu was a monster after we let him out. Unfortunately, his separation anxiety made him a menace so we didn't have a choice.

I peeled a banana for my monkey and he took it to the couch, mollified. Abu had a temper but all was forgiven until the next incarceration. I let Sasquatch in, trying not to wonder what was going on in the bungalow next door. While the coffee brewed, I brooded. It had been such a promising start to the day. How had it gone downhill so fast? And I was pissed about not being able to finish that breakfast burrito, doubly so that Logan had run off to another woman with hardly a word of explanation.

No, I was not jealous. I *refused* to be jealous. Luke was handling my budding relationship with his brother/business partner and Logan was handling me still living with my ex-husband. I could not be the weak link in our little trifecta.

It was all sour feelings about wasted pimento cheese.

A door scraped open at the rear of the house. Celeste emerged, thankfully wearing a bathrobe. My mother's taste in nightwear landed somewhere between desperate house-wife and aging porn star.

"Mornin', baby-girl," she drawled, her Southern accent thicker pre-coffee.

"You're up early." Celeste was a reformed party girl and a hairdresser. Her typical wake-up time was somewhere around ten.

"I have some things to do today." She yawned and stretched.

"What sort of things?" I handed her a mug.

She moved to the pot. "Well, house hunting."

I blinked. "House hunting? Like an actual house, not a trailer?"

She turned and I saw the gleam of excitement in her eyes. "I sort of want one of them cute little tiny houses. John and I talked about getting a kit and putting one together. I guess that's not practical anymore." There was a wiggle in her voice when she talked about her deceased boyfriend.

I put my hand on her arm. "Are you sure you're ready? You know you can stay here as long as you like."

Part of me couldn't believe the words coming out of my mouth. But then, Celeste had turned over a new leaf, going to AA meetings and working extra shifts to save money.

After five and a half decades, my mother was finally growing up.

"Thank you, Jackie. That means so much to me." She smiled, her eyes teary and then looked around the kitchen. "Boy, I can't believe how well this turned out. And how fast."

"Luke was motivated." After years of living in a half-finished construction zone, our amicable divorce had prompted Luke to shake a leg and hire a few professionals to fill in the gaps and finish the house. Seeing it was bittersweet. The fixer-upper had been meant to be our forever home and now it was a weigh station while we all figured out what came next.

"So you're going to put it on the market?" She shook her head as though she couldn't believe that.

"Do you know what a goldmine this is? And an added feature we can honestly say this kitchen has never been cooked in."

"So, what about you. Any plans?"

"Not yet. Renting would be tricky, what with the pet clause." I gestured toward where Abu sat watching the cartoon monkey frolic in the snow.

"The downside of Miami real estate being so valuable is that I'm going to end up overpaying for something nowhere near this nice. Plus, there's the business to think about." The second bedroom had been transformed into our home office.

"Maybe it's not the right time to sell," Celeste suggested.

My gaze flicked to the closed bedroom door. "Luke needs to move on with his life and he can't while he's living in this house with me. We're living in such close quarters that we are totally aware of one another's movements. When the other goes out or when he or she comes back. I seriously doubt he'd bring a date home to seduce on the couch."

"Have you considered moving in with Logan?" Celeste propped herself up on the counter.

My coffee mug was empty, giving me an excuse not to look at her. "He hasn't asked me."

My mother tipped her head to the side. "Jackie, you know he wants to be with you."

"I don't, actually. We haven't really discussed the future." And I didn't say it because it would hurt her feelings, but I didn't want to depend on anyone to secure the roof over my head, not even my Dark Prince. "This is something I need to figure out by myself."

"Maybe we can get matching tiny homes. Side by side. They have these converted cargo containers, they're really cute. Stackable even so you can get a better view."

I couldn't contain the shudder at the mental picture of living in a cargo container. "Mom, one of these days I need to sit you down and watch *Dexter*."

Luke emerged from the bedroom at the same time Logan pushed his way through the front door. He winked at my mother. "Celeste."

She fanned herself and I shoved her toward her bedroom door. "Better go get dressed. You want to look nice for the tiny homes."

"Kiss up." Luke bumped his brother's shoulder.

"Tiny homes?" Logan raised a brow.

"It's basically this century's version of a trailer." I folded my arms over my chest. "And don't think you're getting away with it, pal."

"Away with what?" Logan's dark brows drew down.

I folded my hands over my chest. "You ditched me like last season's wardrobe and now you want to proceed as if nothing happened?"

"It's not for me to tell."

"Is she in danger? Are you in danger because she's living in your house?" God, he was still recovering from the last time he'd been shot. I couldn't go through that again.

19

He scowled. "Don't be so dramatic."

"Oh, *I'm* the dramatic one? You're the one who dragged me out of there without my breakfast burrito."

Logan's lips parted, probably to say something that would make my blood pressure spike, but Luke—ever the peace-maker—cut him off.

"Guys, I hate to butt in but if Corrine is okay, we need to get to work. Our caseload could choke a donkey. She is okay, right?"

He looked to the Dark Prince for verification. Logan nodded, eyes still fixed on me. "She's fine. Though I thought maybe we could leave Sasquatch with her for a little extra security."

"And now you're giving away my dog without asking?"

"She's Luke's dog, too," he snapped.

"And I'll bet you didn't ask him, either. Did he?" My head swiveled to Luke.

He held up his hands. "If it makes her feel better to have the dog around, what's the harm?"

"Fine." Knowing I was being unreasonable, I marched into the office, plunked down behind the desk and started sifting through case files. Luke was right, we'd fallen behind. Not only did we have to finish the yearly inspections in the Sunnyvale complex, but I also had a stack of other complaints ranging from nonpayment of rent to squatters, to funky smells, to checkups on onsite property managers who weren't getting the job done.

Damaged Goods operated as a three-person team. I was the Certified Process Server. It was important when operating in property management that we stayed on the right side of the law, to keep our client's from getting sued and to protect tenant's rights. I was also well-connected and personable, the one who got us admitted into the rentals nine times out of ten.

Luke was Mr. Fixit. He knew more about construction and building maintenance than most of the specialists we came across. He knew how to do everything from unstopping a drain to assessing structural integrity and knew when to call in an expert.

Logan was the intimidator. Sometimes tenants didn't like hearing what we had to say, especially if we had to proceed with an eviction. The Dark Prince's foreboding countenance made the loose cannons think twice about coming after us. He also operated as our emergency medic, which had come in handy on several occasions.

Together we could take on the Magic City one rental property at a time.

If we didn't kill each other first.

---

CORRINE AGREED NOT ONLY to take in Sasquatch but Abu as well, saving me from having to contain his hairy hide and deal with the fallout later. I'd forced a smile and said thank you, all the while feeling Logan's gaze on the back of my neck.

"Call me if you need anything," he'd murmured to her.

"Call me if you need anything, meh meh meh," I hissed under my breath and climbed into the backseat of the Big Black Truck.

"What's going on, Ace?" Luke stared at me in the rearview mirror. "This isn't like you. You're usually first in line to help someone out."

"It's nothing." At least nothing I wanted to talk to my ex-husband about. And, though I was ashamed to admit it, he was right. If I'd met Corrine independently, I probably would have offered to let her dog sit, or hell, move in to keep her safe. Envy green so wasn't my color.

Logan climbed into the passenger's side and didn't say anything. After a moment, Luke turned the engine over and we headed out to job number one.

I flipped the file open to verify the details. "We're headed to a triplex in South Coconut Grove. The onsite manager is Garret Green. Owner is a snowbird and he allows Mr. Green to live in one of the apartments in exchange for keeping the place up year-round."

"So what's the problem?" Luke asked. Logan stared out the window as if he couldn't care less.

"The problem is the second tenant—," I paused to double check the name on the paperwork— "Zamara Diaz, hasn't been paying her rent. The owner hasn't been able to get in touch with Mr. Green and Mrs. Diaz doesn't speak English."

"How old's the guy?" Logan asked as Luke turned onto Dixie Highway. "Is this some old geezer taking up residence in the morgue?"

"According to the paperwork, he's thirty-seven. No more of a geezer than you are." My tone was sweeter than Southern tea.

The Dark Prince grumbled something under his breath, then louder, "I say we check in with Diaz first. Get her side of the story and see if she has a valid reason for not paying rent. Then we can follow up with Green."

"Other way," I said. "If the manager sees us knocking on doors without checking in with him, he might call the cops on us. And also, he's the employee, not just the renter."

"Fine," Logan folded his arms over his chest. "Have it your way."

"Jackie, you said it was a triplex," Luke said before I could snipe at Logan. "Is there anybody in the third unit?"

"Not according to the paperwork. It's where the owner stays when he's in town."

"Then maybe we should talk to the manager while you check with the tenant. Hit them from both sides."

I opened my mouth to agree but Logan said, "I'll go with her."

It wasn't a suggestion.

We pulled into the half circular driveway of the pretty little building. It wasn't oceanfront but you could smell it in the air. The layout was a Mediterranean style building with arched doorways and three one-story units connected by a courtyard with a bubbling three-tier dolphin fountain. Palm trees swayed in the morning breeze. Just another day collecting rent in paradise.

Luke whistled low. "What's a place like this run?"

I blew out a sigh. "More than any of us can afford. Tenant is on the far left, manager on the right."

Luke moved toward Mr. Green's door while I headed for Ms. Diaz's place with Logan breathing down my neck with every step.

I closed my eyes, then raised a fist and knocked on the door. "Property management."

Logan moved off to the side. "Curtains are pulled tight. Maybe she's not home?"

"There's a silver Lexus in the driveway. I doubt that belongs to our onsite manager." I was about to knock again when the door to the middle unit opened.

"Who the devil are you?"

Logan and I turned and faced the man standing in the doorway of the apartment that was supposed to be vacant. "We work for the owner. I'm Jackie, this is Logan. Who are you?"

"Maximillian Radcliff." The man with the upper crust British accent huffed with importance. Too much importance considering he wore only a green and black kimono

23

that ended at midthigh. His knobby knees looked like something that belonged on a stork.

"I thought you said the third unit was empty," the Dark Prince grumbled.

"It's supposed to be. Maybe he's a friend of the owner?" I hissed while pasting a friendly smile on my face. "We'd like to talk to you for a second. If that's all right."

Good old Max made an impatient gesture for us to come in.

Across the atrium, Luke monitored us as we approached the potential squatter.

"I've got a bad feeling about this," Logan grumbled.

"You always say that."

"And I'm usually right. I hope he's at least wearing a banana hammock under that thing."

I barely suppressed a gag. "Mr. Radcliff. We represent the property owner. Can you tell us how long you've been staying here?"

"About six months."

It sounded a bit long for a vacation to me.

"May we come in?" I kicked my smile up a notch to counteract Max's sour milk puss.

Gaining entry to the unit served two purposes. First, we could ascertain the condition of the property, see if anything was broken, like windows or locks. If there were signs of forced entry, we could call the cops and report Max for breaking and entering. Problem solved.

And also, getting inside kept the guy from shutting the door in our face when we asked a question he didn't like.

"I'm sorry who did you say you were again?" Max glared between the two of us.

"Jackie Parker. This is Logan Parker. No relation."

Logan snorted.

"And you work for the owner? Can I see some sort of identification?"

Logan took his wallet out of his back pocket while I retrieved a business card from my tote which also contained my clipboard, notices, and pens. I'd learned the hard way to keep all my personal items in an entirely separate purse so that tampons and credit cards didn't get snatched by irate tenants.

Maximillian had very bad hair plugs which the bright Florida sunshine streaming through the palm fronds did nothing to hide. Other than his stork knees, the plugs and his accent there was nothing remarkable about him. Just a pasty middle-aged British dude hanging out in a kimono.

"All right, fine." He stalked back inside.

The unit was a one-bedroom, one bath with a sliding glass door in the back leading to a large lanai with a built-in fire pit. The kitchen consisted of a stainless-steel refrigerator and wall oven, gas range top and dishwasher. The furniture was obviously new with giant monstera leaf patterns. A big-screen television sat over the electric fireplace. Exactly the sort of high end upgrades an owner would put into his own unit.

Logan had crouched down to look at the lock on the front door.

"What's he doing? What are you doing?" Maximillian scowled.

"His job. Don't worry about him." I stepped in front of Logan, blocking Max's view. "Mr. Radcliff, I hate to tell you this but you're trespassing on the owner's property."

Max puffed up his chest. "I'm renting this property."

Logan rose to his feet towering over the squatter. He didn't like that Max had invaded my personal space. I caught the slight headshake, indicating he hadn't found scratch marks consistent with a break-in. "Do you have a lease? Who are you paying?"

"The owner of course," Max's expression curdled further.

"If you have a copy of that rental agreement, I'd like to see it."

"It's in the bedroom."

"Would you get it, please?"

He turned and stalked away.

"Not your typical squatter," Logan murmured.

I had to agree. "Let's see what he produces."

Max returned with a copy of his lease as well as his bank statement and a photocopy of the check he'd used to put down his security deposit. The lease was for a one-year occupancy of this unit. The check was made out to Garret Green, our onsite manager.

"Mr. Green told you he owned this place?" I asked to be sure.

"I answered an online advertisement." He said it the British way *ad-ver-tis-ment*. "He said it was available for immediate occupancy, fully furnished. It was exactly what I was looking for."

Logan and I exchanged a glance. First, a solid tenant stopped paying her rent and then the owner's unit was being occupied without his consent.

"Thank you for your time, Mr. Radcliff," I said and then took Logan's arm and steered him outside.

"That's it?" the Dark Prince hissed.

"We need to check in with the owner, see what he wants us to do." The lease wasn't valid and our pal from across the pond had fallen victim to a rental scam. I could serve Max with a three-day cure or quit notice to start the eviction process. But the bigger problem was our onsite manager.

"He's not answering the door," Luke grumbled. "I talked to the other tenant. She insists she paid her rent in cash. I believe her." He waved to a middle-aged Hispanic woman who stood on her front doorstep.

"I can tag the door." Even though Garret Green worked for our property owner, he was still protected by the same landlord-tenant laws. We had to post an intent to enter at least twenty-four hours in advance of letting ourselves into his home.

"Do it," Logan said. "Luke, let's get a better look around the property. See if...." They moved to the other side of the fountain until I couldn't hear them.

I rooted through my bag for a pen and the right form. I filled out the twenty-four-hour notice and pressed it to the door.

It was hot.

That was when I smelled the smoke.

## 3

"Get back," Logan had broken land speed records to drag me away from the door. "Luke, get the fire extinguisher."

"On it," Luke ran for the truck.

"Jackie, call 911."

I already had my phone in my hand when we heard the first scream.

"Someone's in there." Logan made to move forward and I gripped him around the bicep.

"Wait for Luke. The door was hot. If you kick it down, you'll make things worse." I had my cell cradled between my shoulder and ear and was trying to talk some sense into the big, strong dumbass poised to charge into a burning building.

"911, please state the nature of your emergency." The female operator had a brisk accent less tone.

"Help!" A child's panicked voice.

"I'll go around back, see if there's another door." Logan shook out of my hold and ran.

"Frigging hell," I spat at his retreating back.

"Ma'am?" The operator prodded.

"There's a fire. We think someone's inside the unit. We need the fire department and paramedics." And then there was my fool boyfriend who needed to play the big damn hero.

"Give me the address."

I rattled it off while simultaneously gesturing to Luke. "Logan went around back. We think someone is in there."

There was a thunderous crash. I flinched, envisioning Logan tossing a patio chair through the sliding glass door.

"*Madre de Dios.*" Ms. Diaz had emerged from her apartment and crossed herself.

"Here," I thrust my cell into her hand. 911 didn't appreciate it when you hung up on them but we had too much going on for me to stay on the line.

"Get the guy out of the other unit." Luke charged around the building.

Sirens sounded in the distance. We'd passed a fire station on our way in and this time of day, traffic was light.

I ran over to the owner's unit and hammered on the door. "Mr. Radcliff? There's a fire."

No answer.

I smacked it harder and kicked for good measure. "Mr. Radcliff!"

Still nothing.

Screw it. I had the right to enter the rental if I thought someone was in danger. A fire in the unit next door posed enough danger to warrant an unauthorized entry. I put my hand on the knob, not really expecting anything, but the door swung open.

I stared directly out at the opened patio door, could see the Big Black Truck. No sign of the Lexus.

I took the two minutes required to search the apartment, but no sign of my buddy. His kimono was draped over one of the pineapple posters in the bedroom. Either he was out streaking or he'd gotten dressed and left.

I exited through the patio door, jumped down the three-deck steps and ran around to the back of the complex to the onsite manager's apartment. I had been wrong. It wasn't a deck chair Logan had used to break the sliding glass door, it was a charcoal grill. The nuggets of charcoal were spread all over the deck. Luckily the door had been safety glass which pebbled on impact so there weren't shards of glass everywhere. Bad enough smoke billowed out from inside the dark apartment.

"Logan! Luke!" I shouted in through the open door. I couldn't see the fire, not through the thick buntings of smoke, but I could hear the roar.

Logan appeared—a child cradled in his arms. She wore a pink nightgown and was otherwise unconscious.

For his part, the Dark Prince was limping badly and smelled like a bonfire but appeared otherwise unscathed.

"Are you all right?" I moved to help him with his burden.

He gave one quick nod.

"Where' s Luke?" I asked as we set her down on a patio chair.

Logan shook his head, crouching over the inert figure. "I don't know. They were cooking up some sort of drug in the kitchen. That's where the fire started. Caught a poster and it spread to the front door. She was hiding under the bed."

"Is there anyone else inside?"

"Not that I saw." His attention turned to the girl, his hand feeling for a pulse. "Jesus, she's even younger than I thought."

It was true, in the daylight the small figure was clearly only five or six. Too young to be left alone, never mind with meth cooking away in the kitchen.

Luke appeared, fire extinguisher in one hand, hamster

cage in the other. His jeans and t-shirt were soot-stained but he looked otherwise unhurt. "I think it's out."

Just in time, too as the fire truck rolled into the lot.

"Are you okay?" I leaned down to touch Logan's shoulder.

He jerked out of my hold. "Fine. I'm more worried about her." He lifted the girl's eyelids. "Go wave the paramedics over here. Tell them she has severe smoke inhalation."

I decided not to get worked up over his commanding tone. He was trying to save a life—he was allowed to be terse.

"I'll go see to the other tenants." Luke set the hamster cage down.

I walked alongside him. "It's just Ms. Diaz. Our maybe squatter disappeared."

He cut me a sideways glance. "Coincidence?"

I shrugged. "He left the front door unlocked. Didn't look ready to go out when we spoke to him earlier, though."

Luke nodded, then jogged toward where Mrs. Diaz stood in her doorway, cuddling a calico cat in her arms.

Our Jane Doe was loaded into the ambulance. "You should go with her," I moved to stand by Logan's side where he watched her being loaded. "Maybe get yourself looked at."

"I'm fine."

I studied his profile carefully. "You keep saying that and every time you do, I believe you a little bit less."

He turned to face me—his expression grim. "I'm waiting for you to tear me a new one."

I frowned at him. "Logan, you saved that girl's life. Why would you think I would give you crap about that?"

One dark eyebrow went up. "You're not mad at me for going in?"

"I'm not thrilled you didn't wait for the fire extinguisher —or the fire department—but I know the man you are. Nothing would have kept you out of that place when you heard her scream." I put a hand on his arm, the small

31

contact I would allow myself when we still had a job to do. "Trust me, I knew what I was signing on for to be with you."

He put his hand over mine and squeezed.

I gestured toward a stone bench by the fountain where Mrs. Diaz sat hugging her cat. She handed me back the phone, which had been disconnected from the 911 call.

I stuffed it in my jeans pocket. "If you won't go to the hospital you should at least sit down. Get off that leg. We're going to be here for a while."

He gave my hand one final squeeze and limped off. Were all men so dense or was it only the ones I worked with?

With the fire out, the guys in the fire department were loading back on the truck.

I introduced myself and handed a man with the hairless good looks of a Bruce Willis a business card. "Do you know what started it?"

"Can't tell for sure until the fire marshal inspects." The guy had a thick Staten Island accent.

"I work for the property owner. If there's some sort of potential fire hazard, we need to know so we can make accommodations for the other tenant." I flashed him my best just a working girl in a tough world smile.

In the end, he verified what Logan had suspected. An illegal gas hookup that had been rigged to an open flame was most likely the source of the fire.

I nodded and thanked him.

Luke made his way over to me. "Good news, the hamster is going to make it." He pointed to the cage where what looked like a fat, furry turd ran on a wheel.

A smile stole across my face. "You Parker brothers are always saving the day."

"What do we do now?"

I snagged my phone from my jeans pocket. "Now, we call

the property owner and I listen to him rant and rave at me over this fiasco."

Luke blew out a sigh. "Are we masochists for doing this job?"

"Probably." I agreed as the phone rang.

---

THERE WAS VERY LITTLE we could do, other than have Luke change the locks on the owner's unit. Legally speaking, Maximillian Radcliff was a squatter. His lease wasn't valid. And once a squatter left the premises, he had no real claim on the place. We would inventory and store all of his personal items for fifteen days and leave a notice on the door regarding where and how he could reclaim it. If he wanted his kimono back, he would have to pay for the moving and storage.

Garret Green was a different matter. The man had been engaged in illegal activity. That didn't spell good news for us. The cops would be notified of the fire and Child Protective Services of child endangerment. I needed to go down to the courthouse to begin the eviction process. It was neither cheap nor efficient and would probably wind up costing our owner several thousand dollars in addition to the cost of fixing the damage from the fire and the lost income revenue. We took a piece of plywood and boarded up the back door but the locks had to stay the same since legally, Garret Green still lived there.

Though he didn't like it, based on what we'd found, the owner agreed to forgive Mrs. Diaz's missing rent. Considering what else his on-site manager had been up to, it was reasonable to assume Green had collected her money and never bothered to hand it over to the property owner.

Logan was conversing in rapid-fire Spanish with the

elderly tenant by the time I got off the phone. He caught my gaze and gestured me over.

The Dark Prince lounged on the bench, reflective sunglasses hiding his ice-blue eyes, looking like a stunt double on break from filming an action scene. "Mrs. Diaz says she thinks the girl is Green's daughter. Her name is Harper and she's six. She plays with Mrs. Diaz's granddaughter when her family visits."

"Any idea where her mother is?"

Logan translated. Even with four years of high school Spanish under my belt, I only picked up every few words. Logan and Luke both spoke the language like natives.

Mrs. Diaz shook her head sadly and then said a few quick sentences.

"No idea." Logan's expression was stony. "She didn't say so, but judging by the girl's age and what we found in there, the mother either abandoned her with Green or Od-ed."

Poor kid.

That would also complicate the eviction process. Courts didn't like to leave children homeless. Of course, if Garret Green didn't materialize, poor Harper would get sucked up into the system.

"Can you tell her that the owner has offered to pay for her to live in a hotel until the fire marshal clears the place tomorrow?" That had been my idea, an olive branch so that the *abuela* would feel safe and not look into breaking her own lease and we'd be left with three vacant apartments. Another expense the owner didn't like, but had reluctantly agreed to.

"I can tell her, but I doubt she'll want to leave," he nodded to the cat.

He was right, Mrs. Diaz had no interest in going to a hotel for the night. Said she would be fine right where she was and she shuffled back inside her apartment.

"I think we should put cameras up." Logan pulled me down next to him. "To see if Green comes back, or the squatter for that matter."

A solid plan. "We should have one in the truck we can rig to a cell phone."

He leaned forward, folding his hands over his lap. "I'd say we should stay and do on-site surveillance but I don't like the idea of leaving Corrine alone at night with her husband in town."

"Are you ready to tell me what's going on there?"

He shook his head. "I can't."

Frustration gnawed at me. "Can you at least tell me why she isn't going to the cops for help?"

He looked up at me so I saw two images of my disheveled self reflected in his opaque lenses. "It's complicated."

I let out a sigh. "Logan, you know Luke keeping things from me is what drove us apart."

"This is different."

"How?"

He wrapped his hands around me, pulling me in close so that he could rest his cheek on my belly and look up at me. "Because it's not about us. I have things going on that I need to see through. Are you going to drop every single thing you started before we began dating for the sake of our relationship?"

I didn't like that answer, mostly because he was right. I wouldn't abandon early commitments just because Logan and I were together. But I wasn't about to admit that he had a point. I put my hands on the sun-warmed stone. "Just tell me one thing. Can Corrine hiding out at your place get you hurt again? Or killed?"

He swallowed. "I'm not going to lie to you. Her ex is not a good guy and there's a reason she doesn't want a paper trail leading to where she is."

I held my breath and waited for him to continue.

"But Jackie, his being in Miami doesn't mean he's here for her or me or anything like that. He has…business interests and this is a large port city. I was being overcautious because you were with me." He threaded his fingers through mine and squeezed.

This was nuts. We were on the job—fresh out of a fire—and yet I was harping on Corrine. I hated that all these petty thoughts kept distracting me.

"I don't like you living with another woman."

His lips twitched and I could tell he fought a smile. "Have I mentioned how adorable I find your crazy possessive streak?"

Glad someone was enjoying it. "Emphasis on the crazy."

He gave my hand another squeeze. "It's temporary. I have someone who is going to help her disappear. You remember Neil and Maggie Phillips, who stayed at my place last Christmas?"

"Of course." Maggie was my favorite non-Miami resident. Together we'd caught a scumbag burglar who'd dressed up as Santa Claus.

"Neil's got contacts. We're just waiting on a few necessary paperwork items to come through and then she'll be gone."

I gave him a level look. "You mean you're waiting for someone to forge a new identity for her."

He chuckled. "I won't confirm that because I don't want to drag you into anything that could cost you your process serving certificate."

"So, you keeping things from me and making time with another woman is all for my sake?"

"That's the second time you've brought up the living situation. Jesus, Jackie. I've been recovering from a gunshot wound."

Even in the afternoon heat, I shivered. "Don't remind me."

"Trust me, you have nothing to worry about. I think of Corrine like a sister. Besides, I'm not thrilled about you living with my brother."

"That's different."

"Yeah, you two used to be married. If you're so worried about it, you and Corrine could always swap places."

His tone was teasing but I sobered at the thought. "We should help Luke with the door."

I made to step away but he grabbed my hand.

"I love you, you know. And I would love for you to move in with me."

My response was automatic, still feeling the same little thrill at being able to own it out loud. "I love you, too."

One dark eyebrow went up. "But?"

Damn the man's handsome hide for knowing me so well. "But, I'm not sure I'm ready…for everything that entails."

"You mean sex."

"No, I mean *everything*. I come with a lot of baggage, Logan. An oversized dog, a badly-behaved monkey and a drama queen mother who wants us to buy matching tiny houses."

He scratched his chin. "That sounds like a special hell."

I glanced over to where Luke fiddled with the door lock on the owner's unit. "And there's the business. We're operating it out of the house. We both got on board with Damaged Goods for his sake. I just don't want to screw up a good divorce by moving too fast."

Logan didn't say anything.

Reluctantly, I let him go. "I'm gonna go get the camera."

I was halfway across the lot when he caught my wrist and turned me to face him. He'd removed his sunglasses and his eyes burned with raw feeling.

"I'm going to break down your walls one at a time until you trust me completely." "That's a big ask," I whispered.

He curled a finger under my chin and forced my gaze to meet his. "We can take it at any speed you need to, as long as we're together."

And that was why I loved him.

The camera was a motion-activated rig that we decided to hook up to Luke's cell phone since it was the newest therefore the least likely to spaz out when an update was pushed through. I held the ladder while he climbed up to the roof of the owner's unit and angled it down while Logan checked to make sure both front doors were visible.

"Where to now?" Luke asked when we were all loaded back in the truck.

I checked my open files. "We've got a choice. Inventory a commercial lot down by the port or start with the twenty-four-hour inspections on the apartment complex in Wynwood."

"I've had enough of crazy tenants today," Logan rubbed at his thigh. "I say we grab a late lunch and start tackling the inventory."

"Sound good to you, Ace?" Luke looked at me in the rearview.

I nodded, though my thoughts were elsewhere. "Can we swing by the hospital?"

Logan turned to face me. "If this is some ploy to get me to see a doctor, I told you I'm fine."

"Maybe I just want to stick to my diet. Really shitty cafeteria food will keep me from overeating," I shot back. "Though they do have those awesome frosted brownies the size of my clipboard."

His expression softened as he saw right into my murky depths. "I'd like to check on her, too."

Physically, Harper was going to be all right. She wore an oxygen mask and a pink nightgown. Her eyes were bloodshot, probably from the smoke. She looked small and scared in the hospital bed.

"We shouldn't overwhelm her." Luke backed up.

Logan and I exchanged a glance.

I gestured to the open door. "You saved her. She might remember you."

"Hey you," Logan approached her first. He'd taken a minute to splash water on his face and somehow looked much less imposing seated beside the child. "Do you remember me, from earlier?"

Her big brown eyes widened and she shook her head. I couldn't see if her lips moved beneath the oxygen mask but she must have said something because the Dark Prince smiled.

Her tenuous living situation was another matter.

A police officer and a woman from family services stood outside the semi-private room.

I introduced myself to them both and then asked, "What's going to happen to her?"

"We'll get her placed in a temporary children's shelter," the woman, whose nametag read Dolores, said. "See if we can locate a relative."

"And if you can't find any?"

Dolores had gone prematurely gray, probably from the stress of her job. "Then a court will probably place her somewhere with a foster home. We do the best we can to keep kids with their families, but it's not always possible."

As it probably wouldn't be with Garret Green, the thieving drug cooker who'd left her alone. I'd been left alone as a young child too and understood firsthand just how scary it could be.

"Is there any chance she'll be adopted?" I don't know why I asked the question, but it seemed fairer somehow if maybe

Harper got a forever family that would love and cherish her. A silver lining to come out of the whole debacle.

Dolores shrugged. "Maybe, if someone really wants her and her father relinquishes his rights. She'd have to be in a foster home for at least six months. She's older than most who are adopted. People want babies to be part of their lives right from the get-go. Are you asking for yourself and your husband?" Her shrewd gaze darted to where Logan sat beside the bed.

"No," I spoke automatically, then frowned. "Maybe?"

*Maybe?* My inner voice shrieked. *Are you nuts? You don't even know which bungalow to live in and you're going to commit to a child? What are you gonna do when you go to work, put her in a cage next to Abu?*

Dolores fished a business card out of her back pocket. "Best thing to do is register to be a temporary placement with the state as a foster place. Plan on nine to eighteen months before you're officially set up. There's a process and I have to warn you, in these sorts of situations, the parents often come back into the picture."

My heart sank. Nine to eighteen months in another foster situation for poor Harper, then six more months to wait out the paperwork. Yeah, this wasn't an impulse buy or even like adopting Abu. Hadn't she been through enough already without being inflicted with my unique brand of cray-cray?

Still, as I watched Logan with her, I felt a pang of longing that wouldn't go away.

## 4

"**C**ome on, lazybones." Marcy pounded on my bedroom door. "You promised we were going to spin class today."

I dragged my sorry carcass out of bed and stumbled to the door to face my soon-to-be-ex best friend. "I liked you better before you decided to get healthy."

Marcy had gone on a self-imposed man cleanse after her last date had gone through her purse. Instead of trying to find "the one," my bestie was focusing all of her efforts on self-improvement and dragging my miserable hide along in her wake.

"You look like hell," Marcy's blonde ponytail bobbed as she took a hit from her trusty water bottle.

"Gee, insulting me doesn't seem like the best way to get me to do what you want." I rubbed my tired eyes.

After our sojourn to the hospital, Luke, Logan and I had spent the rest of the day and half the night trundling through commercial construction equipment, everything from table saws to hammers to forklifts. And that was only *one* of the five cargo containers.

Down the hall, a door opened and Celeste appeared wearing a pink leotard, yellow tights, and an aqua sweatband.

"How do I look, girls?"

"Like you just got barfed out of a Richard Simmons tribute video."

"Oh Jackie," Celeste swatted at me. "Be nice."

I glanced at my Felix the Cat wall clock. "Before eight I can exercise or I can be sociable but I can't be both. There's only so many times a day a girl can fake it."

Marcy eyed me shrewdly and then turned to Celeste. "What dress size would you say Corrine is?"

My mother's crayoned eyebrows pulled together. "Maybe a four?"

"Did you hear that, Jackie? Logan is living with a size *four*."

My mother caught on. "You never know, Marcy. Looking at a fit and trim woman all day might make him appreciate a little junk in the trunk."

"I hate you both." I snarled and reached for my gym bag.

Twenty minutes later I had my size four times three*ish* ass parked on an exercise bike, pedaling like mutant gators were chasing me down.

"And up!" The perfectly proportioned Norwegian goddess picked her firm tuchis several inches off the seat. To my left, Marcy copied her, though with much more visible effort. On the other side, Celeste held her seat and peddled gently like she was on a bicycle built for two.

"Corrine," Marcy wheezed.

I huffed out a breath that sounded like an old man with emphysema and then pushed up. With great strain and struggle, my backside cleared the seat.

"And down," Norwegian goddess didn't alter her speed at all as she gently lowered herself to the seat.

Marcy and I plunked back down.

Two seconds later. "And up!"

"Can't she make up her mind?" I bitched and struggled to elevate again.

"Less griping more work," Marcy huffed.

"I need to tinkle." My mother got down and sashayed toward the ladies' room under the withering stares of the laboring cyclists.

"Dig deep," the instructor leaned forward and peddled as though she was on the final set of the Tour de France and she was neck and neck with Lance Armstrong. "Find your center of power."

"I left my center of power in the nightstand between the latest Jenna McCormick novel and a bottle of KY."

Marcy was too busy sweating and panting to laugh.

See, exercise really did suck out all the joy in life.

An excruciating amount of time later I stumbled from Marcy's car with Celeste traipsing along behind me.

I dropped my keys. "If I bend down to get them I'm pretty sure I won't be getting back up again."

"Don't be so dramatic," my mother said.

"I learned it from watching you."

"Oh, for heaven's sake." She bent and scooped like it was no BFD then held open the door.

On watery legs, I stumbled back into my bungalow and face-planted on the couch.

"You shouldn't have overdone it." Celeste clucked her tongue at me. "Not at your age."

"How's the house hunt coming?" I grumbled.

Two minutes and forty-three seconds later Luke and Logan came in. I know, since I watched Felix the Cat's second hand the entire time.

"What the hell happened to you?" the Dark Prince leaned on the back of the couch to study me.

"Spin class happened," I muttered into the couch cushions.

"You went to the gym?" Luke went to the backdoor to let Sasquatch out. "On purpose?"

"Marcy's going through something. And apparently, girl code demands I go through swamp crotch hell along with her."

"Looks like you hit a few buoys along the way." The Dark Prince was having way too much fun.

I thought about flipping him the bird but that would require movement and I wasn't ready to do anything so drastic.

"You better shake it off. We have all those rentals with twenty-four-hour inspections due." Logan's tone was full of amusement. "Plus, that inventory to finish."

I whimpered.

"Come on, hot stuff. You'll feel better after a shower." The Dark Prince grabbed me by one arm and levered me upright. "At least until the muscle soreness sets in."

He helped me stumble into the bedroom and propped my back up against the bathroom wall, while keeping a hand on me. "If I let go are you going to slide to the floor?"

I thought about it for a beat. "Probably."

He chuckled. "Never a dull moment, Jackie."

"Glad to provide entertainment." My tone was snide.

He leaned over and turned on the water in the shower. When he turned back to me, I saw his dark blue eyes were hot.

"Out," I lifted my hand to point. It only made it halfway up before flopping against my thigh like a dead trout.

He fingered the spaghetti strap on my tank top. "Maybe I should stay."

"Logan," I growled his name.

"If I leave, you'll probably curl up in the fetal position at the bottom of the tub. You might drown. More than a third of all household injuries happen in the bathroom."

"I'm not eighty." I just felt like it at the moment.

His fingertips trailed down my arm and then he laced his hands through mine. "Jackie, I want you."

I searched his face. "Now isn't—"

He cut me off with a searing kiss. His body pressed into mine, demonstrating the physical proof to back up his words. *Behold, exhibit A.*

Logan's heat, his need, scorched me way deep down until I was in danger of melting into a needy puddle on the floor.

He pulled back, rested his forehead to mine. "I know it isn't a good time. I know there are other people, other feelings to consider here. But I need you to know that I'm ready for more. Are you?"

"Now?" I squeaked.

The skin around his eyes crinkled with amusement, probably to my panic. "No. But soon."

"Soon," I repeated the word automatically, a little lost in his scent. Everything about him captivated me. Enthralled me. Beguiled me.

Scared me. "How soon is soon?"

His grin spread. "How about tomorrow night?"

My teeth sank into my lower lip. "That's soon."

His thumb traced along the small indents I'd made. "Come over about six. I'll make us dinner."

Oh, the man was temptation wrapped in desire and topped with a healthy dollop of sin. He knew I couldn't resist a home-cooked meal. Or anything else he had on the menu.

I cleared my throat. "We're wasting water."

"I'll wait in there." He stepped back and chucked his thumb in the direction of my bedroom a devilish gleam in his blue eyes. "Maybe go through your lingerie drawer."

"Pretty sure nothing I own will fit you." I sniped and shut the door in his laughing face.

Terror and desire were an odd combination. I stared at my sweaty, wide-eyed reflection and mouthed one damning word. *Soon.*

---

"THIS IS GONNA BE one of those days, isn't it?" Luke grumbled as he loaded our gear into the truck.

Since we'd started Damaged Goods, the Big Black Truck had been converted into a rolling office. There were the tools of my trade—extra pens, business cards, forms, and clipboards all neatly contained in a file box in the back seat. Luke kept a toolkit and then there were the flexicuffs, flashlights, pepper spray, body armor, taser, fire extinguisher, and extra ammunition for the Parker brothers' sidearms. Plus a change of clothes for each of us in case shit got real.

We'd needed everything we carted around at least once.

"Try to think positively," I muttered while checking my stash of pens. "Maybe no one will shoot at us today."

Luke made a face. "Jackie, only two tenants opened their doors to us on Thursday. We had to post eighteen twenty-four hour notices. Something is rotten in Denmark."

I wanted to say that it was a weekday and that people were probably at work. However, the majority of the people we were visiting in Sunnyvale were on public assistance. If they could have afforded better digs than this particular dump, they would have been gone in a red-hot Miami minute.

Logan jogged out of the house, Sasquatch on her leash beside him. She was a sweetheart most of the time but we'd taken to bringing her along on certain jobs. For one thing, she was huge and imposing and could take down any other canine threat as well as most human ones.

"What about Corrine?" I looked at Logan over my sunglasses.

"She's staying with one of her college sorority sisters through the weekend." He patted the backseat and the big dog scrambled up into the truck, eager for an adventure. "Luke and I dropped her off this morning."

Since it was before my disastrous spin class, it must have been early. "You're sure she'll be okay?"

"Relax, Ace. We've got it handled." Luke got behind the wheel. "If she needs anything, she'll call one of us."

I thought about his words as we drove into Wynwood. "Luke, do you know what the big secret is about Corrine?"

Logan frowned over at his brother, who nodded. "Since I talk to her, yes."

"You talk to her since when?"

Luke shrugged. "I stayed with her while you two were hiding out after the last disaster." He sent me an indecipherable look in the rearview mirror.

"What?" I asked.

"What?" He shot back.

Well, then okay. I wondered if maybe Luke and Corrine were involved. Like making the beast with two backs involved. As far as I knew, Luke hadn't dated since we'd split up, but I sort of assumed he'd been shtupping someone. Guys didn't need a reason to have sex, just a place. And slipping next door was certainly discreet.

I thought about the change in him over the last several weeks. At first, he'd been against my dating Logan and I'd promised to keep my distance for the sake of the respect that still existed between us. Then, when he met up with us in the Keys, he'd admitted that he had a change of heart. In retrospect, his attitude adjustment had been abrupt. And Corrine had been camped out in Logan's place by then. The girl next door, on the run from her big bad ex. It was just the sort of tale to snare my softhearted ex-husband, the hero.

I scratched Sasquatch behind the ears. What if it was more than sex? Cripes, that would be awkward, considering how we'd all begun. I wasn't being fair to Corrine. Deep down I knew it. Hell, I didn't even know the woman. But first impressions are strong. My first impression of her was being introduced to her as Logan's fiancée after he'd been gone for several months. A ruse the Dark Prince had concocted to make me jealous and admit that I wanted him for myself. It had worked.

I'd forgiven Logan for the deception. After all, the man had borne witness to my marriage to his brother for a decade. He deserved to know how much I wanted him. But I'd felt foolish and stupid and needed someone to blame. Someone who'd been in on it. Corrine was leaving Miami as soon as the paperwork came through. Logan had said so. Whatever her involvement was with Luke, it was short term.

At least I hoped that was the case.

We drove in silence until the Big Black Truck bumped into the crappy parking lot outside of the Sunnyvale complex. The asphalt had seen better days and was pitted and scarred from years of neglect. Weeds abounded. Standing water from crappy drainage drew bugs in every size and shape. Best of all, the place smelled like a combination of a dumpster outside a seafood restaurant and a bus station urinal.

"This place is depressing," the Dark Prince muttered and then popped his door. "Who would want to live here?"

"Have you heard about the housing crisis in Miami?" I held onto Sasquatch's harness as we slid down from the truck. "More people than there are places for them to live."

Miami's number one export was its own real estate.

People from other countries paid a pretty penny to snag waterfront views on South Beach or anywhere else where you could even smell the sea breeze. The rest of us got squished inland like an accordion between the tourists, whose money we desperately needed, and the Everglades. Land was one of those things you just couldn't pick up at the local Walmart.

I did my best to keep the dog from slurping out of a stagnant puddle while Luke and Logan debated what they would need going in. The apartment complex held twenty units in a two-story horseshoe shape around a pool that was the color of pea soup. Beer and soda cans floated in its murky depths and refuse littered the cracked concrete. The fourth side held the giant dumpster, the smaller recycling container, and the utility closet.

"It looks even worse than it did on Thursday. Split up or stay together?" I asked as we approached the skanky pool

"We should stick together," Luke said.

"Unless you want to wait in the truck," Logan added in a hopeful tone.

Part of me kinda did. My job was paperwork and I had done it. This complex was a heap and only the truly desperate lived here. With the twenty-four hours up, legally we could use the master set of keys the owner provided us and let ourselves in. That didn't mean the denizens would be happy to see us.

Above us, a curtain was pulled slightly aside as someone watched our approach. "And leave you two to kick down doors and bust heads without me?"

"You could take the truck," Luke suggested. "Don't you need to get to the courthouse to file for Green's eviction?"

I put one hand on my hips. "Okay, what the hell is going on? You two haven't been this riddled with protective nuttiness since you thought I was pregnant."

Logan cut Luke a glance.

"It's possible," Luke spoke slowly, "That we're dealing with gang activity."

I stared at him for a beat. "What makes you think that?"

Logan scratched at his stubbled chin. "The lack of people who opened the door for a start, plus the shitty conditions. Standards like this usually mean rent being withheld and complaints filed but our owner has had none of that."

"Gangs sometimes move into a place like this, already rundown and take over," Luke added. "And they are more likely to resort to violence."

I blew out a sigh. "If that's the case, you need me here to call the police."

Logan shook his head. "Told you she'd be stubborn."

"I'm not being stubborn," I lifted my chin, maybe being a *skosh* stubborn. "Come on. Gang or no, we have a job to do."

Our inspection was for unauthorized changes to the property. The mess by the pool would definitely count as one, but we'd have to ask a few questions and find out exactly which tenant was responsible for the party.

Luke had his hand raised to knock on the door to the first unit when we heard the scream.

"Which unit?" Logan's head whipped back and forth.

"Oh, God!" The voice was definitely female.

"Next door," I pointed. "With the open window."

Logan was closer. He pounded on the door. "Ma'am? We're from property management. Are you all right?"

Another wordless scream.

Luke was fumbling with keys, trying to find the right one. Sasquatch's ears were pinned back to her head and she whined.

"I'm going in." The Dark Prince balanced on his good leg.

"No, wait!" I reached for him, having picked up a particular note in that last cry that made me think the tenant wasn't in imminent mortal peril.

But it was too late. Logan's size twelve motorcycle boot landed just to the left of the cheap brass doorknob with the force of a ninety mile an hour car crash. The flimsy lock didn't stand a chance and neither did the door frame, which splintered as it gave way.

Inside the apartment, a topless woman with breasts the size and shape of watermelons was reverse cowgirl on a man half her size with skin about six shades lighter. She screamed, this time for real and scrambled off him. He gave a strangled yell as she connected with some of the sensitive bits in a less than tender dismount.

"Get the hell out!" The woman didn't bother with clothes, just plucked up a couch cushion to cover the ripe produce. "This here is a private party. What the hell do you think you're doing?"

"I'm sorry," Logan said. "We heard a scream."

"Fool. Can't you tell the difference 'atween a little after-noon delight and a cry for help?"

"We thought someone was hurt," Luke was trying—and failing—to keep a straight face.

"Not until you all showed up." She fumed.

The man groaned from his fetal position on the bed.

The woman plucked up another couch cushion and started beating at the Dark Prince with it. *Whap.* "And look what you gone and done to my door. Now, who the hell is gonna fix that?" *whap.*

"Ma'am," Logan began but she *whapped* him again. Not that I blamed her, I'd give him a whack too if he ma'amed me.

I took advantage of her distraction to assess the condition of the apartment. No obvious structural changes at first glance. The purple dress on the floor was pleather, with lipstick-red fuck-me boots. The guy's expensive charcoal suit was laid carefully over a chair. A pair of fifties sat on the countertop. Hmmm.

"You can't just be barging in here to interrupt my business," she bitched and continued to hit him.

*Whap whap whap.* Technically speaking, that was assault but it wasn't as if we were going to call the cops because Logan was losing a naked pillow fight.

I shuffled through papers until I found the lease for this unit. "Are you Ms. Diedre Plant?"

"And what's it to you?" Ms. Plant rounded on me.

I offered an easy smile pretending we weren't up to our eyeballs in this mess. "Ms. Plant, I'm sorry about the intrusion, but we work for your landlord. Did you get our notice of inspection? I taped it to your door a few days ago. It gives us the right to ascertain the condition of your apartment."

"It don't give you the right to break in the damn door!"

"We'll fix the door," I soothed. "Sir? Do you need help? Logan, check him make sure nothing's broken."

"I'm fine." Diedre's boy toy had crawled out of her round platform bed and was moving toward his pants.

Seen upright, I could swear there was something familiar about him.

"Should we drive you to the hospital Mr...?" Luke trailed off.

"No, I'll be okay, really." Pants on, he plucked up his shoes and socks, shirt, tie and limped out the door with his jacket over his face, obviously not wanting to be seen. Our tenant removed herself to the bathroom.

"That's Councilman Barry Young," Logan muttered in my ear. "I remember all the commercials last election cycle. You think she's a pro?"

Considering he was a politician—I'd bet my left boob on it. "You guys start with the door. I'll talk to her."

"I think I have what I need in the truck." Luke made Sasquatch sit and then headed back to the lot.

I turned to the Dark Prince. "You better get out before she comes back out and hits you with something more solid than a couch cushion."

"I don't want to leave you alone in here. What if she's gone to get a weapon?"

"From the bathroom?" I raised a brow. "She won't talk if she sees you. The door is open, you'll be right here in case she goes bananas."

He gave me that look, the one that said he didn't like it but since we were out of options, he would have to suck it up and deal.

"Just try not to piss her off," he mumbled then left.

Diedre Plant's lease said she worked at the local Publix part-time as a cashier. She'd lived in the unit for about three years. No complaints from neighbors about excessive foot traffic or loud noises. Then again, this was the kind of place where people tended to keep to themselves out of self-preservation.

Diedre emerged from the bathroom wearing a too-small towel that didn't provide much more coverage than the couch cushions. "You still here?"

"I was just wondering how long you've been bringing Johns back here." I nodded to the bed.

"I don't bring all of them here, just the important ones." She plucked her fifties off the counter. "It's not like I can just do it in an alley with a famous face."

Bingo. "Yeah, see here's the thing. Prostitution is illegal in Dade County. When you bring your dates here, you're operating an unlicensed business out of a residential area and breaking the law, both of which are violations of your lease. You've gotta stop."

She narrowed her eyes at me. "You a cop?"

I shook my head. "No, I told you, I work for the landlord. Listen, I'm going to issue you a five-day notice to cure or quit. That means you have five days to stop bringing your work home with you. If we catch you with another customer here, we'll have to move forward with the eviction process."

She narrowed her eyes on me. "I could squish you like a bug."

"True, but you don't want to do that. You seem like a hard-working woman. Just conduct your business elsewhere and we won't have to get the courts involved."

It was a dirty trick, but hopefully I got my message through.

"Have a nice day, Ms. Plant."

She flipped me off.

I stepped out past where Luke was prying up the broken door trim with a crowbar and out into the steamy Florida sunshine. "That's three down, seventeen to go."

Sirens sounded in the distance as I filled out the cure or quit notice for our tenant. Luke finished with the door and then got to his feet. "Did either of you call the cops?"

"No," Logan shook his head while I asked, "Why do you ask?"

Luke gestured with a screwdriver. "Because they're pulling into the parking lot."

Crap, there was no way the cops showing up was going to make the day any better.

"Logan Parker?" One asked. I was shocked to see his partner draw her sidearm.

The Dark Prince looked from the officer to the weapon that was trained on him. I could only imagine what he was feeling, what with having been shot a few weeks ago. "That's me."

"Turn around and put your hands on the side of the building."

Logan complied even as I stepped forward. "What is this about?"

The taller officer, the one without the weapon moved forward, securing Logan's sidearm from his holster. The other had handcuffs at the ready. Ignoring my outrage, he started Miranding Logan. "You have the right to remain silent. Anything you say can be used against you in a court of law. You have the right to an attorney. If you can not afford an attorney one will be provided for you. Do you understand these rights?"

"Yes," Logan met and held my gaze.

"No," I started forward. "What the hell is going on?"

Luke gripped my arm, hauling me to the side. "Call Vasquez."

My phone was already out, the Miami Sargent's number on my top five speed dials. Dismay filled me as the cops perp-walked my significant other to the car.

"I was wondering when I'd hear from you," Vasquez answered, his thick Latin accent filling my ear.

"Do you know why Logan is under arrest?"

"An unidentified tip in an open homicide investigation said we'd find a murder weapon in Logan's house. We did and his fingerprints were all over it."

## 5

"I don't understand," I said for probably the fiftieth time.

Sargent Enrique Vasquez sighed. He was a handsome man with the kind of long dark eyelashes a girl would give an ovary to obtain. Combined with his café au lait skin tone and typical brooding countenance he was what I liked to think of as a hawt cop. And his crush on Logan Parker should have been more than enough to get me a few answers.

"Logan wouldn't kill anybody. You know that. I know that."

Vasquez raised a perfectly sculpted eyebrow. I wondered if he had them waxed. Fixating on the Sargent's grooming habits seemed safer than dwelling on the matter at hand.

Namely one Logan Parker arrested for murder.

"I told you," Vasquez sighed again." My hands are tied. Logan will have to go before a judge and have bail set before you can see him. Only legal counsel is permitted in."

Luke was outside burning through favors and trying to find us a criminal defense attorney. And here I thought that the scabby apartment complex was going to be the worst part of my day.

"I told you he ran when he recognized the guy, right?" I was fairly sure it had come up but damn it all, I wanted to make sure that Vasquez had all the facts. Even if he insisted that he couldn't help us."

"Jackie, just go home. The DA is pushing for a swift bail hearing. I will call you when I hear anything."

"That's good, right?" My time in the courthouse was usually spent futzing around with paperwork. Criminal trials were not in my wheelhouse.

Vasquez hesitated. "Not likely. I think they are going to argue that Logan is a flight risk."

"What?" I slammed my hands down on the crappy chair and pushed myself onto my feet. I don't know why, other than the instinct not to accept that sort of news sitting down. "Why on earth would they think he is a flight risk?"

"Probably because of all the time he has spent traveling abroad. He could disappear with about the same amount of effort you or I would expend getting a to-go lunch," Vasquez intoned. "He spent four months out of the last year overseas."

I blinked "He did?"

"Look, do you know where Logan keeps his passport? If you turn that into the court, it could go a long way to proving he isn't a flight risk."

I shook my head. Boy, was I ever a crappy girlfriend. The man knew my favorite kind of breakfast burrito and I didn't know how many months out of the past year he'd been abroad. "If you let me talk to him, I'm sure he'll tell me."

"That's between him and his lawyer." Vasquez rose as well and then headed out of his office. "I'm sorry, Jackie. My hands are tied. I promise I will call with any updates."

I blew out a breath and stomped out of the precinct. Luke

was perched against the Big Black Truck, his cell phone nestled in the crook of his shoulder.

"No, Mom. I'm sure you don't need to come down here. We'll take care of it."

My lips parted. Marge and Gerald Parker lived in Juniper where Gerald was recovering from recent heart surgery. The last thing they needed was to get worked up over what was going sideways in Miami.

"Okay, I will. Love you too. Bye." Luke hung up, looking exhausted. "Dad knows a few criminal defense attorneys, otherwise I wouldn't have called them."

I put my hand on his arm. "I know. Vasquez thinks the DA will want to deny bail because Logan is a flight risk."

I'd expected to see Luke react the same way I had a few moments ago. Disbelief, seasoned with a healthy dose of outrage. Instead, his expression turned grim. "He has the connections."

"Do you have any idea where he stashed his passport?" I asked as my teeth sink into my lower lip. "Vasquez said that turning that over might be a sign of good will for bail."

Luke frowned. "Maybe at his house?"

I sagged against the Big Black Truck. "Which is off-limits because the police have it taped off as a crime scene. That's what Vasquez meant about why the DA was pushing for a quick bail hearing not being a good thing. Without that passport, the judge will probably deny bail."

"Don't get yourself worked up about it, Ace." Luke put his hand on my shoulder. "The lawyer Dad recommended is on his way down here now. He'll be able to talk to Logan directly. We just need to wait."

"I'm not good at waiting," I grumbled. "You know that."

The corner of his mouth quirked up. "I do know that. Maybe we ought to review some paperwork, just to take your mind off things?"

I shook my head. There was no way I would be able to concentrate until the lawyer showed up and spoke to Logan.

I'd feel that much better if I could speak with Logan directly. Damn it, the sight of him being handcuffed was up there with my least favorite memories, right next to him being shot.

I closed my eyes and sucked in a lungful of humid Miami air. "Okay, let's think about this from a legal perspective. Someone killed Corrine's ex and the murder weapon was found in the house where she was staying. Why isn't she under arrest?"

"Because," Luke murmured. "Corrine didn't kill her husband."

"Neither did Logan." I almost growled. Clearly, Luke didn't want to imagine the woman I was now about 90 percent sure he had been boffing was capable of murder. "Okay, so let's say for argument's sake that you're right and I'm right and that neither Corrine or Logan killed the guy who was alive and well yesterday morning. That means someone else must have done it. Any suspects leap to mind?"

My ex eyed me warily. "Why are you asking me?"

"Because you know the situation better than I do. All I got out of Mr. Tall Dark and Stoic was that her ex was bad news. Bad enough that he was in the process of getting her a fake ID so she could hide from him." I frowned and thought over my phone conversation with Vasquez. "Sargent Vasquez said that an anonymous tip led them to Logan's bungalow. It has to be a setup."

Luke nodded thoughtfully. "So then the question becomes who would set up Logan and why?"

That was a question I had no way to answer.

A black BMW pulled into the space beside the Big Black Truck and a familiar form climbed out. "Are you Luke?" The attorney was a big man in his mid-fifties with that old-timey

59

southern charisma that lent itself to images of large houses with wraparound porches and tall glasses of sweet tea. His double-breasted gray suit was custom-tailored to fit his massive shoulders. His brown eyes sparkled behind rectangular spectacles and he carried a black briefcase.

When Luke nodded the lawyer extended a hand. "Call me Buck."

I'd seen him in action a few times, when my old boss, Stan the Stain, had crossed swords with him in court. Donald "Call me Buck" Buchanan, had bested him every time.

"Buck," Luke took the proffered hand and shook. "This is my wife, Jackie."

I shot him a glance, but didn't correct our relationship status. We had bigger fish to fry.

"Good to see you again, Miz Jackie." The attorney offered his hand to me. I took it and returned his smile and firm grip before asking what I needed to know. "Do you think you can help get Logan out?"

Buck nodded. "I will go talk to him right now. Give me your phone numbers and I'll call you when we have a bail hearing set."

It wasn't what I wanted but given the circumstances, it was probably the best we were going to get. I fished out a business card and handed it over to him.

He slipped it into his wallet and then headed up the steps and disappeared behind the double glass doors leading into the Miami police department.

"So now what, Ace? Work or go home and brood."

I knew what I wanted to do and I knew what I ought to do. Why could the two never meet? "Let's go tackle some more inventory."

"You got everything you need? Clipboard, inventory sheets? Tags? Sharpies?"

I nodded and then Luke opened the door and helped me

into the Big Black Truck. It felt odd, riding in Logan's usual spot. I tried not to imagine him locked in a cell, nervous and wondering what the hell we were doing to help. Especially when the answer was not nearly enough.

The leather seat was hot but not the burn the skin off the backs of your thighs kind of hot that was typical for mid-September. I flicked the air conditioner on high and then stared out the window, my thoughts a jumble.

The last thing I wanted to do was the damn inventory. At the same time, Buck didn't come cheap and while I knew Marge and Gerald would foot the bill, Logan prided himself on paying his own way through life. Even when he scrimped and scraped by.

We were very much alike that way.

"How many stamps does Logan have in his passport, if you had to guess?" I asked Luke.

"More than either of us," Luke braked for a red light and looked over at me. "What makes you ask?"

"Just something Vasquez said. That he could disappear if he wanted to very easily."

"You know he can do that though, Jackie. Think about all the times he's split without a word."

"But I mean that was disappearing from our immediate vicinity. Not falling off the face of the earth."

"I don't know what to tell you, Ace. Logan is his own man and has lived his own life."

He was right about that. I knew it. And deep down I just didn't like it.

Who was my Dark Prince when he wasn't in Miami with us?

And more to the point, was he capable of murder?

"WELL, THIS SUCKS." I gestured to the pain in the ass inventory. "Who the hell needs that many spare computer parts?"

I was starting to feel like the little mermaid trundling through gadgets and gismos, never mind the whose-its and whatsits.

"A tech guy?" Luke shrugged and dusted his hands off on his jeans. "I dunno, Ace. It all looked too dated to be of much use. Mostly landfill and scrap heap stuff."

Night had fallen in all its sticky glory and the no-see-ums were out and almost as ravenous as I was after eight hours in the stifling cargo container. The inventory was taking *for-freaking-ever*. Mostly because there was no cell reception in the cargo container and Luke and I alternated taking breaks so that we could check for any updates.

"The courts are probably closed for the night," Luke said on my fifth dejected trek back inside. "We can go home if you want."

I shook my head. The image of Logan spending the night in jail was driving me a little bit nuts. "No, I'd rather finish this."

We worked for several hours more, Luke calling out an item and brand name if it was available and me filling out the paperwork. The muscle soreness Logan had warned me about was beginning to set in by the time we locked up the cargo container and headed back to Coral Way.

It was a silent ride, both of us lost in our own thoughts.

Luke pulled up in front of the house and we both just sat there. My gaze shifted next door, to the yellow crime scene tape.

"Do you think he could have...?" I asked.

Luke turned to face me. "Are you asking if Logan is capable of killing someone?"

"No." I knew the answer to that and it wasn't the politically correct one.

"Here's the thing, Jackie. I've been turning this around in my head and if there's one thing I know about my brother, he isn't stupid. He would kill to save you or me, of that I have no doubt. But a murder where he uses his own gun and leaves it on his property for the police to find? Something doesn't add up."

I swallowed. "Then we need to talk to Corrine"

Luke's expression was pained. "Jackie, I don't think it will help Logan if you go try and track down a murderer. Let the police and the lawyers do their jobs."

"I hate being left in the dark," I grumbled.

He chucked me under the chin. "I know you do, Ace. But it's just one of those things."

He popped his door but I reached for his wrist. "One other thing. When you introduced me to the lawyer earlier, you called me your wife, not your ex or your business partner."

His brown eyes grew wary. "And?"

"And I'm wondering if that was just out of habit, you know, like a default. Or if maybe there's some reason that you didn't want the lawyer, who is your dad's friend, to hear you say we are divorced."

He blew out a breath and I knew.

"Damn it, Luke. You still haven't told your parents that we're divorced?"

"There's been a lot going on." His tone was defensive. "Dad's surgery and then Logan getting shot."

"We need to tell them." Dear God, why was this my life? What my poor mother-in-law would think of me. "Like now."

"If we call now, they are just going to assume it has something to do with Logan," Luke reasoned.

I grit my teeth together. "Tomorrow then. When Logan is out on bail."

He nodded slowly.

I thunked my head against the headrest. "Your mother is going to hate me."

"My mother thinks you hung the moon, Jackie. I wouldn't worry about it." He took my hand and squeezed. "I will tell them tomorrow. I promise. Come on, let's go inside and deal with your monkey."

I groaned and slid out of the truck. "He is gonna be uber pissed. Paper rock scissors for who lets him out."

"Hell no, I already agreed to do the parent phone call. You get the primate wrath." Luke unlocked the front door and flipped on the hall light.

Illuminating the chaos within.

The place was destroyed. Couch cushions shredded with the stuffing pulled out, Kitchen drawers yanked off the tracks and the contents dumped on the floor, furniture overturned.

Luke was saying something but I was in too much of a daze to understand him. "There's no way Abu could have done all this?"

From back in the bedroom I heard the spider monkey screaming.

"Call the police, tell them we've had a break-in." Luke gripped me by the arm and shoved me out of the house. "I'll go check on the animals."

A break-in. Holy hell, someone had broken into our house.

"Sasquatch. Where is Sasquatch?" I asked. The huge dog should have scared off any run of the mill burglar.

Unless they hurt her.

"The cops, Jackie," Luke snapped and then disappeared inside.

My hands shook as I dialed Vasquez directly.

"Jackie, I told you," He said as he picked up the phone. "There's nothing I can do for Lo—"

"Someone broke into our house." I cut him off.

"When?" Vasquez's tone changed immediately.

"I don't know. Luke and I were out all day." But we weren't the only ones who live here. "Celeste." I turned in a circle, hunting the street for Bessie Mae, my beat-up Barbie blue civic that Celeste drove.

"Where are you now?" There was a rustling sound as though Vasquez was pulling on clothes.

"Outside, on the front lawn. Luke went in to check on the animals."

"Stay where you are. I'll call it in and a patrol team will come by. I'll be there as soon as I can." He disconnected.

From inside I could see Luke, carrying Abu's habitat with the shrieking spider monkey within.

"I called Vasquez," I said as I unlatched the cage door. "Did you see Sasquatch?"

Luke shook his head. "No, I'm going back in to look."

"What if whoever did this is still in there?" I asked.

"What if Celeste is in there?" he countered.

I hesitated. "The car isn't here."

"Call her," Luke advised.

I dialed and waited it rang through to voicemail.

"Mom, it's me. Give me a call when you get this." I kept my voice even. The last thing I needed was for Celeste to start a downward spiral because of a B&E.

"At least take your sidearm." Luke and Logan both had concealed carry permits. It would be a pain in the ass when the cops showed but no way was I going to let him go into the house again unarmed.

Luke ran to the rear of the truck, to the gun safe. He tossed a Kevlar vest to me before donning his own. I could feel his sense of urgency, worried for my mom and my dog. The car not being here was a good sign but Sasquatch....

Armed and as protected as he could be, Luke bolted for the front of the house. A minute passed and then two. I shifted from foot to foot. Sensing my distress, Abu remained quiet in his cage. Sirens blared in the distance as the patrol car Vasquez had promised made their way to our location.

I wanted to call out to Luke. But that was stupid. If whoever had tossed the place was still within, I'd be making them aware of us.

The cops screeched to a stop beside the Big Black Truck and two uniforms emerged. I didn't recognize either of them.

"You Jackie Parker?" The taller of the two men said.

I nodded. "My ex-husband is inside checking for my mom and our dog. He is armed."

The shorter man swore and drew his own firearm. "Ma'am, please stay back."

I retreated from the front door several steps. Maybe encouraging Luke to go in hot after we called the cops had been a bad idea.

"Sir?" The taller officer had also drawn his weapon. "This is the police."

Luke emerged carrying what at first looked like an enormous rug.

On closer inspection, it proved to be Sasquatch.

"Is she—?" My hand flew to my mouth.

"She's breathing. I need to get her to the emergency vet though."

"Where is your weapon, Sir?"

He turned and presented the officers with his back. "My waistband."

After disarming him, the cops waved us away.

"I'm sure the house is empty," Luke grunted as he heaved Sasquatch into the back of the truck. "She was in the back bedroom, on your mother's bed. No blood or other signs of injury."

"Celeste?"

He shook his head.

"One of us should stay here," I said to Luke. "For the police."

It wasn't a question of which of us would leave. I wasn't strong enough to lift the heavy dog.

"I'll call as soon as I hear anything." Luke climbed behind the wheel and a moment later I watched as the Big Black Truck passed Enrique Vasquez's white SUV.

I wrapped my arms around myself to ward off the chill.

What a freaking day.

## 6

"You're sure that nothing is missing?" Vasquez asked as he helped me right the chairs and couch.

"Not that I've noticed."

Abu was sticking close, his little tail wrapped around my throat like a scarf and combing through my hair looking for bugs which I prayed he wouldn't find. Lice was about the only thing that could make this day worse.

The uniforms had left but Vasquez had insisted on staying until Luke and Celeste got back.

"If this was anyone else, I would tell you that there was no way this could be a coincidence, not with Logan sitting behind bars." Vasquez picked up the broken picture frame that had contained my and Luke's wedding photo. He plucked the photograph free of the shattered frame. "Since it's you, I'm going to ask who you've pissed off lately?"

"Gee, thanks." I held out the trash bag I was holding. "Get rid of that before you cut yourself and sue my ass for liability."

He snorted and dropped the frame into the bag, then handed me the photo.

My cell rang and I dropped the bag to pluck it out of my back pocket. "Luke?"

"She's going to be okay." He sounded as tired as I felt. "They tranquilized her but she's waking up. The vet had to flush it out of her system with an IV. They are going to keep her overnight but they expect her to make a full recovery."

"That's good news." My shoulders sagged a bit in relief. "Drive safe."

"Doggie's going to make it?" The Sargent asked.

I nodded and scratched Abu behind the neck. "Do you want some coffee?"

He sighed. "I guess sleep isn't happening tonight. Coffee would be good." He sagged down onto one of the bar stools while I went into the kitchen to make coffee. With the pot perking merrily away, I leaned back and surveyed the space.

Not too bad, all things considered. The couch was righted, the cushions flat but not completely decimated. Several shattered mugs and glasses from the kitchen the glass fronts on several of the cabinets had been shattered, but otherwise, the space looked normal.

"Do you think this was random?" I asked Vasquez.

He shook his head. "No. Between nothing being missing and the dog getting tranqued, I would say whoever broke in here did it intentionally."

"Why though?" I retrieved two of the undamaged mugs and the half and half from the fridge.

"Whoever it was, he knew you had a dog and didn't want to hurt it. The dog might be a message but my gut is telling me this was something else."

I'd had the same thought. "Like they were looking for something."

Vasquez tipped his head to the side. "Any idea what?"

I shook my head. "No, but dollars to doughnuts it's got something to do with Logan's case."

The front door opened. "Jackie."

"Mom," I ran to her and gripped her into a bear hug. "Thank God. Why didn't you answer when I called you?"

"I was at Pinky Bouffettes retirement party. My cell died." Celeste's crayoned eyebrows drew down. "What on earth happened here?"

"Someone broke in. Enrique and I have been doing our best to clean up."

The sergeant nodded to her. "Ma'am."

Celeste looked around. Her expression was dazed. "Someone broke in to your home?"

"That's the trouble with fixing the place up. People think you might have something worth stealing."

"That's not funny," Celeste looked at me. "Are you all right?"

I swallowed and nodded. "Yes, no permanent harm."

Other than the overwhelming invasion of personal space. Someone had been in here. Not just subtly looking for something. The destruction felt almost vindictive. They'd wanted us to know.

"But, but what did they take?"

I shook my head. "Nothing that we know of."

"You mean someone wanted to hurt you?" Her blue eyes went wide. "Do you know who it is?" My mother was working herself up to a full-tilt drama queen meltdown. I could see the wild thoughts happening behind her eyes. Shit, I knew better than to just blurt things out to her.

Vasquez hopped up. "Ma'am, do us a favor and check your room. We need to know if anything is missing."

"Of...of course." Celeste nodded as though in a trance and she stumbled down the hall.

"I'm impressed. You diffused her nicely."

"Not as impressed as I am that your mother knows someone named Pinky Bouffette."

I snorted, but the humor quickly evaporated. "Are we safe here?"

Vasquez didn't offer me any false reassurances. "I honestly can't say. There was no sign of breaking and entering. No scrapes around the locks, nothing broken or signs of forced entry. Either you forgot to lock up—"

"Which I never do," I stated. I'd been living on my own in a big city long enough to be sure of that tidbit.

"Or they had access to a key. Who has them?"

I ticked them off on my fingers. "Me, but mine is right here. Luke, but he had his on him. Celeste, we can check with her, but I'm fairly sure she's got it since she drove Bessie Mae home. The only other one who has access to a key is Logan."

Vasquez sat up straighter. "Does he have his key on him?"

I shook my head. "No, we took the truck to the job and he rode with us. He has a massive amount of keys and doesn't usually carry them around."

Vasquez held up a finger. "Let me make a few phone calls."

I nodded and went down the hall to check on Celeste.

She stood in the door to her room, tears tracking down her face. It wasn't trumped-up drama, but real genuine heartbreak that I read in her expression.

I put an arm around her shoulders. "You okay?"

She shook her head back and forth. "I'm scared."

"Luke will be home soon." I soothed. Though I had no idea where he would sleep, considering the couch had been gutted like a trout.

"It's not just this," Celeste turned to face me. "Ever since John died, I just don't feel safe. Like at any moment, someone could come along and hurt me. Or you."

A lump formed in my throat. Celeste had watched her significant other gunned down right in front of her. It still haunted my dreams too. "I know, Mama."

She smiled a little at that. "You haven't called me Mama in a long time."

I squeezed her a little. "I'll have to do it more often."

We stared at the clothes strewn across the floor for a moment in silence.

"Does it ever get better?" Celeste asked. "Does the feeling like it could all be ripped away from you at any moment ever stop?"

I wanted to tell her yes, of course it did. But that would be a disservice to her heartfelt confession.

"You adjust," I said and let her go to bend down to pick up a pretty floral skirt. "It becomes part of the background. Like ugly wallpaper in the bathroom that you're too busy to do anything about. It's just part of the scenery. You can ignore it."

She righted a lamp that had been tipped over. "Until the next thing happens."

"Yeah," my voice was hoarse. "Until the other shoe drops."

---

I woke up to a face full of monkey butt. Not all that unusual as Abu tended to snuggle up on my pillow during the night. What was a little different than the norm was that Celeste snored from my other side. I'd spent the night in my mother's room so Luke could get a decent night sleep in the master bedroom. Quietly as I could, I displaced Abu. He let out a sleepy chirp of inquiry, but then settled back into his standard early morning coma.

The air conditioning was cranking even with the sun barely above the horizon. I shuffled into the hall bathroom, used the facilities and then went to the coffee pot to start a fresh batch of liquid life. Good thing the intruders hadn't messed with Mr. Coffee. I would have had to cut a bitch.

72

I might anyway. What sort of asshole tranquilizes a dog?

While the coffee perked I went over to my cellphone and scrolled through. There was a text from Vasquez, that had come in after he'd left last night.

*Logan's key is missing.*

That was it. The whole message. I cracked my knuckles as I debated what to do next.

The phone rang in my hands. The number was local but unfamiliar. I swiped the green icon and answered it. "Hello?"

"Ms. Parker? This is Donald Buchanan."

I gripped the phone tighter and skipped the pleasantries. "Do you have some news for me?"

"I do. Logan's bail hearing is set for ten this morning. Do you think you can produce his passport by then? He says that you would know where it is."

I made a frustrated sound in the back of my throat. "Honestly, I have no idea where it is. But we'll be there either way. How is he?"

"Holding up," Buck said. "I'll try to get in to see Mr. Parker again to ask about the passport. I'll see you in court."

I said goodbye and stared at Felix. It was seven-thirty now. I had exactly two hours and some change to figure out where the hell Logan stashed his passport and get it and my happy ass to the courthouse. Damn it, why hadn't he given detailed instructions to his lawyer?

Luke came out of the bedroom, his hair rumpled, his shirt untucked. "Was that Buck?"

I nodded. "Logan told him I would know where his passport was. Why would he say that?"

Luke scratched his chin stubble. "Because he thinks you do know. It can't be in his house. He knows that's taped off for a crime scene and he wouldn't want you to risk going in there."

I leaned back against the counter. "Then where the hell else would it be?"

"Safety deposit box?" Luke suggested. "Did he ever give you a key?"

I shook my head. Damn the Dark Prince and his cryptic hide. "The only place I can imagine is the truck."

Luke slid his feet into sneakers and plucked up his keys. "You get dressed while I start the search."

I nodded and padded toward the bedroom. "Damn you, Logan Parker." Why did everything always need to be so difficult with him?

I made my way into the bathroom and then paused to stare at my reflection in the mirror. Logan had been right. The muscle aches were much much worse. I popped open the medicine cabinet hunting for a pain reliever.

And stared at the faux leather booklet situated right behind it. A passport.

"What the hell?" I murmured. I nudged the pain killer aside and reached for the booklet. My hand shook as I extracted the thing from behind the white and red bottle and then flipped through it. Countries I'd heard of and ones I hadn't. So many stamps. My breath caught as I spotted the image of a somewhat younger Logan, blue eyes blazing out at me. Why on earth would Logan have stashed his passport in my medicine cabinet?

*Because* that insidious little voice in my mind whispered. *He knew you were going to need it.*

"But why, self with all the answers, the medicine cabinet?" I mumbled to my reflection."

*Because he knew you would go looking for pain reliever this morning.*

I swallowed and took a breath. "Now is not the time to freak the hell out. There has to be a sensible explanation as to why Logan would stash his passport in my medicine cabinet."

But how could he have known he was going to need it unless…?

No. I slammed the door on that train of thought. No freaking way was I going to start jumping to conclusions about what Logan did or didn't do. Not until I talked to him.

I let out a breath and headed back into the bedroom, threw open the window and called out to Luke. He poked his head out of the truck window. "What's up, Ace?"

I gestured him over. "I found it."

He looked surprised. "The passport you mean? How?"

"It was in the medicine cabinet behind the OTC medication," I explained how Logan had known I was going to need the pain killer.

"But why would he do that?" Luke said. "It doesn't make any sense."

"I don't know." My gaze darted down the street. Cars drove by, the normal morning commute in full swing. Pedestrians strolled by and all the small hairs rose along the nape of my neck. "I don't think it's a coincidence that someone tossed our house yesterday. I think they were looking for this."

Luke held my gaze for a long moment. "I don't like this, Jackie. If Logan wanted you to hang on to his passport why not just hand it to you and ask you to keep it for him?"

I swallowed. "Because I would ask why and he didn't want to tell me." And I would have kept at him until he gave me an answer.

We stared at each other for a long moment.

"Let's not jump to conclusions," Luke said at last. "We'll get Logan out on bail and then grill his ass like a T-Bone about exactly what the hell is going on."

I let out a slow breath and then nodded. "It's the best plan we've got."

And that wasn't saying much.

"BAIL IS SET at one million dollars." The judged banged the gavel.

My lips parted at the number.

There was murmuring in the courtroom. Clearly, I wasn't the only one stunned by the figure. The DA had made a few salient points, like that Logan had military training and had a connection with the victim's wife who hadn't appeared. Buck had been just as persuasive though, citing that Logan Parker owned a property management business and had family in the area, was a trained medic and was willing to turn over his passport.

I looked to where Logan sat wearing a suit that was too tight at the shoulders. It was better than an orange jumpsuit, but still, he looked...wrong sitting up there next to Buck.

I'd seen evil up close. I knew what it looked like. Logan didn't belong there.

He didn't react as the officer came forward to put the cuffs back on him. He hadn't looked over at me once since he'd come in. I winced when he leaned heavily on the back of his chair to take the weight slightly off his bad leg.

"That's outrageous. Even though they have his passport?" I seethed.

Luke made a patting motion. "It's okay. Mom and Dad can post a bail bond. Logan won't run."

I released a breath. "Right. I guess you ought to call them."

Luke slipped out of his seat. I watched as Buck packed up his files and then hurried to catch up with him. He opened the door for me and ushered me out of the courtroom.

"What happens now?" I asked the attorney.

"Now I take what Mr. Parker has told me and start building a plausible defense case."

"Luke is arranging for the bond. Is there anything I should be doing?" I asked, shifting my weight from foot to foot. "To help I mean."

But the lawyer shook his head. "Right now, the best thing you can do is keep living your life. Mr. Parker specified that he did not want you involved with this case."

I blinked at him. "What?"

He held up his hands. "His exact words were 'make sure Jackie doesn't get dragged into this'."

I stood there, stunned. He wasn't serious. Like I was just supposed to go on about my day while my significant other, the man I loved and who claimed to love me, was on trial for murder in the first?

God, if any of them knew he'd stashed his passport in my medicine cabinet, words like premeditation would be tossed around like confetti.

I walked down the courthouse steps and over to where the Big Black Truck idled with the engine on. Luke was on the phone and I waited for him to gesture me inside.

"No, Mom. I still don't think you need to come here." Luke rolled his eyes toward the roof of the truck. "You're better off where you are. I'll keep you posted. Okay. Okay. I love you too. Bye."

He hung up the phone and scowled at me. "What's wrong?"

"Logan's attorney just told me that Logan wants me to stay out of this." I grumped and fastened my seatbelt.

"He's worried about you," Luke said and shifted the truck into gear. "He doesn't want you to get hurt."

My heart hurt. I guess that didn't count though. "Does he know about the break-in?"

"No, but I told Buck about it. He said he was going to touch base with Sargent Vasquez."

"So where to now?"

"Mom said she was going to wire us the money for the bail. After we pick it up we'll find a bail bondsman and get Logan out of lock-up."

"And then maybe we'll get some answers," I grumbled.

Luke blew out a breath. "Jackie, I know you hate secrets, even if they are for your own good."

I bared my teeth at him in a snarly expression. "Hate is too mild a word. I detest when you and your idiot brother decide what is best for me and leave me in the dark. I'm involved with both of you."

He looked over at me.

"Financially speaking," I added. "Because of the business."

"Right."

The more I thought about it, the more my temper flared. Logan hid his damn passport in my home without my knowledge. And someone had broken in.

Someone who didn't want Logan to be released on bail.

"Take me home," I snapped at Luke.

He glanced over at me, his expression wary.

I shut my eyes. "Sorry. Would you please take me home while you deal with springing your brother from lockup?"

"If that's what you want."

What I wanted were some damn answers. I felt impotent, out of my depth. "Yeah, I think so."

Luke made a U-turn and headed back towards our neighborhood.

I stomped up the steps and headed inside. It was too quiet without Sasquatch's nails clicking on the bamboo. Tears filled my eyes but I ruthlessly brushed them away.

Celeste's bedroom was empty. Out tiny-house hunting again probably. I headed into the master where Abu screamed from inside his cage in the middle of tossing feces at the wall behind my dresser.

"You are such a pain in my ass," I told the monkey. From past experience, I knew that I'd have to haul the entire enclosure into the bathroom before I let him out. "You don't think I have enough shit to deal with?"

He chittered merrily, obviously having no problem with the poopy suit or my black mood.

I lugged the cage into the bathroom and got the water running. An hour later I had a clean monkey, a freshly scrubbed tub and had just finished wiping down the walls when the front door opened.

"That was fast," I said as Luke entered the bathroom.

He shrugged. "Not much I can do until the bondsman calls me. You feeling better?"

"Oddly yes. It's amazing how much better I feel after bathing my monkey."

Luke smirked. "That sounds dirty as sin."

"Not half as dirty as Abu was." I pointed to where the spoiled little fiend was watching a cooking competition on the flat sofa cushions. "So now what?"

"Now, we tackle some paperwork."

"Fun," I grumbled.

"It's either that or go back to inventory."

It was one hundred and ten degrees in the shade. No way did I want to spend the afternoon sweltering inside a cargo container full of industrial flotsam. "Paperwork it is."

I sat in my usual spot behind the desk while Luke sifted through invoices. I scrolled through my music library and found some eighties hard rock which was our standard listening while doing the billing soundtrack.

Luke sang along, off-key and completely unself-conscious.

I stood up to stretch my back. "I like this,"

"Like what?" He asked, gaze still fixed on the case file he was reading.

"That the two of us can hang out like this." I smiled. "You've always been my guiding star."

I'd been expecting a return grin. What I got instead was a sheepish expression. Luke set down the folder and sighed. "Jackie, there's something I need to tell you."

Well, that didn't sound good. At all. "Are you hooking up with Corrine?"

His jaw dropped. "Are you kidding?"

"What? It's a valid question. You said you had spent some time with her."

"Yeah as in coffee and a few sit-coms. Jesus Jackie, is that really what you think of me, that I would take advantage of a woman who was on the run from her ex?"

I cracked my knuckles. "When you say it like that it sounds bad."

He made a disgusted noise in the back of his throat.

"Luke, I'm not accusing you of anything, really. It's just that you seemed different lately, in a good way. More at peace. You said you'd been spending time with Corrine, so I put two and two together—"

"And came up with sixty-nine?"

I noticed he hadn't denied it. "So, are you? Seeing her?"

"I'm not dating Corrine."

I relaxed a bit a moment before he added, "But I have been sort of seeing someone else."

"Ha," I ignored the little pang in my heart and instead plastered a triumphant grin across my face. "I knew something was different. Anyone I know? How long have you been involved? Where did you meet?"

Luke shifted his gaze away. "I'm not ready to play twenty questions with you. It's...strange."

*As strange as me dating your brother?* The question sat on the tip of my tongue and I clamped my teeth over it before it could escape. Luke and I were in a fairly decent place, mostly because we'd been as open and honest with one another as we could be. There hadn't been any games between us. We respected one another's boundaries. He was asking me to back off, telling me he wasn't ready to talk openly about a potential new relationship. Though my curiosity was on par with my hunger, I needed to respect the line he'd drawn in the proverbial sand.

"Okay, I hear you. But I just want to make sure you know that you can talk to me. We're still friends, right?"

He smiled and nodded. "Right. So tell me why you dislike Corrine."

My eye twitched. "Who says I do?"

"Let's see," he began ticking reasons off on his fingers. "You're defensive every time her name is brought up. You didn't want to lend her Sasquatch, and you didn't go out of your way to befriend her the way you do with every other person."

My phone rang, Sargent Vasquez's handsome face illuminating the screen. "I should get this."

"You are so busted," Luke's even white teeth flashed.

I rolled my eyes heavenward and then answered. "Jackie's house of humiliation. Can I tell you about our two-for-one special?"

Luke snorted.

"Maybe later," Vasquez drawled in his Cuban-American accent. "I just wanted you to know that I have been trying to get in touch with Corrine."

My left eye twitched and I put a hand to it. "And?"

"And according to Logan's statement he says he and Luke dropped her off early yesterday morning at her friend's house in Tampa. The friend, Becky, corroborates."

"That's what they told me." I pressed my palm into my eye socket wondering if he would get to the point.

"She's not there now," Vasquez said.

"You're sure?" I sat up straighter.

"Positive. The friend said she went out for a jog around sunset last night and never came home."

## 7

I sat in the back of the Big Black Truck, my usual position as I waited to catch sight of Logan. Luke and I hadn't spoken since the lawyer called to confirm that the bond had been posted and Logan was free to come home.

Until trial of course.

Many people streamed in and out of the police station but I saw none of them. My mind was whirling. Logan had hidden his passport in my medicine cabinet. A few hours after that he'd been arrested and a few hours after that Corrine had gone missing and someone had broken into our apartment.

On the seat beside me, Abu chirped. I'd decided that instead of locking him up again I would bring him along with us. After all, this was supposed to be a short trip, pick up the Dark Prince and then bring him home and nail his ass to the wall.

Metaphorically.

What the hell was taking so long? I worked a hangnail on my thumb and wondered where the hell Corrine was. Dead? Or on the run after killing her husband and framing Logan for it? Had she been the one to toss our house, looking for the passport? She had access to his keys, being his tenant and all.

The problem was that I was worried Luke was right. That I was letting my jealousy and dislike of Corrine color my judgment. Surely Logan would have some idea of who had killed the man we'd spotted in Miami Beach less than two days ago? He would have figured Corrine would be the number one suspect. Significant others always were in murder investigations.

Finally. I saw the Parker brothers heading down the steps. Logan wore the same jeans and black t-shirt he'd been wearing when the police picked him up. Luke wearing a white t-shirt looked like his photo negative. I let out a sigh of relief as I saw them. Logan wore his reflective sunglasses and the windows of the Big Black Truck were heavily tinted.

I could still sense his gaze on me.

Abu screeched as he approached the door and climbed in. I frowned as I saw Luke staring down at his phone instead of taking his usual spot behind the wheel. "What the hell is he doing, updating his Instagram? Just sprung my broheim hashtag #crimedoesntpaykids hashtag #mugshotMondays.

"He's giving us a minute. I asked him to." The Dark Prince turned in his seat to face me.

"Why?" I folded my arms over my breasts and glared at him. "Want to tell me to stay out of the investigation some more?"

A muscle jumped in his jaw. "That's for your own well-being."

"You honestly think I don't know that?" If I had been able to reach him I would have slugged him. Big dumb jerk.

"Look, this situation is complicated," he began. "And it isn't my story to tell."

My blood boiled and I held up a hand. "You know what? I

don't want your explanations. You must know something, otherwise, you wouldn't have stashed your passport in my medicine cabinet."

"I'm sorry about that," he murmured. "I didn't want it to be a thing but I thought just in case."

"So you knew someone would come looking for it? That my house, that was just finished a few days ago, would be trashed?"

He paled beneath his tan. "What?"

So no one had told him. "Someone showed up while Luke and I were on the job yesterday and tossed the bungalow."

His head shook back and forth. "It might be a—"

"If you say coincidence, I will jump over this seat and strangle you."

"Jackie, I'm sorry. I never thought someone would break into your home."

My temper bubbled over. "That's right, you didn't think, you just did whatever you felt you should do not bothering to ask for help. Well let me tell you, that was pretty fricking stupid. You are a jackass, Logan Parker. Did you know they tranqued Sasquatch? What if they, whoever the hell you aren't telling me about had shot her instead? What if Celeste had been home? Or Luke, or me? Huh? Did you give a moment's thought to anyone other than Corrine who you are so fucking busy protecting while you let the rest of us twist in the wind?"

His lips parted but before he could say anything the driver's door opened and Luke hauled himself behind the wheel. "I just got an alert from the triplex video feed. Garret Green is there."

I stared at Logan, my blood boiling. Being angry with him was so much easier than being scared for him. Maybe I had been unfair in the things I'd said. But how could he not see that he'd already dragged me into this situation?

"Guys?" Luke said. "Did you hear what I said?"

"Are you allowed to work?" I asked the Dark Prince.

He turned in his seat. "I'm not under house arrest, if that's what you mean."

"Then let's go," I thumped back against the seat and folded my arms over my chest.

Luke fastened his seat belt and then pulled out into traffic.

My knee jogged restlessly as we made our way through midtown. Garret Green must be desperate, an idiot, or both to return to the triplex after the fire. Then again, junkies often returned to familiar territory.

Finally, we pulled up into the gravel lot. Abu scrambled up my arm just as I was about to insist he stay in the car. His tail wrapped lovingly around my neck as though not wanting to be parted from me.

"Fine," I told him. "Just try to stay out of trouble."

"Vests?" Luke asked Logan.

The Dark Prince nodded. "Probably a good idea. Jackie, maybe you can go check on Mrs. Diaz. Make sure she is okay."

"I don't speak Spanish. Does she understand enough English that I can explain what's going on without freaking her out?"

Logan nodded. "Yeah."

It was busywork to keep me safe, but I didn't mind. Wearing Kevlar in one-hundred-degree heat was not my idea of a good time. I waited while the guys strapped themselves into their gear and then headed for Garret Green's front door before moving to Zamara Diaz's apartment on the far side of the fountain.

I rapped softly at the same time as the Parker brothers did. No answer at either door.

"Mrs. Diaz?" I turned my back to the Parker brothers so I

could peer through the glass panels alongside the door. "It's Jackie Parker. We met the other day, remember?"

There was the sound of shuffling feet and then the lock snicked and the door opened a crack. A gush of cool air escaped. The unit must be turned down to sixty degrees.

I took a final glance across the fountain to where Luke stood. Logan must have circled around back in case Green tried to escape through the back. They were doing their thing and waiting this one out with Mrs. Diaz and her sub artic apartment sounded like a mighty fine idea.

I pushed the door open. "You really shouldn't turn the temperature down so low," I said as I pushed my way into the dim interior. "It makes the unit work overtime to keep up…." My voice trailed off as I saw the twitchy form of Garret Green. He wore loose cargo shorts that had seen better days. They were spattered with white paint. His gray t-shirt had small holes and he wore socks and Crocs on his feet. And he also held a scary-looking firearm which was pointed right at Zamara Diaz's head. The elderly woman had been tied up with duct tape and her eyes were wide with terror.

"Shit," I said.

"Where is she?" Garret's bloodshot eyes fixed on me as he bounced on his toes. "Where's Harper?"

"Harper's safe." I used my most soothing voice. "We took her to the hospital. If you put the gun down, we would be happy to take you to see her."

He was shaking so hard he was practically vibrating in place. "You're lying. I checked the hospital. She wasn't there."

Double shit. "Look, that was two days ago. Maybe someone—"

He closed in on me the barrel of the firearm waving wildly. "Stop lying! I hate lying bitches. Her mother was a lying bitch."

I pressed my lips together. Abu's tail wrapped more

securely around my neck. I don't know if he sensed the danger we were in or he was just cold. With spider monkeys, it's hard to tell.

"Tell me where she is or I swear, I will shoot you."

It was at that moment that Zamara Diaz's cat decided to make a cameo. He strolled around the corner from the hallway, the way cats always do as if surveying their territory. The cat took one look at Abu and arched his back. Abu shifted from one shoulder to the other.

"Stop that," the motion aggravated Green. "What's he doing?"

Meanwhile, the enormous feline hissed.

Abu screeched in response.

"Make him stop!" Green clamped his free hand over his ears with the barrel of the weapon still aimed at me. "Shut him up!"

The cat charged forward at the same time Green shifted back a step. His foot landed on the cat's tail.

"Rawwwrrr!" The noise startled a spooked Abu who lept from his perch on my shoulder to the pass thru between the kitchen and the living area. The cat took off after him, tripping Green in the process. Green lost his balance and I lunged, shoving the firearm up toward the ceiling.

There was a deafening boom as the weapon discharged. Mrs. Diaz screamed behind her gag. Plaster rained down on our heads as we struggled for control of the gun.

Green wasn't a big man but he was strong. What he lacked in balance he made up for in sheer determination.

"Bitch," he called me. "You lying bitch."

Then he called me *the* word. The word that men just shouldn't ever be allowed to say to a woman. The C U Next Tuesday word.

I shoved my knee into his crotch so hard that I was fairly sure Harper would never have any siblings.

Green actually turned green and curled up like a shrimp. He dropped the weapon in favor of cupping his junk and I snagged it.

"Jackie?" It was Logan, barreling through the door most likely summoned by the sound of the gunshot. "Are you hurt?"

I shook my head. "Check on her. I need to find Abu."

Luke came in a moment later and bound Green's hands in Flexicuffs. He had his phone nestled between his ear and his shoulder as he called the police to report the incident.

Abu was huddled on top of the fridge between a box of cereal and a cluster of bananas. The cat had made her way up to the counter where she prowled back and forth, her tail swishing eagerly.

"Nice kitty," I said and reached to pick her up.

She spit and swatted at me, gouging my arm with her claws. "Damn it. When the hell did my life morph into an episode of wild kingdom?"

Logan came over and scooped the cat up. He carried her down the hall and I heard the sound of a door opening and shutting. He returned with a bottle of hydrogen peroxide and a few cotton swabs.

"Here, let me see that," He reached for my arm.

I snatched it away. "Don't touch me."

"Jackie," his tone was pleading.

"Fine." I held out my arm, turning my face away so I didn't have to see the blood.

His touch was gentle as he cleaned out the scratches. "When was your last tetanus shot?"

"I don't know." I narrowed my eyes up at Abu who was still perched on top of the fridge. "Come down from there, troublemaker."

He chittered and wagged a finger at me before turning his attention back to the bananas.

I sighed. "Once upon a time I wouldn't have believed this was even possible."

"Which part? Having a firearm shoved in your face or the fact that you disabled an armed gunman with a knee to the crotch?"

"More like the fact that I want to knee you in the crotch." I pressed my lips together.

Logan finished wrapping the scratches and then smoothed his thumb over my wrist. "Please, don't be angry with me. I promise stashing the passport was just for safe-keeping. I never thought anyone would break into your home in search of it."

I held his vivid blue gaze. "You need to tell me what's going on, Logan. I won't tolerate being left in the dark. Not with you."

He nodded slowly. "I will."

"Tell me the truth. Did you kill Corrine's husband to protect her?"

He licked his lips. "If I said yes, what would you do?"

My lips parted but I didn't know how to respond. So I shook my head. "I don't know. I guess I'm hoping to hear that Corrine used your gun and shot him in self-defense."

"Because you could live with that answer?"

I yanked my arm away. "It is not up to you to decide what I can and can't live with. You say you know me. Well since this whole thing began I'm wondering just how much I know you."

I didn't wait around to hear his reply. Instead, I stood on tiptoes and snagged the banana Abu was mangling and then stepped over Green's curled body and walked out of the apartment.

## 8

Harper, it turned out, had been released from the hospital and placed in a temporary foster situation. I thanked the social worker and let her know about our run-in with Green. In addition to theft, fraud and property damage to the units, he was also to be charged with attempted kidnapping and aggravated assault.

It wasn't ideal for poor Harper, but I had to trust she was safer where she was.

We secured the empty triplex by installing new locks. With the criminal charges against Green pending, we could proceed with evicting him. Zamara Diaz had decided to go stay with a friend in South Beach while repairs were made to the units. I don't think even our owner could blame her.

"We'll be able to get new tenants in here," I told the distraught owner over the phone. "Even if Mrs. Diaz does decide to break her lease."

"Thank you, Jackie. I appreciate the way your team handled the situation." The man had a gruff Boston accent. "Maybe I'll just sell the whole thing. It's not worth the headache. My wife would rather get a trailer on the beach."

"Let me know what you decide to do. A few of the real estate brokers I know would sell their grandmas for a commission on this place."

I hung up the phone and saw Luke walking toward me. "You all right?"

I nodded. "Can we go home now? I don't think I have it in me to tackle any more inventory."

"How about we go pick up Sasquatch. The vet just texted and said she is good to go. Logan and I can tag the third unit."

Logan was skulking inside the truck.

A few hours away from him, at home with my dog and my monkey sounded like exactly what I needed. "I like that plan. Then you can do the grill him like a T-Bone thing you mentioned earlier."

"About that," Luke hesitated.

I blew out a breath. "Oh, come on. You're not backing down on this, are you?"

"He made a mistake, Jackie. He's human. You've forgiven me for a lot worse than hiding a passport. Remember when I moved Logan in without telling you?"

I grimaced.

"It was a small thing, the passport. I asked him if he knows who broke in and he said no."

"And you believe him?"

"Logan doesn't lie."

I opened the door and loaded Abu without answering. Logan did lie, but not the way normal people did. He lied by omission and by distraction. He lied because he never revealed the entire truth of the matter.

*What would you do if I said I did kill him?* He'd asked.

I honestly didn't know. Would it be a dealbreaker for our relationship? Would I throw out the fresh start I'd been desperate to have?

Would I stop loving him?

We drove in silence to the vet's office. I waited in the car with my monkey while the Parker brothers retrieved Sasquatch. Abu started jumping up and down, chirping with glee at the sight of her. She lept over my file box, turned around once and then settled herself in the middle seat, curled up as though she were as exhausted as I was.

We headed back to the house. Logan and Luke insisted I wait in the car while they checked it out and after the last few days, I was happy to oblige. They reemerged just as Celeste pulled up in Bessie Mae.

"Logan, it's good to see you." My mother embraced the Dark Prince like they were long lost loves.

I rolled my eyes and walked past them into the house.

"Give me a minute." It was Logan's voice and I wasn't surprised when he caught up to me in the door to my bedroom.

"Logan," I began, letting my fatigue carry in my voice. "I can't—"

He kissed me. Like full tilt bending me back in a movie type of action. He kissed me until I was breathless and my knees went weak. My traitorous body responded and I had my arms wrapped around his neck, my fingers tunneling through his hair. He still wore the Kevlar vest but even with the extra layer, I could feel his body burning with need.

The same need that was eating me alive. The one to be near him to know him to be sure of him.

"I will fix this," Logan said when he finally pulled back. "No matter what it takes, I will fix this between us."

I was too out of breath to respond.

"Dinner. We're going to do dinner here tonight. Just you and me." His eyes were sapphire flames.

My mouth went dry.

"Nod if you're on board with this plan."

93

I nodded. I don't know why. Maybe because I have masochistic tendencies. Maybe because I thought he might change his mind and let me help him.

Maybe because deep down I knew that I didn't care if he had shot Corrine's ex and a thousand other bad guys. He was mine and I wasn't going to let him get away from me without a fight.

"Good. I'll see you in a few hours." He stroked a thumb over my cheekbone and then he was gone.

I huffed out a breath and sank down onto the edge of the mattress. "What the hell is wrong with me?"

A knock sounded on my door and I looked up to see my mother wearing banana yellow pedal pushers and a white peasant blouse. She wore chunky yellow hoop earrings, yellow sandals and carried a—you guessed it—yellow tote. "Hey, baby girl. You want to talk about it?"

I shook my head.

"Not even over German chocolate cake?" She pulled a pink bakery box out from her yellow tote.

"Is that from Hazel's?" I asked.

"Where else?"

"Could I have the cake without baring my soul?"

She snorted and flipped open the lid. The chocolate shavings had been formed into little curly cues of happiness. I breathed it in and sighed. "Fine. Let's take it to the counter at least. If Abu sees me eating in the bedroom he'll never let me live it down."

Celeste shook her head. "You have a very strange relationship with that monkey."

Unsure if she was talking about Abu or Logan, I shrugged and then dragged my weary carcass into the kitchen where I retrieved two forks and the last two undamaged mugs for milk.

"No clean glasses?" My mother eyed the mugs.

"It tastes better out of ceramic." I sipped my mug milk and then sliced the cake into quarters.

"Should we save some for the guys?" Celeste raised an eyebrow as I portioned up one segment of the cake.

"They don't deserve any," I said around a mouthful of ooey-gooey goodness. Hot damn, that cake was fabulous.

Celeste took a delicate bite and then had a sip of milk. She blinked in surprise. "You're right, it does taste better."

"Hashtag #mugmilk. It'll be the next Dolly Parton Challenge."

We got down to the serious business of eating then. My mom didn't screw around when it came to dessert. Everything else maybe, but not chocolate cake.

When we were done, she took the plates to the sink. "Okay, so now that I've bribed you with cake, tell me what the hell is going on."

I sank onto a barstool. "It's the Parker brothers."

"Both of them?"

Slowly, I nodded. "I knew what I was signing on for with Logan. Or at least I thought I did. But he and Luke have this whole secret swirling around Corrine and now Logan is out on bail and awaiting trial."

For a drama queen, my mother could really be a stellar listener. She didn't gasp in shock when I told her about the Dark Prince being arrested. Her hands didn't fly to her face when she heard that he'd stowed his passport in my medicine cabinet without bothering to tell me. The part about his lawyer warning me not to mix in got a raised eyebrow, but that was it.

"It all comes back to Corrine. Logan must be covering for her. It's the significant other nine times out of ten. And he's just the sort of noble jackass that would try and help."

"Do you think he and Luke helped hide the body?" Celeste asked.

I shrugged. "I don't know what to think. I mean they were acting normal right up until Logan got dragged away in handcuffs. And I keep bugging Luke but he's all, well, it's Logan, what did you expect?"

"What did you expect?"

I scowled at Celeste. "When did you turn into a shrink?"

She shrugged. "I'm not. But it's one of those things that I have to wonder about. You and Logan are together now. What did you expect, that he would immediately tell you all his secrets?"

"Kind of."

"Baby girl, relationships don't work that way. It all comes down to trust. Logan trusts you. More than he does his own brother it seems. He left the passport for you to find."

She had a point.

"Do you trust Logan? And I'm not talking some big, over-arching blind faith kind of crap. This is about do you trust him to tell you what he thinks you need to know?"

I blew out a sigh. "It's not that simple. We work together. He put my life and yours and Luke's at risk. Sasquatch got tranqed." I stared down at where the big dog had sprawled herself across the rug. Her tail started thumping against the bamboo when she noticed me looking her way. I reached out with a foot and scratched her enormous side.

Celeste raised a brow. "So how should he have handled it?"

"He could have stowed that passport in a safety deposit box and given me the key."

"What if there wasn't time?"

I frowned. "What do you mean?"

"Well, it seems that you just spotted Corrine's ex in Miami the other day, right? And for whatever reason, Logan felt the need to stash his passport after our spin class, when you were sore and he knew you would discover it. That wasn't a lot of time."

"I guess. But I don't understand why he felt the need to hide it if he didn't do anything wrong."

Celeste shook her head. "I don't know, Jackie. If you want the answers, you're going to need to get them straight from the dark horse's mouth."

"The Dark Prince's mouth."

"Whatever. You two have a date tonight?"

"It seems silly, with everything else that is going on. And I'm not in the mood."

Celeste slapped her palms down on the table. "Nope. I am not going to let you get away with putting this off. You will only regret it later. You need something to help get you in the mood."

"Like?"

"Come on, what you need is a facial."

"A facial?"

"It's on me. You want to do something to feel feminine before your date, right?"

"I don't know." But Celeste was already reaching for her phone. "Let me see if Tansy is available this afternoon."

There was no stopping Hurricane Drama Mama when she got going. We headed out to Bessie Mae and I slid behind the wheel, inserted the key and cranked the engine over.

Nothing.

"Oh, I meant to tell you it has been leaking a little oil lately." Celeste wrinkled her nose.

I blew out a sigh. "Great, now what?"

"What about Mr. Murphy's car? You have keys for that, right?" She nodded to the big white land yacht that was parked in Logan's driveway. He'd purchased it from Mr. Murphy along with the bungalow.

"Yeah, I've got keys."

The nice thing about driving Mr. Murphy's maroon Oldsmobile was that the air conditioning worked. The downside was parking the behemoth sedan resembled docking an ocean liner at the Port of Miami.

"Keep your shirt on," I grumbled at the tool in the Toyota who laid on the horn as I tried desperately to parallel park between an Escape and a Volvo without hitting either one. The spot had looked large enough on the first pass, but every time I cut the wheel, the car seemed to grow like Pinocchio's nose post fib. It didn't help that my range of motion was seriously impaired from muscle soreness.

"Try again," Celeste encouraged.

Curb check. The rear tire on the driver's side lifted like the vehicle was trying to do an impossible yoga stretch. The dick in the Corolla zoomed around the front end, flipping me the bird as he went.

Ah, city living at its finest.

Finally, the boat was docked and I was sweating buckets as we made our way into Curly Cue's, the beauty parlor where my mother had worked for as long as I could remember.

The walls were bubblegum pink that had faded as everything did under Miami's relentless sunshine. Little white and gold curlicues had been stenciled along the walls and around the door. It was a tacky, retro beauty parlor whose average patron collected social security.

"Maybe this is a bad idea," I hedged. "We could go grab a late lunch instead."

"And spoil your appetite for dinner? Hey, Alfonz." Celeste waved to the slightly built Cuban receptionist who worked part-time styling here.

"What are you doing here on your day off?" He smiled at us, displaying perfectly even white teeth.

"I brought my daughter in for a facial. Tansy, Jackie's here."

"How you been, doll?" Tansy was a robust African American woman with gorgeous skin. I felt confident letting her work her mojo on my face. Today she wore a lime green tunic over hot pink tights and bright yellow hoop earrings. Gold eyeshadow had been smeared liberally across her lids and her shoes were pink ballet flats. She had long nails each stylized with a purple and gold pansy. She looked like a bird of paradise. If I ever wore that combo of colors someone would toss me in the looney bin.

"Your mama said on the phone that you've got a hot date." Tansy winked and gestured to her station.

"He's cooking for me," I settled in the reclining chair.

"I love me a man who can cook." She wrapped the Curly Cue signature pink plastic cape around me and then frowned as she studied my complexion. "What in the sweet bye and bye you been using on your face, Brillo pads?"

"Not exactly."

She planted her hands on her hips. "What's your skincare regime?"

"Little of this, little of that." I hated to admit that I didn't actually have a skincare regime, other than to splash water and body wash on it while in the shower.

She tutted and then dipped a cloth into the steaming bowl of water. "First we got to open up them pores. Get the crud out. I gots this stuff, it's an old family recipe. Smells like the devil's crotch rot but does it ever work miracles on aging and sun-damaged skin."

"Gee, when you sell it like that, how could I refuse?"

The cloth was hot and I couldn't exactly breathe comfortably through it, but Tansy scared me a little so I kept my trap shut.

"Do you drink enough water?" She eyed me suspiciously.

"Define enough," I mumbled through the mask.

"Hydration is the best thing you can do for your skin. I been telling Doris that we need to get some nice lemon water in here. Or maybe that fancy kind with the mint leaves and berries. Why on my last vacation…."

I let her prattle on, my mind wandering back to Corrine's disappearance.

Had it been voluntary? And did Logan know she was missing?

"Jackie, would it be okay if we move you over to one of the empty stations?" Alfonz approached me. "Tansy just got a call for another facial coming in five."

"No problem."

"Thanks, doll. Good luck on your date." He winked at me.

Once Tansy's Pansies secured the charcoal mask in place, she guided me to a chair by the front window. "Now, I'm gonna get you some cucumbers and you need to put them over your eyes for a good five minutes at least, you hear? By the time I'm done with you, you'll be a new woman."

I nodded and she left to sacrifice a perfectly good vegetable for the sake of my puffy eyes.

I stared out onto the street, people watching. It was less fun than playing the tourist vs. native game with Logan, but then everything was more fun with Logan.

My phone buzzed and I plucked it out of my bag. "Speak of the Dark Prince," I murmured when I saw his face on the screen. It was an amazing shot, with him in profile with the setting sun behind him. He looked like a god.

I cringed glad he couldn't see me as I picked up the call. "I was just thinking about you."

"Something dirty, I hope."

"No. Just that life is more fun when I'm with you."

I could hear the smile in his voice when he murmured. "Right back atcha, hot stuff."

What's up?"

"We're making decent progress at Sunnyvale, though we're going to need you to serve some cure or quits. Most interestingly, a brass stripper pole needs to be removed from one unit."

I grinned at the image. "Never a dull moment."

"I miss you," he breathed. "It's not the same going out without you."

Satisfaction warmed my heart even as the beauty shop's AC hardened the sludge on my face. "That is the nicest thing I've heard all day."

"Are you feeling better?"

"I am actually." Getting up and moving certainly helped. Not that I would ever tell my mother that she'd been right.

"Good. We're still on for tonight, right?" He sounded both uncertain and hopeful.

I bit my lip. Tansy returned and handed me the cucumbers. "Now put them over your eyes. I mean it, girl, don't make me get rough with you."

"No, Ma'am." See? It really isn't a term of respect, just something people say instead of "you bitch".

Logan's low chuckle made my girl parts shiver. "Where are you and, dare I ask what you're supposed to put over your eyes?"

"Curly Cues. Celeste roped me into a facial, complete with cucumbers. I feel like an idiot."

"I bet you look cute though."

I licked my lips, then grimaced as I tasted charcoal goop. "So, you still want to…tonight? I thought maybe with everything going on you would want to postpone?"

He turned the question back around and lobbed it at me. "Do you want to postpone?"

Yes. No. Maybe? I didn't know how to respond so I looked out the window.

"Holy frigging hell," I breathed.

"What?" The Dark Prince asked.

But I'd already hung up, darting out into the street to catch up with Corrine. I exited the salon running at full speed. She wasn't paying any attention as she headed down a narrow alley across the street. A moment later a man followed. Large, well over six feet tall wearing sunglasses. People paused to look at me as I dodged traffic to follow them, gray face, pink cape and all. The stares told me I probably looked like a homely supervillain.

I'd just reached the mouth of the alley when I heard the gunshot.

## 9

Another shot rang out. Instinct had me and half the pedestrians in hearing range kissing pavement. Footsteps echoed and someone lept over the top of me, running for all he was worth. I heard an engine roar and looked up in time to see a silver Audi peel out and do an illegal U-turn in traffic.

Shoot, I hadn't gotten the plate.

"What's happening?" A woman wearing a big floppy beach hat and walking a yapping little dog on a pink rhinestone leash asked.

I pushed myself upright. "Do you have a cell phone?"

When she nodded I told her to call 911. "Tell the operator there's been a shooting."

I didn't wait to see what she said, instead I ran down the alley to see if there was anything I could do. Ice formed in the pit of my belly.

There wasn't. No body, no blood, no sign of anything amiss. I went all the way to the end where a six-foot chain-link fence topped with barbed wire blocked the opening from a repo yard. No way out.

My hands shook. Damn it. What the hell was going on?

The sound of approaching sirens permeated the bustling afternoon. I withdrew to the mouth of the alley to wait, since I was a witness.

A crummy witness at that. Damn it, why hadn't I gotten that license plate? I'd been so intent on cornering Corrine that I'd developed tunnel vision.

"Jackie?" Celeste had come out of the beauty parlor. "The police are on their way."

I exhaled and nodded. "You think I have time to get this crap off my face? It's starting to harden in the sun."

She opened her mouth but before she could answer a patrol car pulled up by the alley.

I had my ID and the paperwork ready. Standard procedure would have the uniformed officers tape off the crime scene so the physical evidence would be preserved before they started canvassing for witnesses to make statements. But in addition to hardening, Tansy's miracle crap was also making me itch. I really wanted to get it off as soon as possible.

"You better get back inside," I said to Celeste as the officers approached.

"I'll call Logan," she bolted back into the beauty parlor before I could tell her not to bother him.

By the time I explained who I was, what I had been doing —looking for a friend— what I'd seen and what smelled like hot garbage—the miracle mask—my face felt like it was on fire.

"My mother works just across the street," I said and pointed to Curly Cues. "Would it be okay if I wait over there?"

The uniform nodded. "We have your card. Someone will contact you if necessary."

I hobbled across the street and collapsed in the chair I'd vacated.

"Get it off," I begged Tansy who was already waiting with a bowl of hot water. "It freaking burns."

She cussed a blue streak as she rubbed in vicious circles. I hissed in agony. Her eyes grew bigger and bigger and she began shaking her head and muttering under her breath.

"What?" I barked. "What's wrong?"

My mother came up behind her. "Oh, Jackie. Oh, baby, no."

"What?" I shrieked, horrified by their reaction.

"You're kinda…scorched." Celeste bit her knuckle as though forcing other words back.

"Scorched?" I had visions of a trauma ward with people wrapped up like mummies. My skin felt tight and achy but no longer as if I was a heartbeat away from spontaneous combustion. "Turn me toward the mirror."

They eyed each other.

"Mirror!" I barked like a total psycho. All the patrons of the beauty shop were staring at me now. One little girl started to cry.

Tansy winced but pivoted the chair until I could face my reflection.

I stared at the mess that had been my face. The skin was red. Not just one shade of red either. Some parts were more pinkish while others appeared almost maroon. It didn't even look like me. Tansy had kept her word—she'd transformed me into a new woman.

I started to laugh.

"What's wrong with her?" Celeste hissed.

Tansy's head shook back and forth. "Maybe it seeped all the way through to her brain?"

A few tears leaked out leaving cooling trails against my

skin. I couldn't stop the hysterical outpouring of emotion. If I kept up like this beauty and fitness were going to kill me.

"It's a chemical burn," Tansy said slowly. "What in the sweet by and by were you thinking to leave it on so long?"

My histrionics cut off abruptly. "I thought it was an old family recipe! I didn't know it would take half my face off!"

"Aloe," Tansy flapped her hands like she was trying to make the pansies take flight. "We need to get some aloe on that."

"Do you have any?" Celeste asked.

Tansy shook her head. "Maybe you should stay out of the sun. Anybody got a big hat?"

One of the stylists did. It was pink with a white and pink polka dot band and a plastic daisy on the left side. Not exactly the kind of accessory to aide my anonymity.

"How long before I go back to normal?" I asked Tansy.

She shrugged helplessly.

Perfect.

I took a deep breath and tried to gather my calm. Okay, this was Miami. Half the people out there had sunburns. It probably wasn't as bad as I thought.

I looked at the sobbing little girl and she screamed. Nope, not as bad as I thought. It was worse.

"You still want to go to lunch?" My mother asked.

I picked up my shoulder bag. "After having my face transformed into ground chuck, I've lost my appetite."

---

I'D FULLY INTENDED to go back to work after the disastrous facial. I'd taken a long hot shower, which helped relieve some of the muscle soreness but made my face sting. I'd sat down on the bed for half a minute and when I'd woken up, it was dark and delightful scents were coming from the kitchen.

Logan was cooking for me. Looking to butter up to me no doubt.

I was still in my silky bathrobe and I headed into my closet to piece together just the right outfit. In the end, I chose a green maxi skirt with a slit up the side and a pink and green floral blouse which I enhanced with a truly excellent push-up bra. From the savory scents wafting in from the kitchen, Logan was bringing his A-game. I could do no less.

Unfortunately, between lobster face and bed head I wasn't exactly up to his fighting weight.

Maybe I could just hide in the bedroom until he left. Maybe my face looked better, now that the sun had gone down.

I moved into the bathroom and flicked on the light. And hissed.

Fire engine red.

I braced my hands on the sink. Okay. There was still the hiding option.

A knock sounded on the outer door. "Jackie? You coming out soon?"

"No," I answered and then stuffed a fist in my mouth.

"What's wrong?" The doorknob rattled.

I flew into the other room and shoved my shoulder into the door, keeping it securely lodged in its frame. "Nothing."

"You're acting weirder than usual."

"Am not. I'm always this weird." Just not always this red. "Maybe we should just reschedule."

"For when?"

For however long it took for skin to grow back.

He was silent a moment. "Is this about the passport thing?"

"No."

"Bullshit." Logan slapped the door with an open palm so that it rattled in the frame. "Look, I made a mistake. I get it, but it was just supposed to be a precaution. I never would have left it here if I thought they would toss the house. Do you really think I would put you in harm's way?"

I didn't. "Logan, it's just not a good time right now."

"Why? Tell me why it's never a good time for us."

I couldn't let him think I was pushing him away. "Just, give me a few minutes, okay?"

"Fine," he snapped.

I swore and eyed the window, debated going out it. There was the possibility that the ol' family recipe might have made me glow in the dark though.

I returned to the bathroom, debated the wisdom of using foundation to at least fade the tomato hue. One stroke with a soft make-up brush had me hissing and vowing never to do that again. Fine, red it would be.

The hair was easier, I just twisted it up in a clip. After applying just a dab of pearly pink lip gloss, I slid my feet into sandals with comfy stretchy straps that wove halfway up my calves and then headed out to do battle.

Logan was inspecting the fridge. He had changed out of his standard blue jeans and a black t-shirt to a white button-down and tan slacks. His jawline was clean from his standard five o'clock shadow.

His intense blue gaze swerved directly to my bedroom door when he heard the rattle of the knob. How had I ever thought his eyes were icy? When I looked into them now all I saw was blue heat.

And at the moment amusement.

"This is why you were hiding?" He slid the fridge door closed. "What the hell happened to you?"

I lifted my chin, trying to feign a confidence I didn't feel. "Tansy at Curlie Cues happened. She put this stuff on my face and left it on too long. Way too long."

He started to laugh.

Tears jumped into my eyes and I covered my face. "I'm hideous, but you don't have to laugh at me."

"Hey now." The laughter cut off abruptly and he moved around the counter and pulled my hands away from my face. "Look at me, Jackie. It's okay. I'm sorry, I didn't mean to laugh at you. I'm relieved because I thought something was really wrong."

"Something *is* really wrong." My hands flapped in the air like nervous birds.

"Does it hurt?" He gripped my hands again so I couldn't conceal the mess from his probing stare and bent down to inspect the train wreck that was my face.

"Only when I touch it." Or looked at myself in the mirror. "Tansy gave me aloe to put on it."

"Aloe is good."

"I made a little girl cry and scream," I sniffled.

"It is startling. But it'll get better. I still think you're the most beautiful thing I've ever seen."

"You're just saying that because you fucked up."

"I'm saying it because it's the truth, red face and all."

We were caught up in a moment, neither of us moving or speaking, just staring at one another. My heart pounded as it had when he'd taken me on his motorcycle. The same giddy energy pulsed through my bloodstream. This was real, after all this time we were really a couple.

"You look...." He swallowed, his gaze roving over my body.

"You like it?" I twirled in place, letting him get the full effect.

He turned away without saying anything and a pang of disappointment went through me as he moved to the stove. But instead of resuming cooking, he took the pan off the heat, shut off the burner and put it in the oven before striding back over to cup the back of my neck in his rough palm.

"Like is too mild," he murmured, his other hand sliding to my clip.

"Don't," I pleaded as he unfastened it, letting the wild riot of slept-on hair fall free. "It's a mess. I'm a mess."

"I like you a mess." And then his lips brushed over mine in a welcoming sort of caress, which made me forget all about the state of my hair.

It was a long, thorough kiss. The kind where I could only clutch the back of his arms and hold on for all I was worth. He was careful not to touch my face as he explored my mouth.

Just when I feared we'd both suffocate, his lips lifted from mine and held my gaze. "So, you've had a day."

"Says the guy out on bail," I wheezed. "Whatcha cooking?"

"Nothing that can't wait." He dipped down and kissed me again.

My hands slid up to his shoulders so that I could pull him in even closer. With my wits scattered, I forgot all about the fear and stress of the last twenty-four hours.

That is until the sound of breaking glass.

Logan moved like lightning. One second I was in his arms and the next he was shoving me toward the back door. "Run!"

"What?" I asked even as I smelled the smoke.

Someone had tossed a Molotov cocktail through our front window.

## 10

We stood in the backyard for the second time in two days as rescue personnel swarmed over our property. Abu sat on my shoulder and Sasquatch sniffed around at half a tennis ball that had been caught up in the lawnmower at some point. Logan had made sure to get all of us out to safety before running for the front yard as the sound of screeching tires headed for the intersection that led to the freeway.

"I didn't see who it was." He huffed when he returned to me. "Neighbors either."

"My house." A tear slid down my cheek.

Logan reached out and wiped it away, his expression full of regret. "I know. I'm sorry."

I wondered if that regret was seasoned with guilt. "Who would have done this?"

He didn't answer.

Luckily, even with the accelerant from the bottle of cheap vodka, the fire department contained the blaze to the front rooms. My bedroom and the living room caught the worst of it. From the back, it looked as though nothing had happened.

From around the corner, wearing a pair of wrinkled khaki pants and a blue shirt strode Enrique Vasquez. "Was there anyone else home?"

"No," Logan said. "Celeste left a little while after I got here and Luke had a date."

"He did?" I asked. "With who?"

"He didn't say." Logan shrugged.

"Do you have any idea who would have done this?" Vasquez asked the Dark Prince.

Logan's jaw clenched and he said nothing.

"Could you give us a minute?" I asked the detective.

He studied Logan and then me and nodded once. "I'll be nearby."

I waited until he was out of earshot. "Was this the same person who ransacked my house yesterday?"

"Probably not the same person exactly," Logan said.

"But the same person made the call?"

He scrubbed his hand over his freshly shaven chin. "I didn't know this was going to happen, Jackie."

"I know you didn't. But you have to tell me what the hell is going on. Otherwise, how can I protect myself?"

He swallowed.

"Logan, did you kill Corrine's husband?"

Slowly he shook his head back and forth.

"Did you help someone else do it?"

Again a single head shake.

"Then who were you hiding the passport from?"

"It's a long story."

My temper snapped. "That's not an answer I can live with. My monkey, dog and I are currently homeless."

"My house—" he began gesturing to the bungalow next door.

"Is an active crime scene."

He swallowed. "I can fix this. You just need to have faith in me."

"I do." I pinched the bridge of my nose. And then yelped when I remembered the chemical burn. "But I just wish you had a little faith in me. That you would tell me about what is going on instead of keeping me in the dark all the damn time."

Logan opened his mouth and then closed it again. I waited for a beat and then headed over to Vasquez. "Did you find any sign of Corrine earlier?"

He shook his head. "But you were right, there was a bullet embedded in the concrete. Someone fired off a round in that alley. Ballistics has it now, I'm waiting to hear back."

I swallowed and eyeballed the house next door. "Listen, is there any way you can pull a few strings so we can hole up at Logan's place? I have nowhere else to go. Renting a room with these two is too damn difficult." I gestured to Sasquatch and Abu.

Vasquez looked at me with sympathy. "Sorry, kid. You know I would if I could."

I blew out a sigh. "Fine. Then can I borrow your cell? I need to get a hold of Luke and mine was in my bedroom."

I intentionally kept my back to the charred remains of the space that had been so peaceful and serene only an hour ago.

Vasquez handed me his cell, then gestured for Logan on the side while I dialed Luke's number.

"Hello?" my ex shouted into the phone.

Latin fusion music blared in the background. "Where the hell are you?"

"Downtown," he hedged.

"Well, you need to get up here ASAP. Someone just tossed a Molotov cocktail into our front window and your brother is being a dick and I have nowhere to put my monkey."

One of the nearby uniforms snickered. I glared at him and he turned away in a hurry.

Luke didn't reply for a long moment there was nothing but the music in the background. Then, "Are you joking? Tell me you're joking."

"I wish. Sorry, I don't mean to be that pain in the ass ex-wife but things are looking pretty effing grim here."

"I'll be there in a few," Luke said and hung up.

I handed the phone back to Vasquez.

"Do you think this might have something to do with the shooting earlier?" Vasquez asked me.

"Which one?" I asked at the same time as Logan said, "No."

The Dark Prince glowered at me. "What do you mean, which one."

"Jackie spotted Corrine earlier and a man following her into an alley. There was a gunshot but no sign that anyone was hit."

Logan stared at me for a long minute and I could see the gears in his head clicking over and over. "That's why you hung up on me earlier. You thought you saw Corrine."

"I did see her," I practically snarled.

Sasquatch whined at me.

"Someone shot at you and you didn't bother to tell me?" Logan got in my face.

"Guys," Vasquez said.

"No one shot at me." My hands were fisted on my hips as I faced off against the Dark Prince. "There was a shot in my general vicinity."

"This is Florida," Logan threw his hands in the air. "There's always going to be a gunshot in your vicinity. But normal people don't go charging toward it."

"Guys," the Sargent tried again.

"Normal? What the hell is that supposed to mean?" My hands curled into fists at my side.

"You go running off after some woman who you think might be Corrine even though I've told you she isn't here. You get shot at *multiple* times a day, your house was just fire-bombed." Logan gestured from the monkey perched on my shoulder to my bright red face. "Exactly what part of that do you consider normal?"

I drew back a fist and punched him. I didn't mean to, it just sort of happened. The rage and frustration bubbled up like a soda can that had been shaken and then had the top popped, until all the feelings just fizzed right out. There was no clear intention, no decision like, *gee, I ought to punch the jackass for that remark.* My fist took on a life all its own.

I got him right in the nose. There was a sickening crunch and blood sprayed. Logan stumbled back, clutching his face. Abu screeched and scrambled off me even as the momentum sent me sprawling to the ground, right into a pile of Sasquatch poo. *Squish.* So much for my pretty outfit.

All around us the cops were shouting and scrambling.

A pair of well-worn sneakers appeared about an inch from my own nose. I looked up into the chocolate brown eyes of Sargent Enrique Vasquez.

"Are you going to slap me in handcuffs?"

"Are you going to hit anyone else?" He tilted his head to the side.

"No."

He sighed and offered me a hand. "I think you've been punished enough for one night."

---

LOGAN STAYED on the far side of the driveway, as far as possible from me until Luke appeared. Vasquez had pulled a few strings and gone into Logan's house to retrieve a t-shirt and pair of athletic shorts so at least I didn't need to parade around in the poo outfit. I'd changed in the darkest corner of the yard, my face red from more than just the chemical burn.

Every time I looked to where Logan sat, an ice pack held to his swollen nose, a stab of guilt went through me. I'd hit him. No, I'd freaking *slugged* him in front of witnesses. And not just any witnesses. Police. They were well within their rights to charge me with assault and battery and throw my sorry butt in jail.

Why had I done it? Stress? Yeah, having my home fire-bombed was stressful. So was being held at gunpoint and watching Luke and Logan tear-ass into a burning building. So why had the straw that broke the camel's back been Logan saying I wasn't normal?

Maybe because deep down, I feared he was right.

I wasn't normal. Not for a process server. Not for a thirty-something woman. I had been married to one brother and was dating the other. I slept with a monkey in my bed and my ex slept out on the couch. I was afraid to sleep with Logan. My life just wasn't right.

But I'd been trying to fix it. I thought I had fixed it, or at least patched the gaping holes well enough so that nobody could see what a mess I was.

I moved to approach Logan just as the Big Black Truck parked across the street. Luke scrambled out, followed by Marcy.

"Hey," I waved to the two of them.

"Are you all right?" Marcy rushed to my side while Luke went to check on the Dark Prince.

I nodded and swallowed, then shook my head. "Not really."

"Aw, honey." She wrapped an arm around my shoulders. "It'll be okay."

She smelled of the expensive perfume she'd bought herself for her birthday and was wearing a pretty swishy skirt and a cold shoulder peasant top.

"You look nice," I sniffled.

"Thanks."

I had too, other than the face, at least before I fell in dog shit. Now I looked and smelled like the homeless person I was.

"Don't worry, you can stay at my place," Marcy said.

Marcy's place was a studio apartment with a Murphy Bed. The only door was to the pokey bathroom. Sasquatch could probably lie down by the front door and have her tail touch the rear wall. I tried to imagine cramming all of us in there and shuddered.

"Thanks," I sniffed. "Maybe I'll just board the animals."

Abu chittered as though he understood my intention.

Luke jogged over and Logan followed at a more sedate pace. Luke frowned when he saw my face. "Was that from the fire?"

I shook my head. "Earlier mishap."

"We're going to Mom and Dad's house," Luke said.

I frowned. "In Juniper?"

"They have plenty of space. And it's easier than finding a place in Miami."

Easier maybe, but we'd spend half the day sitting in traffic commuting from one to the other. Then another thought struck.

I met Logan's gaze. "What about your bail terms?"

He shook his head. "Can't. I'll get a motel room."

My lips parted but I didn't know what to say. That he should come anyway? That would get his happy ass tossed back behind bars. That I would stay with him? Maybe smack him around some more.

"There's another option," Marcy hesitated.

I glanced over to her.

"You could stay with Gertie. There's an apartment over the garage. Small kitchen and, full bath private entrance and everything."

Gertie was Marcie's shut-in older sister. Saying she was odd was like saying the ocean was big. In other words, a massive understatement.

"Would Gertie be okay with that?" I asked, gesturing from me to the guys, to the monkey. "We're kind of a three-ring circus act on wheels."

"She's doing better." Marcy insisted. "Her new medication has been helping. Though she doesn't like large dogs."

Sasquatch might be a problem then.

I took a deep breath and then made the call. "Okay. Luke and I will take Sasquatch to his parent's house and then we'll come back and crash at Gertie's place."

Logan's lips parted and I waited for him to speak, to argue, but he just shook his head.

Vasquez came over. "I talked to the fire marshal. You should be able to get back inside the place tomorrow evening, grab whatever you need."

I nodded and gave him an update on our plans.

He looked to Logan's broken nose and then turned back to face me. "Are you sure that's a good idea, the three of you living together?"

I tried not to take offense because I knew he was just doing his job. "If it gets too tough, I can always stay with Marcy."

He nodded. "Call me when you get a new phone."

We piled into the truck, the Parker brothers in the front, me squished between Marcy and Sasquatch in the back.

It was a silent, almost defeated air that filled the interior as we drove to Gertie's house. It was an older place in Coral Way, larger on a bigger piece of property. Built back before the population of Miami had mushroomed out. Marcy exited with Abu on her shoulder. Gertie was my number one monkey sitter. I doubted she would have a problem with him.

The rest of us on the other hand....

I froze. We were one short. "We forgot about Celeste."

If my mother showed back up at home and saw the wreckage from the fire, she would flip the hell out.

"I need to call her."

"Relax, Ace." Luke met my gaze in the rearview mirror. "Marcy called her on her way over. She is going to stay with Tansy. Said you should call her as soon as you get settled."

My shoulders sagged in relief. "Wow, you really thought of everything. Called Celeste, went to get Marcy—"

Logan made a choking noise. "He was already with Marcy."

"What?" That made no sense. "I thought you said he was on a date?"

"I was." Luke's voice was soft, as though waiting for a bomb to go off.

It hit me then like ten tons of brick from the sky. Marcy's pretty flirty dress. The Latin music in the background, the fact that she had been with him and her overly helpful attitude. *"You're dating my best friend?"*

"You're dating my brother," Luke shot back.

"And look how well that's going," Logan grumbled.

Luke sighed. "And this is why I didn't want to tell you. I knew you would overreact."

My mouth opened and closed a few times but actual speech wasn't happening.

Marcy, the traitor, bounced back over to the truck. "Okay, we're all set." She frowned at the three stony faces, one flushed red, one burned red and the third covered with blood. "Um, is there a problem?"

119

"No problem." I ground out.

"Do you want us to give you a lift?" Luke asked.

Marcy shook her head. "I'll call an Uber after I get Logan settled. See you later."

Logan popped his door and reluctantly, I did the same.

We stared at each other for almost a full minute, neither of us wanting to be the first to break the silence. I could go in with him. Luke didn't need me to ride shotgun all the way up to Ft. Lauderdale and back just to drop off Sasquatch. For a moment I thought he would invite me to stay, that he'd beg me not to walk away and tell me that he was sorry.

And then I would be free to do the same.

He heaved out a breath and turned away.

I got into the truck and narrowed my eyes on Luke, who turned the engine over.

"Do not freaking start, Jackie."

"I can not believe you. My best friend."

He laughed, the sound completely devoid of humor. "Was it better when you thought I was sleeping with Corrine, who you hate?"

"No."

"So what, you're allowed to move on but I'm not?" The streetlights flashed as he merged with traffic heading for the interstate.

"That is *so* not what I'm saying. You and Marcy have intentionally kept me in the dark."

"Because it's all about Jackie, right?" Luke seethed. "How everything makes you feel, never mind the carnage you leave in your wake."

I reared back. "Luke—"

He held up a hand. "You didn't want to be married anymore. And that's fine. I get it. But now you're tanking things with Logan and I have to wonder, what the hell is it all for, Jackie? What's the endgame here? Are you going to keep screwing with us until the end of time?"

It was a damn good thing he was driving or I would have bloodied his nose to match his brother's. "You know, I sometimes forget that you and Logan are related and then you go and act like an ass and then the family resemblance shows up."

"I don't want to fight with you anymore," Luke said. "That's why we got divorced, right? So we didn't need to keep fighting?"

"Exactly." I reached out and clicked on the radio. A sappy love song played and I flipped the station until I found some Industrial rock music. No more love songs for me anytime soon.

We drove several miles before Luke muttered, "And I'd appreciate it if you didn't mention Marcy to Mom and Dad."

I frowned. "Because they're still dealing with news about our divorce?"

Luke blew out a breath. "No, because I still haven't told them we're divorced."

## 11

I gripped Sasquatch's leash in one hand while Luke rang the bell. Nerves flitted around in my stomach in a horrible riot until I felt on the verge of tossing my cookies all over the pretty Azalea bush beside the front porch. I had been less nervous when Luke had introduced me—his then white trash girlfriend to his upper-crust white bread folks than I was now. Maybe because back then, Luke had been all sweetness and reassuring.

Now he was the sneaky ex who was shagging my bestie behind my back. And hadn't bothered telling his parents that we were divorced.

"Damn it, Luke." I bitched at him. "This is just the sort of situation I wanted to avoid."

He said nothing, just stood there with his jaw clenched. Sasquatch whined, clearly upset that her humans weren't happy.

Footsteps sounded on the other side of the door and then Marge appeared. "Oh Jackie, you poor thing." She squeezed me tightly and it took everything in me not to sob. Would this be the last hug we shared?

Marge Parker had known that Logan had feelings for me while I was married to Luke. We'd talked about the situation, lest the hairy details. She was the kind of genuine and reassuring woman that you could tell anything to and she would roll with the punches. Except Luke was right, our odd situation had gone from ancient history to current events and Marge and Gerald had missed a few steps.

Like that I returned Logan's feelings. That Luke and I, while still living and working together, had transitioned from man and wife to friends.

I glared at him over his mother's shoulder. I wasn't feeling too friendly towards him at the moment.

Marge smelled of vanilla and warmth. Not the overly fragrant kind that was incorporated into perfume. No, she smelled like the genuine vanilla she used in her fabulous triple chocolate chunk cookies.

"Your poor face," she said with sympathy as she touched her cool hand lightly to my cheek. "Was that from the blast?"

"There was no blast, Mom. It was a fire. Jackie didn't blow anything up." The *this time* went unsaid but I still heard it.

"No, it's a chemical burn. It looks worse than it feels."

Sasquatch wagged her tail and Marge bent down to greet her grandpuppy. "Hey there. Who's a pretty girl? Sasquatch is a pretty girl, that's who."

I loved my dog but she looked like a cross between Chewbacca and Big Foot. No one else called her pretty except when they added the word scary afterward. Marge looked up from scratching a very contented K-9 on the butt and Sasquatch was doing a little tap dance in ecstasy. "Where's Abu?"

"We left him with Marcy's sister."

"Oh, you could have brought the little stinker. I just bought bananas and George refuses to eat them even though the doctor said he should get more fruit in his diet."

123

"Dad around?" Luke propelled me over the threshold and shut the door.

"He's gone up to bed already, though I doubt he's asleep." She looped her left arm through one of mine and then snagged Luke by the other. "Between what happened to George and now this thing with Logan and a fire on top of it, I'm starting to wonder if this family will ever catch a break."

I shot Luke a speaking glare over the top of her head.

"Well, at least no one was hurt. That's the important part. I have your room all ready for you."

"We were actually going to head back tonight," I began.

Marge waved me away as though the idea of heading back to Miami was obscene. "You need a hot meal and a good night's sleep. I've got the guest room all made up."

I opened my mouth to protest but Luke talked right over the top of me. "Sounds great, Mom. We're both beat."

"What the hell, Luke?" I hissed as Marge bustled down the hall to the kitchen. "Not only did you not tell her, but now we're sharing a room?"

"Look, I will tell them, tomorrow. I don't want to wake Dad up. And don't tell them about the Molotov cocktail. They're already in a state over Logan."

My molars were being ground into powder but I forced a smile as Marge extracted a cold chicken from the fridge. "How about some chicken salad? I found this great recipe on Pinterest for a batch with slivered almonds and cranberries. Even you could make it, Jackie. No cooking required."

"Except hopefully for the chicken." Luke pulled up a stool and sat down at the large island.

Marge extracted a jar of mayo and a head of frilly green lettuce from the fridge. "She could get one of those pre-cooked chickens from the grocery store. Chips?"

I nodded, not because I really wanted chips but because I

felt the need to cram something into my face before I said something I shouldn't.

Marge was right, the chicken salad was awesome and I thanked her for her thoughtfulness in printing out the recipe even as I knew I would toss it the instant we left the house.

We ate in relative silence, with Marge filling us in about her hot yoga class, her water aerobics class and her Mediterranean cooking class. "It really is the best way to eat for heart health. Olive oil, fresh fish."

"I read that somewhere." Luke paused in the act of adding extra mayo to his sandwich.

"Well, you and your brother need to start thinking about these kinds of things," Marge warned. "George's heart problems could very well be hereditary and you're getting up there in years."

"Boy, I'm beat," Luke stretched, showing off his well-toned abs for his mother's benefit. It was so unfair, both Luke and Logan were perfect specimens of health and vitality. I'm pretty sure I'd packed on five pounds looking at the jar of mayo. The extra weight all settled in my lower half, where it would make nice with the cake I'd eaten earlier.

"Oh, let me snag you a few extra towels. Fresh out of the dryer so they'll be nice and hot."

I fed the last of my sandwich to Sasquatch and Luke wordlessly took his plate and mine over to the dishwasher. I stared around at Marge's beautiful black and gray kitchen and thought of my own, much more modest one. It had been done. Finally complete. And now it was a sooty, charred ruin. Tears stung my eyes.

Luke put an arm around my shoulder. "You okay?"

I sniffed and shook my head.

"I know you're worried about him, Ace. I am too."

A lump formed in my throat. I'd never found out what

Logan had been cooking. Damn it, how had everything gone to hell so fast?

Maybe Luke was right to wait to tell his folks about us. Marge had enough stress. As much as I hated the thought of keeping the secret, I couldn't deny that I needed her homey warmth after such a shock.

Marge returned with a load of warm out of the dryer towels. "Here you go. You left some clothes here from the last time you stayed. Do you need anything else?"

"We're good. Night, Mom." Luke kissed her on the cheek.

I gave her another hug. Even though Celeste was much better than the party girl she had been when Luke and I had first been married, Marge Parker was the first maternal figure I had ever really known. And the idea of disappointing her with the news of our divorce made something in my chest wither up and die.

Luke closed the door and blew out a breath. "Before you start, I thought it would be better for you and Logan to have some time apart."

I nodded. "One of us should call him though."

Luke took out his phone and offered it to me. I shook my head and reached for a towel. "I need a shower."

I tried not to listen to his conversation, even turned the shower on, but the door was hollow and Luke was a loud phone talker.

"No man, I think she's all right." Pause. "It's just a lot to deal with."

I braced my hands on either side of the counter and stared at my reflection. What a mess.

And I wasn't just talking about my face.

---

LUKE WAS WAITING with the phone when I emerged dressed in a pair of too-tight sleep shorts and a tank top with a built-in bra.

"Woah, headlights," Luke smirked.

I covered my arms over my chest. "Shut up, it's not like I had a ton of choices and the air conditioning is cranked to sixty-two." Probably because of Marge's hot flashes. She was always either sweating or freezing.

"He wants to talk to you." Luke did one more appreciative sweep of my body before handing me the phone, which I had to uncross an arm to take.

He smirked at my rack and I gave him the finger. His laughter echoed in the tiled bathroom.

"Hey," I said to Logan because there was no doubt in my mind who he was.

"You okay?" His voice rumbled in my ear.

"Other than turning into a human popsicle, yeah. You?" I snagged a knit blanket off the back of an armchair and wrapped it around myself.

"Gertie came by. Didn't say a word. Brought me Abu and a few dozen bananas. I'm still not sure if they're for him or for me."

"Probably both." I settled back on the bed. "How's your nose?"

"Hurts."

I winced. "I'm so sorry. I don't know what came over me."

"I do and it's mostly my fault. I know you have...issues."

"No, I don't."

He snorted.

"Okay. Maybe I have a suspicious mind but that proves useful in my line of work." Serving people with notices they didn't want to receive meant that you had to outsmart the sneaky ones.

"But not in a relationship." I could tell in the change of

tone that Logan was stretching out onto his back. "Look, Jackie, if you don't trust me, then I don't know what the hell we're doing here."

"Me? You're the one who is keeping me in the dark about everything."

"I know and like I said, I'm partly to blame. But your insecurities about Corrine are becoming a problem."

"Logan, the last I heard she was missing right on the heels of her ex being murdered. I thought I saw her. I went after her. Don't make a federal case out of it."

"And you're sure that's all it is?"

I sank deeper into the chair. "Maybe there's a little more."

" I don't know what to say other than I don't have feelings for her. But it's up to you to believe me."

I was quiet for a long moment.

"About you staying with Luke…" he said.

"Don't tell me that bothers you? We're divorced."

"Divorce doesn't mean feelings end," Logan said in a soft voice.

"No, they don't. But Luke has moved on."

"I wasn't talking about his feelings."

I sucked in a sharp breath.

Logan chuckled darkly. "It's probably best that I'm an hour plus away or you'd be winding up to hit me again."

"No, I wouldn't," I said and forced my hand to unclench from a fist.

"I do love you, you know," the Dark Prince murmured.

"Sometimes you have odd ways of demonstrating it." I clutched the phone, not wanting to let him go. "Logan?"

"Yeah?"

"I do trust you. Really. But I need to know you trust me. I saw her earlier, right before the gunshot. It wasn't some jealousy-induced fantasy. I saw Corrine. Do you believe me?"

There was a long pause and I was afraid he wouldn't answer.

"How about if I say that I believe you believe it?" He asked.

"That is such a cop-out," I snarled and he laughed.

"Okay, Jackie. If you need me to believe you saw Corrine in some random alleyway even though I know for a fact she is no longer in Miami—"

"Where is she?" I gripped the phone tighter. "Do you know?"

"We'll talk about it tomorrow. And don't let my brother ogle your assets." Logan grumbled and hung up.

I stared at the closed bathroom door and thought about what Logan had said. He wasn't wrong, I did still have feelings for Luke. Mainly they were residual, the leftover feelings you have when you break up with someone you'd been with for a long time. I cared for Luke but I belonged with Logan. But I still wanted to see Luke happy, safe and secure. His wellbeing mattered to me.

As did Marcy's.

"Damn you, Logan Parker." I snarled at the inert phone. "I know what you're trying to do."

"What was that?" Luke emerged from the bathroom, scrubbing a towel over his wet brown hair. He wore a pair of low slung sweats and nothing else. I was gratified to realize my pulse didn't quicken any more than it would at the sight of a half-dressed man who happened to be ridiculously ripped.

"Nothing." I set the phone on the bedside table and then propped myself up in bed. "Are you serious about Marcy?"

His lips parted. "I'm not sure how to answer that."

"Honesty is the best policy."

Luke made a face. "I like spending time with her. If it was

just Marcy, that would be one thing but she comes with…
baggage."

I winced and he held up a hand. "Not you."

The light dawned. "You mean Gertie."

He snagged two of the pillows off the massive four-poster
and bent to make up a pallet on the floor. "She's very devoted
to her sister. Which I admire and respect about her but it
makes it hard to get to know Marcy as an individual."

I nodded. "I get it."

Luke looked surprised. "You do?"

"Yeah. Marcy is amazing. But you just got out of a serious
relationship. And her situation with Gertie is intense. It
makes sense that you're hesitant."

He stared at me for a beat. "I really do like her, Jackie."

"I know you do." Luke wasn't the sort of guy to lead a
woman on, especially a woman who was connected with his
ex-wife. "I'm sorry I freaked out. I still feel very…protective
of you."

His eyebrows went up at that. "I'm surprised you are
admitting that."

"Honestly, I was pushed into it by a very biased third
party."

Luke chuckled darkly.

"It's not just you though. Trust me, I would much rather
see you with Marcy than Corrine."

He smiled then and it was a genuine smile. "Okay. For
what it's worth, I still feel protective of you too. I don't want
to see you arrested for domestic assault."

I blushed. Luckily, the color was hidden by my horrible
burn. "It was a fight that escalated. A one-time thing."

"What it is that is between you and Logan…it's intense."

That was one way of putting it.

Luke lay on his pallet and after a minute, I leaned over
and snapped off the lights.

"Hey, Ace?" His voice drifted out of the darkness.

"Yeah?"

"Do you ever regret being married to me?"

Oh good, an easy one. "No Luke. I don't. We had trouble, sure, but being with you made me who I am. And I like who I am. Red face, neurotic mind and all."

"I like who you are, too." There was a rustling of fabric as though he had turned on his side, trying to dodge the inevitable.

"Oh no. You're not going to get off that easily." I snapped.

"What?" Luke sounded mystified, which I knew was an act.

"Same question. Do you regret being married to me?"

He blew out a breath. "I regret the choices mostly. That I chose to stay in the service and leave you behind. That I didn't push when I realized there was something between you and Logan way back when. But do I regret being with you? Never."

My lips creased up in a smile. "Okay. That's good to know."

"Go to sleep, Ace."

I knew good advice when I heard it.

## 12

"That went better than I thought it would." Luke was all smiles as we headed back to Miami. I half expected him to hop out from behind the wheel of the Big Black Truck whistling a merry little tune and then click his heels together in some old-timey skit.

"Speak for yourself," I grunted and sipped from the giant travel mug of coffee Marge had packed for me. She hadn't met my eye as she handed it to me and a huge ball of ice had formed in my stomach.

"Oh, come on, Ace. Dad didn't drop to the floor with another heart attack and Mom didn't go tearing her hair out. It's over. A load has been lifted."

Maybe for him. He was their son no matter what and I was the woman who had broken his heart.

"Why didn't you tell them about you and Logan?"

I knocked my vintage sunglasses down so I could peer at him over the top. "Are you serious?"

He shrugged. "Why not? They might have been relieved."

"I thought about it." It was true. I had briefly considered telling the senior Parkers about my relationship with their older son. But I realized that while Gerald and Marge sat there looking all crestfallen that there was no way I could add to the load. To anyone on the outside of our bizarre little dynamic, it would look strange, like I was trading one brother in for the other.

I'd imagined Marge grabbing her dust mop and running me right out of the house.

"They have enough to contend with." I murmured as we turned onto Gertie's street.

The Dark Prince sat on the steps leading down from the apartment with Abu perched on his shoulder. The instant he saw me slide out of the truck, the monkey scrambled down and rushed over to me.

"Mom sent you chicken salad sandwiches and apple date bars." Luke handed Logan the giant bag full of leftovers.

Logan's gaze was on me. For my part, I was trying to look anywhere but at him and the dark swollen mess I had made of his nose.

"Everything okay?" Logan asked.

"Sure." I'd had the foresight to snag my clipboard and was busy sorting through our open caseload. "We have a meeting with the Fire Marshal at two and your lawyer at four. You guys feel like doing some inventory or do you want to give the apartment complex another go?"

"Is there a third option?" Luke grumbled as Logan unwrapped one of the sandwiches.

"Not if you want to stay out of debt." I'd called the insurance company first thing and was told that I wouldn't be able to register a claim until the police filed a report on the arsonist.

"I say we finish up at the complex," Logan had already downed one sandwich and was busy unwrapping another. "Did you tell her what we found there yesterday?"

When Luke shook his head Logan continued, "It was even

more of a mess, clearly another party. We talked to several of the tenants but no one is willing to talk about what goes on there after dark. I think our best bet is to finish the inspections and then plan on camping out there at night just to see who shows up."

Another long day. "Okay then. Let's roll."

Logan had been right. The apartment complex did look even scuzzier than it had the last time I'd seen it. There were piles of god only knew what as well as clothing floating in the pool.

"Jackie, you need to get a pool guy over here and get that thing drained," Logan instructed. "People could get sick swimming in there."

While I scrolled through my contacts looking for the pool service, Luke and Logan headed up the outside stairs to the top floor.

The pool service sent me to a random voicemail. I left him a detailed message about who I was and what we needed and asked him to give me a call back. That done, I tiptoed my way around the debris and made my way over to the rickety staircase.

"The inspection notice is still on the door here," Luke said as I joined them on the stairs.

I shrugged. "We've given them the required amount of time. Go on in."

Logan slid the key into the lock and opened the door, calling out that we were with property management.

The stench hit us like a wall. I threw my arm up to cover my nose and mouth and tears formed in my eyes. "What the hell is that?"

"Hello?" Luke called out. "We work for the owner and—"

"Shhh, did you hear that?" Logan put a hand on his brother's arm. "Listen."

I heard it that time too. There was an obvious noise, like a groan.

Logan cursed. "You carrying?"

Luke had already pulled his sidearm. "Yeah."

"Jackie, call 911," Logan said an instant before the Parker brothers disappeared into the apartment.

I did and gave the operator the address adding, "I think someone is hurt but I don't know who or what. Please send the paramedics."

"Shit," the noise came from inside.

"What?" I called out.

Luke reappeared and a chill shot through me when I saw his hands were covered in blood. "Logan needs his first aid kit."

"Describe it to her while I get it." Shoving the phone at him, I moved for the stairs, glad I had on sneakers and jeans, even if they were both a smidge too tight.

I ran back down to the truck and retrieved the small red duffle bag that stored all of Logan's medical supplies, flung it over my shoulder and then rushed past Luke who was trying to describe the situation to the 911 operator.

The interior of the place smelled even worse and was dark, the lone window covered by a blanket that someone had tacked up. There were piles and piles of stuff everywhere. Paintings, books, papers, clothing mixed in with electronics, dirty paper plates, jars of half-filled liquid. Trails were woven through like a maze with stuff piled five feet high on either side.

"Logan?" I choked out. The smell grew worse as we went.

"We're in the bedroom. Be careful in the hallway, it gets bad."

I coughed again. How could it possibly be worse than this?

I found out a few minutes later as I spied the overflowing

garbage cans. Flies buzzed around them. Rotting food and bread spilled out from the kitchen. There was another of those little trails that led to the small sink. Bugs skittered when I switched on the light and I could hear something move beneath the nearest trash heap. "Please don't be a rat." I breathed. "Or a snake."

I continued on. According to the property owner, the largest unit was only 600 square feet. I felt as though I had hiked the Appalachian Trail by the time I made it to the small bathroom.

More stuff filled the combination tub/ shower and spilled over in front of the toilet. The toilet was clogged with god only knew what.

My sneaker squished in something that may or may not have been human waste. I gagged and covered my mouth, glad that I had skipped breakfast.

Logan stumbled his way out of the single bedroom. "Get some gloves on."

"How bad is he?"

"He's not good. He impaled his leg on a broken spring and he's been in here for days."

"Days?"

"Because of the hoarding." Logan shook his head. "He couldn't manage to get out on his own."

The smell intensified as I moved into the doorway of the bedroom. Logan had shoved the window open as far as it would go....but still.

The man on the bed was pale and the smell coming from his leg was worse than the kitchen and the bathroom combined.

"Jackie," Logan's tone was gentle. "The gloves."

"Right." I shook my head and scanned the place to find a place to set the medical bag down so we could get what we needed. The only flat surface other than the bare mattress was an upside-down milk crate. I kicked some shoes and clothing and papers out of the way. There was a squeak and I barely bit back a scream.

"It's okay," the Dark Prince soothed. "Go outside if you can't take it."

I didn't want to leave him alone in this nightmare, not even long enough for Luke to come back in. My skin was crawling just from being in the place. "I'll be fine." I fumbled with the latch and Logan moved to my side to get his own pair of gloves.

"That smell is gangrene." Logan kept his voice down so that the man who lay on the bed babbling incoherently couldn't hear.

"Will he lose the leg?"

"He'll be lucky if he doesn't lose his life." Logan moved through the crap toward the bare mattress. "Sir? We need to get you out of here and to a hospital."

"No hospital," He shook his head back and forth.

"Listen to me," Logan snapped. "This is serious. You could die if you don't get on antibiotics right away."

I stood back, too afraid to move, to touch anything or do anything that might impede Logan's progress. Despite the heat, the tenant was shivering, his body doing its best to rid itself of the horrible infection that had sunk its claws in. The man's eyes were glazed with fever. He didn't look to be more than twenty-two or three. And there he was, rotting from gangrene.

Days, Logan had said. We had been here days ago. First tagging the door, then when the police had arrested Logan. Why hadn't we started with this apartment?

Logan was still talking to the man, slow and soft, his tone soothing.

"Jackie, what's his name?" Logan asked again.

I wracked my brain. "Tom Atkins."

"Tom," Logan said. "Tom. Stay with me, buddy. Okay?"

Tom was shaking his head, his filthy blond hair matted. His teeth chattered and his eyes were glazed over.

"Tom, I'm going to get you patched up and we need to leave, to get you some help."

More incoherent babbling. It sounded almost like a prayer.

I watched as Logan wrapped the injured leg in bandages. He didn't bother sterilizing the wound, either because he thought it would be useless effort or because there was no hope of anything being so sterile in this place.

I could see Logan's frustration building but we couldn't forcibly remove the tenant or even lay hands on him.

I put one gloved hand on Logan's shoulder. "Let me try."

Logan backed up and I crouched down until I could meet Tom Atkin's scared and confused gaze.

"Hey there." I smiled at him. "My name's Jackie. You're Tom, right?"

He sniffled and then nodded.

"How about we go for a little walk in the sunshine, Tom." I held out my gloved hand to him.

"My leg hurts." He sounded more like a scared kid than a grown man.

"I know. We're going to have a doctor check it out. He'll be waiting outside. Logan and I are right here in case you need help. But it's not safe for you to stay here. And I really want to help make you safe, Tom. Okay?"

Nodding often got people I was trying to convince in the mindset to say yes to whatever I was proposing. And my head bobbed up and down as I spoke.

Tom sniffled and then he nodded too. "Okay."

He took my hand and I let him set the pace, limping on the endless slog that took him to his front door. Logan was right behind me. He would pause to rest against a wall and more crap would shift beneath our feet. He cried and stuffed his free hand in his mouth. I winced when I saw how filthy it was but didn't recoil.

And then we were out in the blessed fresh air and sunshine. I felt as though I had been locked in a mine for a week.

The paramedics arrived and took over Tom's care, setting up an IV to help with both the antibiotics and the severe dehydration. We watched, helpless as they carried the man out into the bright sunshine and down the stairs. He held my hand until he was loaded into the ambulance.

"Good job, Jackie." Logan had taken off his gloves.

"Was it?" It didn't feel that way. I thought of my reluctance to come here and tackle the problem yesterday. Maybe if I had been with the guys, we would have gotten to Tom sooner.

I flipped through his rental agreement.

"What are you doing?" Logan asked.

"Looking for the next of kin." His parents were listed as living in Jacksonville. I called and left a voicemail telling them I worked for their son's landlord.

"He can't be on his own here," Logan said. "The hoarding behavior is too bad to leave him on his own."

I looked at him, then at Luke. "That means we are going to have to clean the place out."

But Logan was shaking his head. "No, we need specialists in full hazmat suits. There's biowaste and god knows what else. Hell, we should all probably have a course of antibiotics after being in there."

"Are you serious?" I asked Logan as Luke locked up the apartment.

"No. Yes. I don't know. God, how could no one notice what was going on in there?"

I shivered even in the bright Miami sun. "I don't know."

Logan shook his head, his face haggard. "I don't know what to think anymore, Jackie. His throat was raw from screaming. The walls in this place are paper-thin, someone must have heard him."

He turned away and slammed his fist into the stucco wall.

"Not your fault," I put a hand on his shoulder, felt the corded tension there. "Logan, this isn't on you."

"We were right here. Yesterday and the day before. And two days before that." He swallowed. "It will be a miracle if he survives, and even if he does, that leg is done for."

The police took our statements individually. I told them that we worked for the owner, who would be lucky not to lose the building after what had happened on his property.

Luke joined us, having used the hose in the courtyard to wash up. Logan handed him some antibacterial wipes. We all wiped our hands our shoes and the medical bag. Still in shock but with nothing better to do, we moved on to the next apartment. We all held our breath and waited as Luke slid the key into the lock and turned.

The unit was blessedly vacant.

"What's the name?" Luke asked.

I checked the rental agreement. "Danielle Fogerty. A student at the University of Miami."

Logan checked the closets. "All her stuff is gone."

That made me feel a little bit better about the state of humanity. I'd hate to think that some college girl had blithely gone on about her life with the sound of Tom screaming for help one apartment over.

"The apartment we found him in was the end unit," I mulled as we locked up. Crime scene tape had been pulled across the door to 220. "And it looked like the tenant ran from that one as well."

"Both female," Luke nodded toward the trashed courtyard. "You think they were scared off by what was going on here?"

"Only one way to find out." I flipped to Danielle Fogerty's rental agreement and looked up the number associated with her former address. "Her folks live in Destin. Chances are they know where she is and maybe even why she moved out."

DANIELLE FOGERTY'S mother said she had just heard from her the day before and she told them she had moved in with her boyfriend.

"We just have a few follow up questions regarding her rental."

"I told her not to leave," her mother sniped. "Told her that having a continuous rental history established is important and that this would negatively impact her credit. But she insisted, said it was true love."

True love or fear for her safety. If it were up to me, I wouldn't mention to a soul that a college student had broken her lease because her parents landed her in a shithole that was crawling with lowlifes, and degenerates. But this was why I wouldn't make a good landlord.

"Could you give me the boyfriend's address, please?" I interrupted Danielle's mother mid-rant about irresponsible entitled millennials.

"Jesus," Logan said as I hung up the phone. "I haven't even met this kid and I feel for her."

"Not too many mom's out there who make Celeste look like a prize." I took the opportunity to extract a compact mirror and the small bottle of aloe from my bag to apply it to my burned skin.

The address was in Coral Gables, not too far from the University of Miami. Luke navigated the truck on to the

Dixie Highway heading south. Luke's phone rang and I answered. "Jackie Parker with Damaged Goods."

"It's me," Sargent Vasquez said.

"Enrique, I have a job you know," I huffed.

"Is it as a cadaver dog? Because I heard you found another one."

Cop humor was a strange thing. It allowed those of us who saw the worst of the worst to keep functioning when the compassionate part of us wanted to curl into a safe little ball and never leave our room again. Making light of the dark allowed a callus to form over the soft part of the human heart and get a little distance from the true horror of what people were capable of. Definitely a better crutch than booze or pills.

"Not a corpse." Though the poor guy probably wished he was at various points over the last several days.

Vasquez grunted. "I just wanted to let you know I've pulled a few strings and Logan's house should be cleared by the end of the week."

"That's great news," I repeated what he said to the Parker brothers. Logan grunted and Luke shrugged.

"They're excited too," I told Vasquez.

"Do me a favor and stay out of trouble." Sargent Vasquez said and he disconnected.

"He makes me sound like I'm starring in an episode of *I Love Lucy*. "Jackie, you got some 'splaining to do."

Still nothing.

"I'm trying here, guys." I snapped. "What's up with you two?"

"We'll talk about it later," Logan said.

Luke's hands tightened on the steering wheel, a sure sign he was stressed and wanted to say something but didn't know what. Unlike the Dark Prince, my ex had a habit of thinking things through before he voiced them.

We pulled up in front of the apartment building. It was a Spanish style with red-tiled roof, big white archways and open breezeways between units. Head and shoulders beyond the apartment complex we had just come from.

"Luke, maybe you should wait in the car. We don't want to overwhelm her." And I wanted to divide and conquer.

"Why doesn't Logan wait in the car?" Luke kvetched.

I chucked my thumb at the Dark Prince. "Do you think he'll listen any better than I usually do?"

"Point taken." Luke settled in and fiddled with the radio.

"What's up?" I asked Logan as we moved past scantily clad college students.

"Luke thinks I should stay home and hideout. One of the cops who showed up was giving me a funny look."

"So?"

"He was probably there when I was arrested."

I blew out a sigh. "You know how cops are, total gossip-mongers."

Logan turned to face me so I could see myself in his reflective sunglasses. "You don't think I ought to hide out in my house?"

Even though we were on the job, I threaded my arm through his. "Not unless I get to hide out with you."

His lips twitched.

"Seriously, Logan. I don't think you should stop living your life because of this. You didn't do anything wrong, right?"

His expression closed up.

"Right?" I asked again.

"Come on, let's go talk to this girl." Logan walked away, leaving me standing in the hall.

What the hell had the Dark Prince done?

## 13

Our missing tenant was a pretty brunette with oversized glasses. Her hair was held up by a pencil and she wore cut-offs and a pink tank top that wouldn't contain my left boob.

"You know you are in violation of your rental agreement." I felt like a bit of a heel saying it, but that was part of the job.

She nodded and shot Logan a nervous look. We were doing our good cop, bad cop routine, with me being the *I just want to help a sister out* one and him being the big, scary enforcer type. The broken nose really added to the ambiance.

Or maybe it was the chill that had gripped my spine when he'd refused to answer my question about him doing anything wrong.

"I know, but I just didn't feel safe there anymore."

"When did you leave?" Logan asked.

Her nervous gaze shot to his. "Last week. Monday I think."

"Did you contact anybody, let them know you were heading out?" I kept my tone gentle and sympathetic.

"Only my mom. Look, do I need to pay a fee or something?"

"You wouldn't consider going back there?" I asked.

She shook her head. "It's too far away from campus and I don't want to be around the people who hang around that place."

"You're talking about the other tenants?" Logan asked.

"I don't think they live there. At least most of them don't. They show up and party. Sometimes it gets pretty wild."

"Okay, just so you know, by leaving you are forfeiting your security deposit. And this will also be a black mark against your rental history."

She nodded. "That's okay. This is my last semester anyway."

"What did we get out of that?" Logan asked as we headed back through the breezeway towards the parking lot.

I blew a stray lock of hair out of my eyes. "Not much more than we already knew. She's scared to go back and nothing we can do other than what we already planned to do, stake out the complex and see who shows up at night."

We climbed back into the truck and then headed back towards Coral Way for our meeting with the fire marshal.

The house looked even worse in the daytime. I slumped a bit as I stared out the window at my home.

"You are both very lucky," he said to me and Logan. "That bottle was pure accelerant. Whoever tossed it meant to cause maximum destruction."

"Can we go in?" Luke asked. "We need some items."

He nodded. "Just to grab a few things, sure. The damage is mostly contained to the front rooms. But the structure is sound."

Logan took my arm as we headed for the rear entrance.

"I should call Celeste." I stared into her room. "Ask her if she needs to get anything."

"I'll do it," Luke volunteered.

I walked further down the hall. The living room was barely recognizable. The couch beyond saving. I moved to the bedroom door and took it all in.

The space looked like a weird optical illusion. One night-stand intact, as was the dresser. The other blackened. The bed hadn't gone up but the fire and water had ruined the flooring in that half of the room. Soot and ash-covered most everything.

"Damn," I sniffled.

"How about you focus on what you need." Logan threaded his fingers through mine.

What did I need? My home not to be a charred mess. For Logan to explain why the hell this had happened so I could rid myself of the sickening sense that our time was running out.

"Abu's enclosure. I said. "It's on the dresser."

"I'll take it out to the car while you pack."

He left and I breathed a sigh of relief. I wanted to lean on Logan but it didn't seem right. Not when I was fairly sure he was neck-deep in whatever had caused this.

I hauled two duffels out of the walk-in closet and filled them with clothing and then hauled them into the bathroom. I grabbed toiletries willy nilly, uncaring of what I took. Then made my way to the office.

Luke had stashed his stuff in the closet but he had his duffel ready to go. "Anything we need out of here?"

I blinked and then stared at the desk, unable to think.

"Ace, you okay?"

I shook my head, then shrugged. "I don't know."

"How about we leave it for now, other than the laptop," Luke said gently. "You have all our open cases and contacts for our clients in the truck, right?"

I nodded.

"Celeste is working but she said we could pack up her stuff and drop it by Curly Cues."

Again, I forced a nod. "Logan said you told him he shouldn't be working with us."

"That's not what I said." Luke ran a hand through his hair. "At least that's not what I meant to say. I just suggested that maybe it would be better if he kept a low profile."

"But—"

"Look around this place, Jackie." Luke huffed. "Someone did this to our house. I don't know if it was a message to Logan or if they were trying to kill him. What I do know is that whatever he's involved with, it's bad and it landed on our doorstep."

"If that's how you both feel," Logan said from the door to the office.

I held up a hand. "Not here." It was too depressing to have the acrid scent of destroyed dreams stuck in my nose. "Let's get Celeste's stuff boxed up and then we can go back to Gertie's and talk this out."

We worked in silence. Celeste had adopted a minimalist vibe since being evicted from her trailer and we had her bedroom packed up in under an hour. Everything smelled like smoke, but there was no helping that.

The Big Black Truck was packed to the gills by the time we headed toward the downtown area. Celeste met us out front, saving me from the disgrace of having any more children burst into tears at the sight of my face.

"You sure you're all right?" My mother hugged me.

I nodded. "How about you?"

"I think I found a tiny home this morning. Can you come by tonight? I get off work at seven?"

"We have a work thing tonight. How about tomorrow?"

When she agreed we finished loading the trunk of her car and then piled back into the truck, aiming for Gertie's place.

"You gonna grab Abu?" Luke asked me.

"No." I loved my monkey but he was a pain in the ass, as well as a major distraction. "We're heading back out in a bit to meet up with Buck anyhow. Better not to yank him back and forth."

The apartment over Gertie's garage was a one-bedroom with a pull-out couch. According to Marcy, their parents had converted it for Gertie's sake so she could try living on her own.

"So how come it is empty?" Luke looked around at the clean lines and the dormers that extended the living space. "She could make some good money here."

"Can you imagine Gertie with a tenant?" I shuddered at the thought.

It still didn't explain why Marcy didn't live in it, other than the fact that my friend needed a bit of distance from her sister.

Logan popped open the Tupperware and handed out the apple date bars. I took one but Luke folded his arms over his chest and waited.

Logan sat down on the dingy floral sofa. "I don't know who threw the Molotov cocktail. But I'm fairly sure I know who he works for."

I leaned back onto the barstool and waited.

"Emmanuel Gutierrez is the son of a very powerful man. He's your typical entitled rich boy sadistic asshole. He was," Logan corrected and looked at me. "When I saw him the other day, I was worried he'd recognize me. I wanted to be able to take you and get out of the country fast. That's why I stashed my passport in your medicine cabinet."

"And what, leave Luke and your folks without a word?" I asked.

"If it kept them safe, yes." His eyes begged me to understand. And I did.

"Why not just tell me that?" I raised a brow.

"Because it was only a suspicion. I didn't know for sure that he was going to be a problem and I didn't want to freak you out without cause. Corrine was getting ready to disappear and he had only ever seen me once. He didn't know my name so the chances that he would recognize me or come looking for me were slim. Like I said, it was just a precaution."

"So Corrine killed him," I said.

"She couldn't have." Logan shook his head.

"Why are you being so damn stubborn about this?"

"Because if she was going to kill him, she would have done it a long time ago." Logan exploded up out of his chair. "You don't know what she's been through."

"Because you won't tell me," I hollered back.

"It's not my story to tell, how many goddamned times do I have to say it?"

I got in his face. "You won't tell me shit. Vasquez won't tell me shit. Buck won't tell me shit. Guess where that leaves me, Logan? In the fucking dark waiting to catch a bullet and I don't even know what direction it is coming from!"

Luke got in between us, always the peacemaker. "Speaking of Buck, don't you have a meeting with him?"

Logan sank back onto the couch and rested his forehead on his clenched fists. "Yeah."

I turned to face my ex. "Luke, would you give us a minute?"

He chucked a thumb at the door. "I'll go wait in the truck."

I waited for the screen door to slap closed and then knelt down in front of Logan. "This stalemate needs to end."

"I know." He sounded miserable.

I put my hand over his. "I don't want you to go to jail. I don't want anyone to get hurt. You're in over your head, Logan. Please, let us help."

His Adam's apple bobbed and he covered my hand with his own. "I made a promise. That's not something I'm okay going back on."

I stood up and moved toward the door. "You have until we get downtown to decide what it is you want to do."

Buck's law office was on the fifteenth floor of one of the skyscrapers downtown. I shifted in my seat as Luke drove into an underground parking garage. These stupid things made me nervous.

Buck greeted us in the reception area. He shook hands with Logan first and then Luke. His eyes went wide when he took in my face.

"Miz. Jackie. You're looking…uh…well."

"Thanks for seeing us." I ignored Luke's cough and Logan's snort and followed the attorney into the conference room.

Buck sat across the table from the three of us. Logan sat in the middle with Luke on his left and me on his right.

"Tell me what happened," Buck had a cherrywood dish of pens with the law office's logo printed on them sitting in the middle of the otherwise empty table. *Chambers, Buchanan & Dunn: Attorneys at Law.* He extracted one and prepared to take notes.

Logan shot me a sidelong glance.

"I'll wait outside if you want," I offered and held my breath, praying he wouldn't take me up on it.

He let out a slow breath and shook his head. "If this goes to court, you'll hear it all anyway. About a year ago, I got a call from an old Navy buddy, Chris. He was being deployed and asked me to look in on his sister. He hadn't heard from her and didn't have the leave to do it himself. So, I agreed to visit them in Ecuador."

"Ecuador?" I didn't bother to hide my shock.

"That was quite a favor," Buck commented.

"I wanted to get out of Miami for a bit for, uh personal reasons," he murmured.

I squeezed his knee under the table.

Buck nodded and gestured for Logan to continue.

He took a deep breath and then pushed on. "They lived in a remote area outside a small village and Chris didn't have an exact address. It took me almost a week to track down someone who recognized Corrine from her photo and pointed me to their home. When I finally got there, Emmanuel Gutiérrez claimed Corrine was back in the States visiting a friend. He told me he would pass any message along to her. I said her brother would appreciate it if she contacted him as soon as she got back then I left."

Buck nodded but I wasn't so accepting.

"You went all the way to Ecuador and then took no for an answer?" That didn't sound like the Logan Parker I knew.

The corner of his mouth twitched. "No, but I wasn't about to argue with him while he was flanked by two no-neck bruisers sporting assault rifles. I pretended to leave and holed up in a nearby mission. I paid a local kid to keep tabs on the place. A few days later he came and told me that *el jefe* had left. So I went back and over the compound wall."

"Big frigging hero," I muttered. "You could have gotten yourself shot."

Buck frowned at me before turning his full attention to Logan. "Was Mrs. Gutiérrez in residence?"

"She was." Logan's jaw was tight. "Her face was so swollen I barely recognized her. Apparently, he hadn't liked that a gringo had come and asked about her, a friend of her brother or no. So, he beat the hell out of her as punishment."

I closed my eyes, feeling like the world's biggest bitch. Poor Corrine.

"She was isolated from most people and barely spoke the language and none of the villagers spoke English. Even if they had, they wouldn't cross *el jefe*. She had nowhere to turn, no one to ask for help. He'd done a fantastic job alienating her from friends and family in classic abuser fashion."

Luke cracked his knuckles. "When she told me about it, she said at the time, she thought she deserved it. The bastard really got in her head."

Logan nodded. "I tried to convince her to come back stateside with me, promised to help her hide. She refused though, and in the end, there was nothing I could do except insist that she call her brother if she needed help." His voice was ragged and I squeezed his knee again, knowing just how much it had hurt him to leave her behind.

"You keep calling him *el jefe*," I said. "The boss, right?"

"Yeah, although usually the people who said it were referring to Emmanuel Gutiérrez Senior." He looked to the lawyer. "They ran two businesses. The one on record was exporting bananas. The one you won't read about was human trafficking."

Trafficking. No wonder my Dark Prince had freaked out when he spotted Gutiérrez.

"Is there evidence of this anywhere on record?" Buck asked.

"I doubt it. He had people in place in every agency from border patrol to homeland security and plenty of money to pay off anyone he didn't own. When I spoke to Chris, he said he was going to contact someone at the DOJ, see what they could do."

"If Gutiérrez was arrested for trafficking, Corrine would be more likely to leave." This came from Luke.

"But the wheels of justice don't exactly move at warp speed. Two months ago, Chris died in a car wreck." Logan shook his head sadly. "She came to his funeral, without Gutiérrez. When I approached her, she admitted she was ready to leave. I had her pose as my fiancé and brought her to Miami, where I knew my brother would help me keep her hidden until we could set her up somewhere out of her husband and father-in-law's reach."

Buck was frowning. "Tell me what happened the night of the shooting."

Logan relayed the same story he'd told us earlier. Home at three, fell into bed, Corrine woke him up, claiming she no longer felt safe in Miami, knowing her ex was in town. He and Luke drove her to a friend's house just north of Ft. Lauderdale.

Buck took notes and listened to the entire spiel then gestured to me and Luke. "You two are willing to testify that you were with him at the time of the murder and supposed dumping?"

We nodded.

Buck set his pen down and steepled his beefy fingers. "Okay, here's what I know. Emmanuel Gutiérrez and his family are under investigation for human trafficking into the US. They have been under suspicion for debt trafficking."

I raised a hand. It was a stupid thing to do but Buck just smiled at me. "You wondering what that is?"

At my nod, he said, "Imagine you're living in abject poverty. Maybe you go to school, borrow money, anything and everything to keep your family going. But you can never seem to make ends meet. Then some guy comes along and says, *"Hey I have this nice cushy job waiting for you in the states. Travel expenses in to the country are covered. We'll get you in, and all you need to do is show up at this place on this date."* Sometimes the person has a legitimate passport or work visa, if not the recruiter will get things lined up."

"Sounds too good to be true," Luke murmured.

"It is," Logan confirmed. "When the victim shows up, he or she is essentially imprisoned, any of their documents taken away. They are then forced to work to pay back the cost of their transit. If they refuse, the lives of the family back home are threatened."

The scene he was painting of modern-day slavery was horrific. "And Corrine's husband was involved in all this?"

It was Logan who answered. "According to Corrine, her ex brokered deals in and around the Port of Miami all the time. Paying people to look the other way as he smuggled his latest crop into the country."

Buck steepled his hands. "You asked me to do everything I could to keep Corrine out of it, Mr. Parker. But I have to tell you, without her testimony, your chances aren't very good. We need her to back up your story about the abuse as well as her husband's criminal activities."

Logan was shaking his head.

"I know you want to protect her," Luke said to his brother. "After what she went through, I don't blame you one bit. But this is a murder charge, Logan. You can't screw around."

"If Corrine comes forward, she's putting herself right in the crosshairs. She's more afraid of her father-in-law and from what I know of the man, I can't say I blame her."

I faced Buck. "If Gutiérrez is such a bad guy, isn't there any way to prove that there were other people who might want him dead?"

"If it goes to trial. Honestly, I'm hoping with Corrine's statement and the investigation into the Gutiérrez family's activities, I can get the DA to drop the charges."

"But Corrine's gone missing," I said. "Either she ran or she was taken but we don't know where she is."

Buck let out a deep sigh. "And without her testimony, you don't have a case I can win."

## 14

B uck's words bounced around in my skull. *Not a case he could win.* I was still in shock from all that had been revealed and was unaware we were headed back to Gertie's place until Luke swung into a drive-thru to pick up dinner. The sack of tacos left a grease stain on my lap. I couldn't muster enough energy to care.

Without Corrine's testimony, Logan would go to jail for murder.

"You look beat," Logan said as we trudged up the wooden stairs. "Maybe you should stay behind from Sunnyvale tonight—"

I shot him a poisonous glare and he held up his hands.

"It was only a suggestion."

I was tired. Too much high-octane emotion like fear and anger was hell on the vivacity. I handed Logan my phone. "I'm not really hungry, think I'll go shower and lie down for a little while. Do me a favor and keep that thing out of earshot for the next hour."

Without waiting for a reply, I dipped into my carryon for yoga pants and a tank top and closed myself in the small bathroom. I toed off my sneakers and then removed my grease-stained jeans and t-shirt before stepping under the spray.

The water pressure in the shower wasn't the greatest but I emerged, clean at last into the small, dark bedroom.

It smelled musty, in that pleasant way some older homes sometimes did. I'd been struggling to get the smell of the hoarder's apartment out of my nose all day. Even the acrid tang from my bungalow hadn't fully chased it away. The roofline of the garage created a steep slope on the wall the queen-sized bed was set into and the lone window was more of an octagonal-shaped porthole. I did my best to towel dry my hair, then hung the towel on the command hook on the back of the door, along with my dirty clothes. Might as well put them on again when we went out. When Sunnyvale was over I would burn them. Not bothering with the lamp, I climbed onto the dented mattress and curled onto my side, staring out at the gloaming.

Five minutes passed and I was still wide awake when someone knocked lightly on the door. A moment later a sliver of light shone in from the main area. "Jackie?"

I rolled onto my back. "What's up?"

Logan pushed his way into the room. "I thought we could talk."

"About what?" There were so many topics I wanted to avoid, so many things I thought I should say or do or feel. But there was just nothing left in my head.

"You and me." Logan slipped into the room.

"I don't want to talk."

He paused a few feet away. I noticed he was favoring his bad leg.

I reached a hand toward him. "Come lie down with me."

He waggled his eyebrows. "This isn't the place I thought we should be when we consummate our relationship."

I snorted. "Don't be an ass, I don't have the energy to banter with you right now. I just want you to get off that leg for a bit."

His expression softened. He toed off his boots and then stretched out on the mattress beside me. I didn't look at him, my gaze locked on the slanted ceiling.

"Who the hell uses words like consummate anyhow? You sound like one of my mother's romance novels."

The mattress shook as he chuckled. "Actually, those were my mother's romance novels. She likes historicals, especially Regency. I read a few of the ones she had lying around while the leg was healing up. They're sort of addictive."

I'd seen the stack by the bed in the guest room. A grin stole across my face at the thought of him reading *The Dastardly Duke's Dalliance*. "Logan Parker has a secret romance-novel fixation. Who would have thought?"

We were silent for several minutes and then he said, "Are you still angry?"

I sifted through my feelings hunting for a truthful answer. "Honestly? I don't think so. I know you had good intentions."

"The road to hell is paved with those bastards." Logan laced his hands beneath his head.

I debated it a moment, then decided that his warmth was too alluring and I needed the comfort too badly. So I rolled until I snuggled into his side. He hesitated a moment, then let out a long breath. "Jackie, I'm sorry. I didn't mean to ruin everything."

I put a hand over his lips and shook my head. "Just don't. I'm too exhausted to hash it all out."

He kissed my fingertips. "Then get some sleep."

When I opened my eyes an untold amount of time later, Logan had shifted to face me. My head was pillowed on his left arm and his right hand caressed the length of my arm in long sweeping strokes.

Our gazes locked.

"Better?" He raised a dark brow.

I inhaled and then nodded. "Yeah. Go ahead and say whatever it is."

He propped himself up on one elbow and looked down at me. "I'm sorry. I should have handled all of this stuff with Corrine differently. Bringing her here was stupid, keeping her here as long as I did was even more stupid. I knew that but...."

"But?"

"It was petty on my part but...I wanted to make you jealous."

"It worked," I muttered. "Too freaking well."

The skin around his eyes crinkled. "Yeah, it did." But then his smile vanished. "But it brought all this stuff to your doorstep. It's gutted me that you have been in danger because of decisions I made months ago."

I reached up so I could touch his face. "We can't change the past, Logan. No matter how much we might want to. All we can do is go on from here and deal with what is."

His blue eyes searched every inch of my expression. "And you want that? Want to have a future with me?"

I nodded. "I think I always have. But...it scares me. We've made so many mistakes and—"

His lips sealed over mine in a hungry kiss. The intensity bubbled up and over. All the fear and the trepidation, the hesitancy I'd been feeling was shoved aside as I let myself be thoroughly and completely kissed by my Dark Prince.

His tongue swept into my mouth and his hands roved over my body in greedy glides. Logan slid the strap of my tank down my shoulder as I reached for his belt. Every touch was a demand, choreographing our desperate need for one another.

Too much had happened. And not enough. The future wasn't guaranteed.

But we had the moment. We had each other.

It was enough. And then some.

---

"So that's consummation," I murmured into Logan's chest sometime later. "Gotta say, I'm a fan."

He chuckled, his hand toying with the wild array of curls. "Glad to hear it."

"Should I ask if Luke is in the other room?" The place was small and we hadn't exactly been quiet.

"He went out. Didn't say where. I think he knew we needed some time to ourselves."

"Luke's good like that." I sighed and snuggled deeper into his embrace, glad we had the place to ourselves for a little while longer.

"We're going to make this work, Jackie." Logan murmured. "No matter what it takes, I am determined to make you and me happen."

"We're already happening," I pointed out.

"That's not what I mean. It's not about the murder either." He lifted one hand up and ran it through his dark hair.

I propped myself up so I could look down at him. "So, what do you mean?"

His palm wrapped around the nape of my neck. "I want it all with you. The house. A couple of kids. The damn monkey I know you will never even consider living without. Everything."

My lips parted but no sound came out.

"I know it's probably too soon for all this." He made a sound in the back of his throat. "Or maybe too late. I'm no great catch what with the looming trial and all. But I want you to understand where I'm coming from."

"Logan," I managed to squeak his name out. House and kids? The day before I had punched him in the nose and now he was talking about some sort of Norman Rockwell action? "It's so much and Luke literally just told your parents about our divorce. It's so soon…." I made vague circles with my hands encompassing everything that existed outside of our little love cave.

He caught my flailing hand and brought my knuckles to his lips. "But it's *right.* That's the important part. You are my one and only priority, Jackie Parker. We go as fast or slow as you want to go as long as we go together. Got it?"

I let out a breath. "Yeah, I think I do."

And then he kissed me again and heaven help me, there was nothing sexier than the Dark Prince determined to make a point.

"We need to get up and go back to work," I murmured sometime later. "As much as I don't want to see whatever the hell is going on over at that damn apartment complex."

"Come shower with me." Logan urged me out of the cocoon of covers.

"Are you kidding? That shower is like a coffin. There is no way we will both fit in there at once."

His jaw set at a stubborn angle but I also saw something in his eyes. Something that looked a lot like fear.

What would Logan be afraid of?

Then it registered. "You're worried I'm going to sneak out again. Like I did the last time after…," I gestured to the bed.

A muscle jumped in his jaw. He held my gaze steady and didn't deny it.

So, I wasn't the only one haunted by our past. It occurred to me that for all his seeming invincibility, in his own way, the Dark Prince was just as insecure about our relationship as I was.

What did he give me that made me feel better? Reassurance. Honesty. I owed him the same.

I wrapped my arms around his waist and rested my chin on his chest. "I promise you, Logan Parker. No more running or hiding or any of it. It was a mistake. I was young and scared and I didn't know what a good thing I had right in front of me. Believe me, I have learned. I'm in this to win this. To win you. So you aren't getting rid of me that easily."

He let out an uneven exhale and his arms went around me. His eyes closed and, at that moment, I wish I had even a sliver of artistic talent because his expression, one of shame and relief and joy was something worth carving in marble.

"Okay?" I asked.

"Okay," he said. "Let's get to work."

---

I HAD no idea where Luke had been during our interlude and figured it wasn't my place to ask. Logan had been right, I needed to confront my hodgepodge of feelings regarding Luke, Corrine and everyone else I had been focusing on to avoid confronting what mattered.

Clearing Logan's name.

"Let's say Corrine did leave on her own. Do you have any idea where Corrine would go?" I asked the Parker brothers as we sat in the Big Black Truck across the street from our apartment complex.

"She doesn't have any family left," Logan said. "Chris and Corrine's mom passed away from cancer several years ago and their dad hasn't been in the picture for years."

"Grandparents? Aunts, uncles? College friends?" She

wasn't on Facebook, an oddity in and of itself in the current day.

"No. I think if I hadn't offered her an out, she would have gone back because she had nowhere else to go."

So no family, no friends, no easy answers. "The person you dropped her off with in Ft. Lauderdale?"

"Becky. They were in a sorority together." Logan said.

"What about marketable skills?"

"None that I'm aware of." Logan turned to his brother. "You?"

Luke shook his head. "She said once that she had a BA in business, but the only job was waitressing."

"What about the father-in-law," I said to Logan. "How much of a factor would he be in her decision to run?"

"Huge. She was more afraid of *el jefe* than she was of her husband."

"So hearing that Emmanuel Gutiérrez was dead from the police might be what prompted her to run."

"She was waiting on paperwork." Logan sipped from his coffee cup. "She didn't feel safe in Miami. With Gutiérrez being murdered here, this would be the first place *el jefe* would look. That's why I was sure you wouldn't have seen her here."

"When you say paperwork, you mean a new identity, right?" Leave it to the Dark Prince to start up his own version of the witness relocation program.

"It's not my—" Logan began.

"—secret to tell," I finished with him. "Yeah, I'm fairly certain I have heard that somewhere before."

Luke's gaze met mine in the rearview mirror. "He won't say it but I will. Yes, Corrine wanted to disappear, she told me as much."

"Dude," Logan snapped his head toward his brother.

"Dude," Luke shoved him. "She knows most of it already."

"Dudes," I leaned forward and pointed to the apartment complex where fifteen motorcycles had rolled right on past the hard-scrabbled parking lot and into the rubbish-strewn courtyard. "I think this is what we've been waiting for."

One by one the bikers dismounted. One by one they took off their helmets.

"Shit," Luke breathed. "Am I seeing this?"

Though several of the streetlights had been burned, or in some cases shot out, there was enough light to make out the features of the gang members.

All of them were female.

There was a dumpster alongside the utility room. Five of the bikers strode to it and heaved it over. The thing thudded to the ground and garbage spilled forth some of it into the pool.

"They're trashing the place." Logan leaned forward, studying the doors. "No one is coming out of the apartment complex."

"This is what our college student was afraid of. Why she broke her lease." I already had my phone held to my ear, calling 911. The cops must have the address memorized by now.

There was a thunderous crash as the recycling bin beside the dumpster went over. The tinkle of shattering glass reached us even with the windows rolled up.

"This isn't some wild party," I said as I watched the destruction. There were a few plastic chairs scattered around the pool and the bikers were kicking them into the pool. "They want to trash the place."

Logan reached for the door handle. "I'm going in."

"Are you insane?" I gripped his arm. "Those ladies are dead set on wrecking this place and you want to get in their way?"

"I just want to talk to them." Logan looked to his brother. "You backing me up?"

With Logan out on bail, he couldn't use his conceal carry weapon, not without making his situation worse. If Luke didn't go, Logan would be approaching a biker gang hell-bent on destruction with nothing but his bare hands.

I could see the indecision on Luke's face and then he nodded slowly. "I've got your six."

"Jackie—,"

I was already out the door. "Screw you, Logan Parker. If you're going over there, I'm going over there."

It was our job after all. No matter how much it sometimes sucked canal water backward.

We didn't try to conceal our approach. The gang was too busy kicking over planters and bashing out light fixtures to notice us right away. Three of them were spraying graffiti on the stucco wall surrounding the apartment complex. Not gang tags that I recognized, but it was still destruction of property.

Logan approached the one holding the can of spray paint. "You better leave, the cops are on their way."

"Who the fuck are you?" The woman who was almost as tall as Logan and twice as wide, looked him up and down. Her lip curled back and I saw she had a horrible snaggle tooth. The look she was giving him was not the same kind most women gave the Dark Prince. There was no desire, no hunger. No, Snaggle Toothy Ruthie was sizing him up for a fight.

I stepped in front of him. If she wanted a piece of him, she'd have to go through me. Which admittedly, wouldn't be hard. But Logan didn't need an assault charge dogpiled on top of his current clusterfuck. "We work for the property owner. You are trespassing and destroying private property."

"That's funny." A tall, slim woman with her hair all

buzzed except for a bright red rooster tail towered over me. "You say we're trespassing? But we were hired to do a job. So, I say we have every right to be here."

"What job?" Luke took up the spot beside me, drawing their attention from me.

"Why prettying this dump up, of course." Rooster Tail held out her hands and spun in a circle. "What, you don't like our landscaping?"

Several of the gang members guffawed.

"And what about the people who live here?" I asked. "You're terrorizing them."

That stopped them cold. Snaggle Toothy Ruthie glowered down at me. "Terrorizing? This place is abandoned."

"It isn't. At least twelve of the units are occupied."

Snaggle Toothy Ruthie glared at me. "You're lying."

I was about to ask her to go knock on a door, but knew that bringing tenants into this mess wasn't a bright idea.

Sirens called out in the distance.

Rooster Tail glared at us. "You really did call the fucking cops."

Luke had his hand carefully placed by his sidearm so it was in easy reach. "You better head out then."

She curled her lip and then mounted her hog.

I caught her by the arm. "Wait. You said this was a job. Who hired you?"

She tried to shake me loose, but I held on tight. "Better ask your boss who'd have a bone to pick with him."

Then she shoved me, hard. Snaggle Toothy Ruthie had snuck up behind me and added another push to speed my momentum.

I stumbled on the cracked concrete and teetered, arms pinwheeling. Logan lunged for me but I lost my balance and fell.

Right into the pool. My pool guy hadn't managed to make

it out yet, so I didn't break my neck on impact. Cackling laughter and the roar of motorcycles was the last I heard before I went under. The slap of cold, filthy water hit me like a punch and expelled all the breath from my lungs.

Luckily it was the deep end. There was a slickness on the surface and the water smelled foul. My head went all the way under. I flailed, forgetting how to swim and losing track of which way was up. My mind shrieked that I was going to catch some horrible flesh-eating bacteria from the filthy pool.

Strong arms wrapped around me and then Logan hauled me up to the surface. I gasped in air and he shoved me harder toward the concrete side and the rickety ladder there. The sound of sirens and flickering blue lights illuminated the courtyard as the distant rumble of a dozen motorcycles faded into the night.

Ignoring the ladder, which looked like a tetanus hazard, Logan dragged me toward the edge of the pool where Luke was waiting to haul my sodden carcass out of the cesspit.

I lay on the filthy concrete and tucked my knees up to my chin. Logan pulled himself up and knelt beside me. His hands checked my skull, probably hunting for injuries.

Intense blue eyes held mine. "Are you hurt?"

Physically, I was undamaged. Mentally, I'd gone around the bend.

"I think I changed my mind about the shower," I told Logan.

He patted my hip. "You've been covered in worse. Today even,"

"Don't remind me."

"Look on the bright side, Ace." Luke crouched beside me. "You can now tell people you scared off a motorcycle gang."

I coughed and rolled onto my side. "Cross that one off the bucket list."

## 15

"So, here's what we know. Someone has a grudge with our property owner." Fresh from the shower and with my hands wrapped around a steaming mug of hot chocolate, I studied the Sunnyvale file. "I called and left a message but he isn't picking up."

"An ex-wife maybe?" Luke asked.

He and Logan were busy devouring the pizza Luke had gone out to get while I decontaminated. I had no appetite, the stench of the stagnant pool still lodged in my olfactory senses. The hot chocolate was all I could manage.

"Nope, he is a widower." I'd done a preemptive Google search to see what I could unearth. "Relatively recent."

"Pissed-off girlfriend?" Logan folded the slice of pizza up into a tube shape so he could consume it faster than his brother, who was on his fourth slice. Sibling rivalry at its worst.

I glowered at the two of them. "One of these days, your metabolisms are going to tank and you won't be able to eat like that and still fit through the door."

"What can I say? Swimming makes me hungry." Logan winked at me, the cheeky bastard.

"You're sick, you know that?" I shook my head but then sobered. "The bikers were hired to trash the place but were never told the apartments were rented. I think whatever the hell is going on has more to do with the property itself."

"It's Miami real estate," Luke pointed out. "Maybe we need to find out if anyone has made any offers to buy the complex. If the tenants are frightened and breaking the leases, they aren't paying rent. Enough vacancies would force our guy into selling and doing it at a discounted rate."

I leaned back into the couch. "Any news about our hoarder? The parents never got back to me."

Logan shut the empty pizza box. "I called the hospital while you were draining the hot water tank and found out that he's stable for now. No visitors other than medical personnel."

"Didn't he have a job?" Luke asked. "Boss or coworkers? Someone who would've missed him?"

A moment later I had my answer. "He's an independent science fiction writer. Works entirely online." Not at all surprising. I had yet to meet a mentally stable writer.

"So no one would miss him until his next book came out," Luke grumbled.

Logan snorted. "If then."

"We can't take this guy on as a project." Luke scrubbed a hand over his face. "Last time I checked we are already neck-deep in both inventory and this apartment complex, plus your own little extracurricular research which we all know Jackie will be diving into at the earliest opportunity."

I shrugged. No sense denying the truth.

Logan pressed the heels of his hands into his eye sockets as if he were fighting a headache. "Okay, here's what I think.

We make a few more calls on Thomas's behalf. And maybe we focus on the inventory for a day."

"Count me in." A long, hot day in a cargo container might be exactly the kind of thing I needed to clear my head.

Luke made his way to the bathroom to take his own shower. Logan and I sat in the living room, each lost in our own thoughts.

"You're going to look for her, aren't you?" It wasn't a question.

I tucked my feet up under me. "Logan, you heard what Buck said. We don't have a choice if we want to keep you out of prison."

He propped his chin on his fist and stared out the window as the sun broke over the horizon.

"Listen, the way I see it, she either got scared after you were arrested and ran or someone took her. Either way, she's out there alone and unprepared. You said that her father-in-law is a big baddy, right?"

"The worst," Logan agreed. "I'm sure he's the one responsible for the Molotov cocktail."

I put my hand on his arm. "Then we need to tell Vasquez everything. He's a cop, he has the resources to put out an APB."

He looked over at me and took a breath. "I didn't believe you. When you said you saw her back here in town."

Even though the words stung, I shrugged. "I get it, I was acting like a jealous lunatic about her."

He offered a tight smile. "Kinda the same way I've acted like an ass about you and Luke for all the time the two of you were married?"

"No," I shook my head. "Not the same. You were trying to protect your brother. I was just being an insecure nutjob."

He tilted his head to the side. "I like the way you see me in a good light, attributing positive motives."

I laughed and shook my head. "Trust me, that is not always the case."

"It is when it matters." He reached for my hand and threaded his fingers through mine. "I know you've got my back. And there isn't anyone else I would rather have guarding my six."

"Not even Luke?"

"Nah," he touched his nose. "You hit harder than Luke."

"I heard that!" Luke called as he made his way from the dinky bathroom to the bedroom to dress.

"You were supposed to." Logan chuckled and then grinned at me. "And you were upset. Someone had just tried to burn your house down and it was my fault. I was scared. We both lash out when we're scared."

I shook my head. "Still, it's like the first thing we learned in kindergarten. No matter how upset someone makes you, you don't hit. So I'm sorry and next time, I swear I will use my words.

His grin turned wicked. "Make them dirty words and we're square."

"I need to get the fuck out of here," Luke said but he was smiling. "Get dressed, Ace. Inventory awaits."

I headed into the bedroom where my small stash of clothing was piled on the lone nightstand. My heart had lightened somewhat. If Luke, Logan and I could untangle our messy love lives and be happy for one another, anything was possible.

Once dressed I snagged my cell phone and headed out onto the small balcony.

"You didn't find another body, did you?" Vasquez said when he picked up his cell.

"No, it's about Corrine." I briefly explained the situation concluding with, "I need you to help me find her, Enrique."

"Just because she wasn't where she said she was going to be doesn't mean she was taken."

I worried my lip and debated how much I ought to tell him about Logan's getting her paperwork. "Look, I think she's in Miami. I know that was her by Curly Cues and I have the second-degree burns to prove it. Can't you just spread the word around the watercooler and have people keep an eye out. Shouldn't she be a suspect? Her husband was an abusive ass-muppet." Logan wouldn't be happy but I might as well work in Corrine's case for self-defense.

The Sargent grumbled something in Spanish before switching back to English. "I will check with hospitals and put her description out to a few of our patrol cars as a person of interest. But Jackie, I need more to go on."

My mind was already clicking ahead. Perhaps I could get Buck to get me a look at the police report on the murder. Logan had me and Luke as alibis and if we could prove that Corrine killed her husband and ran it should be enough for reasonable doubt.

But I wanted more. I wanted his firebug father to pay for torching my beautiful bungalow and tranquing my poor dog.

I frowned. Why would whoever worked for Gutiérrez senior bother with a tranquilizer dart? I was sure people who dealt in human trafficking situations weren't above shooting a dog. Someone had gone to a lot of trouble to take Sasquatch out of commission but not permanently harm her. At first, I had just been so grateful that she was all right that I hadn't stopped to think about the why of it.

"Jackie?" Vasquez said, snapping my focus back to him. "I'll see what I can do."

"You and me both," I muttered and hung up.

"I DON'T KNOW, ACE," Luke grunted as he moved an empty barrel out of the way so we could inventory the stuff behind it. "Why do you keep harping on this? We should just be glad Sasquatch wasn't hurt."

"I called the vet. In order to successfully tranq a dog her size someone needed to know her approximate weight. Too much would have killed her, not enough and they would run the risk of her not going down. From the bad guy's perspective, it would have been a hell of a lot easier to shoot her. Someone who cared about Sasquatch went to the trouble of arranging that."

"So, you're saying it's someone we knew." Logan paused in counting boxes of roofing nails to jot a number down on the clipboard.

"Here, give me that, you always mess up the order." I snatched the clipboard out of his hands. "Someone who knew Sasquatch at least."

"Most people who see her are afraid of her." Luke pointed out. "Thirty-seven boxes of Spanish tile."

"What the hell were these guys building?" I muttered. "It's like a hodgepodge of building materials. Not enough for anything and so many different kinds."

"Fly by night construction company." Logan had moved on to bags of quick-drying concrete. "They bid on foreclosures and either fix what is there or throw up something new on the land and sell it for a hefty profit. My bet is the stuff has been lifted off of other construction companies over the last several months."

"And they stored it all in shipping containers on someone else's land and then stopped paying rent?"

"That probably wasn't the best plan," Luke agreed. "They're probably in too deep with whatever their current project is and fell behind on the rent here."

"Or the property owner found out about their shady dealings and had them evicted." Our job hadn't included the eviction portion, just the property inventory.

From somewhere outside a large motor started up.

Logan and Luke exchanged a glance and then looked at me. "Did the owner say anything about somebody doing work here today?"

I flipped through the pages to the time table and schedule the owner had given us. "No, it's clear through next week."

"I'll go check it out," Luke moved to the door of the cargo container.

Five seconds later, "Logan, Jackie, you better get out here."

"Come on," Logan grabbed my hand and hauled me along in his wake.

The cargo containers on the commercial property were aligned in a row on a flat semi-circle of land surrounded by a thick chain link fence. The only way in or out was through the massive chain-link gate which we had closed behind the Big Black Truck.

Ten feet beyond that a giant forklift rumbled down the gravel drive.

"Those are my things!" The guy behind the wheel had bloodshot eyes and wore a grubby white t-shirt.

"He's not slowing down." I took an involuntary step back.

"Luke, your sidearm?" Logan asked.

"In the truck." The same truck that sat in the path of the maniac driving the forklift.

"Shit, he's not gonna stop." Logan breathed. "Luke, give me the keys. Jackie, stay the hell back."

Luke fished in his pocket and extracted the keys to the Big Black Truck. Logan ran for the truck. Flung open the door and cranked the engine over even as the forklift closed in on the gate.

With the driver's side door still hanging open Logan

threw the truck into drive and laid on the gas. The truck shot forward even as the forklift hit the closed gate. The screech of twisting metal mingled with the sound of the roaring lift.

"It's my stuff!" The whacko screamed.

"Jackie, call 911." Luke ran forward, making some sort of hand signal to Logan.

I shook myself and extracted my phone from my back pocket and dialed.

"911, what's the nature of your emergency?" A male voice with a soft Cuban accent asked.

"There is some maniac with a forklift. He just rammed through the gate." I rattled off the address to him and added, "He looks strung out."

"Ma'am keep your distance."

The tread of the forklift had gotten tangled in some of the wire so the thing was no longer surging forward.

"Come on, pal," Luke shouted above the roar of the engine. "Just come down so we can talk!"

"She took everything," the guy sobbed. "All my money and left."

And there I thought I'd been having a crap week.

"Ma'am, you still there?" 911 guy said.

"Uh, yeah. This guy is seriously having some sort of breakdown."

"Is anyone injured?"

"Not so far. What the hell are you doing?" I shouted just as Logan scrambled over the side of the wrecked gate, pulled himself up into the cab of the forklift. His elbow connected with the crying man's face. The guy's eyes rolled back in his head and he slumped in his seat.

"Scratch that, one unconscious maniac." I glared at Logan, even as I breathed out a sigh of relief.

Logan shut off the engine and then he and Luke worked

to move the driver down from the forklift to the ground. In the distance, sirens blared.

"Okay, I think we're good here," I said. "I'm Jackie Parker and my team is Damaged Goods. We work for the property owner and we have the driver under citizen's arrest." Always good to make it clear that we were the good guys.

"I'll let them know. Be careful." The man said and disconnected.

I ran for the Big Black Truck and snagged the first aid kit before joining the Parker Brothers. The man on the ground wasn't unconscious but all the fight had gone out of him.

Logan was examining a tear in his pant leg where blood was oozing forth. "Good thing I had a tetanus shot after the bullet wound." Always Mr. Bright Side.

I glared at him even as I fished for the alcohol wipes.

"She took it all. This stuff is all I have." The guy on the ground reeked of cheap whiskey.

"Well, this wasn't a smart way to go about getting it back," I snapped. "Now not only do you need to pay back rent you're going to have to fix the fence. And you have destruction of property on your record."

I didn't call him a dumbass, but I thought it really really hard.

"I got him," Luke told his brother. "Get yourself cleaned up."

I guided Logan over to the truck and made him sit on the running board and roll up his pant leg. My hands shook as I ripped open the packaging to the sterilizing wipe.

"That was so freaking stupid," I snapped at him. "What if you had gotten a shoelace tangled up in that tread? You could have lost a leg!"

"Then I'd have more of your tender mercies to look forward to," he hissed as I applied the alcohol wipe to the cut.

"Shut up, Logan Parker. You giant—"

175

He kissed me, effectively cutting me off midtirade.

The fight went out of me and I melted against him, heart still racing.

"I'm fine, Jackie. Really." He twisted his calf so he could see the line of red. "It's not deep. Won't even need stitches."

I sagged against him, all the adrenaline leaving my system in a rush. "What about him?"

"We got him on the destruction of private property, possible theft, and my guess is a DUI as well, once the cops check his blood alcohol levels. I don't think we need to add attempted manslaughter to the mix."

I looked to the mangled fence, the flashing of police lights, the forklift that was tilted like a windmill and shook my head.

"So much for the boring day."

"It's never a boring day with you, Jackie Parker." Logan rested his chin on top of my head.

I let out a sigh. "And we still have one cargo container to do."

Logan leaned his chin on my head. "Lead the way, my lady."

"You really need to lay off the Regency romances."

He laughed and the cops looked over at us like we were nuts. I recognized two of them from the night of the fire-bombing.

Damn good thing I didn't care what anyone thought about our screwy relationship. And that Logan didn't own a forklift.

## 16

"The good news is, we don't need to finish the inventory," I said as we headed back to Gertie's place. "Since the property kept in those storage containers was stolen, neither our owner nor the guy with the forklift can lay claim to it."

"So, what's the bad news?" Luke asked. I noted that his white t-shirt was just as trashed as Logan's black one.

"Our property owner refuses to pay us."

Logan swore. "Are you fucking kidding me? We've spent days sifting through that shit in a hundred-degree heat."

"We could always take him to court." I leaned my head back against the seat, glad that the AC in the truck was top notch. I had sweated through my clothes so many times they were stiff on my body. Combined with the dust that the forklift had kicked up, this set of jeans and tank were most likely headed for the trash.

Logan grimaced. "Not really feeling like more time in court is the way to go."

"There's got to be something we can do," Luke popped the top off a beer and handed it to me.

"Well, I sort of have an idea." After holding the icy bottle to my forehead for a few seconds I passed the bottle on to Logan.

"On a scale of one to ten, exactly how illegal is this plan?" Logan took a swig and leaned back against the counter.

"Not illegal. Immoral maybe…and definitely uncouth."

The Parker brothers exchanged a look and then stood side by side, arms folded over their chests and glowered. They looked like hunky bookends.

"Okay, so we need to crash an event," I said. "We corner him, make our case, threaten to make a scene. He'll have transferred the money into our account before you can say extortion."

Luke narrowed his eyes. "What kind of an event?"

"A dinner party. A charity event that a local artist is hosting at her private estate." I'd spotted the invitation in his office when he'd booked us for the job. "Apparently his wife owns a gallery downtown and she's dying to get this artist to sign with her."

"Won't they refuse to let us in?" Logan asked. "Or call the cops?"

"Not if we're careful." It came out as more of a question.

Logan pinched the bridge of his nose. "Okay, if there is even a chance this will get my bail revoked, I'm more of a liability than an asset."

I looked to Luke and cast him a hopeful smile. He threw his hands up in the air. "What should I wear?"

"That charcoal suit I bought you last April."

He shook his head. "It's at the house. I'll have to make a few calls and see if I can get in. What about you."

I already had my phone in my hand. "Mama Celeste's closet." There were a few benefits to having a mother who marched to the beat of her own drummer, like she never let any one shame her into wearing age-appropriate clothing.

Celeste picked up on the first ring. "I just finished my last appointment and Bessie Mae is all fixed. Do you want me to pick you up or should we meet at the park."

"The park?" Mental forehead smack. "Oh, the tiny house thing."

Logan snickered and I kicked him in the shin.

"You forgot," Celeste sounded hurt.

"It slipped my mind." I checked the clock, missing my Felix the cat. Had he survived the fire? I hadn't even thought to check when we'd been at the house. "Listen, if we make it quick, we can squeeze it in before we head over to your storage locker. I need an evening gown."

"Really?" The cheer had returned to Celeste's voice. "Oh, this sounds like fun."

Maybe someone somewhere was mentally disturbed enough to think that shopping for a tiny house followed by an evening of party crashing sounded like fun, but I wasn't that far gone. "You know where Gertie lives, right?"

We agreed that Celeste would pick me up in fifteen minutes. I flew into the bathroom and suds and scrubbed. The good news was the burns on my face had started to fade. Clean and, in the right sort of low lighting favored by older people at a swanky diner party, I would look almost normal.

Or maybe I was just hoping that was the way it would play out.

I was standing in a pair of lacy boyshorts and a demi bra, deciding what to put over them for the tiny house venture when Logan entered the room. The way his gaze fogged over and his lips parted was most gratifying. Right up until he scowled and said, "I still say this is a bad idea."

"The party-crashing or the borderline blackmail?" I found a pair of cargo capris and hefted them up over my hips then trundled through the mess looking for a clean tank.

"Take your pick." The Dark Prince reached for me but I

danced away.

"I swear, if you get smudgy fingerprints on me I will deck you again."

"It might be worth it." His eyes had turned to blue flames.

I swallowed. "I love the way you look at me."

"And how is that?"

Like there was nothing wrong with me. Like I was the most beautiful woman he had ever seen. Like it wasn't physically possible for him to ever get enough of me.

"Like I'm something special," I said.

His gaze met mine. "You know you are."

I shrugged and then found a clean cream-colored tank that didn't look too horrific with the black bra straps banging out. "I'm just a girl with a job to do. Keeping us financially solvent is a big part of that job." And finding Corrine was the other.

"Keep telling yourself that, Jackie." He muttered. "Just do me a favor?"

I raised a brow.

"Don't get arrested."

"Deal." I patted two fingers to my lips and then pressed them to his. "You look like hell, Logan. Better take the night off and rest up for later."

Logan continued to eye-fuck me as I made my way through the main living area, snagged my purse and sandals and headed down the steps with a huge grin on my face.

Bessie Mae waited across the street. My mother sat behind the wheel, her blouse unbuttoned almost to the point of indecency as the vent billowed the fabric of her shirt out.

"Hot flash," she explained to me. "Menopause is a beast."

"Anything that begins with men is a beast," I settled myself in the passenger's seat and buckled up. "We better get going before you get arrested for public indecency."

Celeste did a little waving thing over her face then

checked her mirrors and pulled the car back out into traffic. "I wake up in the middle of the night and have to change the sheets like a child who wets the bed. How am I ever going to make it through the summer?"

My sunglasses were lost at the bottom of my bag. "I don't know. Maybe you could go somewhere nice and cool. The mountains maybe."

"Jackie, this is Florida. The closest thing we have to the mountains is Space Mountain."

"Take a vacation. Haven't you ever wanted to see anywhere else? Alaska maybe?"

"By myself? What would I do?" Celeste looked totally floored by my suggestion.

My mother had been born in Jacksonville and spent her entire life in the sunshine state. Until that moment, it hadn't occurred to me just how limited she might be.

Or how I was exactly like her.

"Maybe I could come with you," I said.

Her expression lit up. "Really?"

If we got paid for the inventory and managed to somehow salvage the sale of the house, I would have the money. "Really."

A grin split her face. "What about Logan?"

"He's not invited. Just us girls." The more I thought about the idea, the more I liked it.

Logan wanted my everything. The house, the kids and even my monkey. I wanted to work to live and not live to work.

I smiled at Celeste. "Okay, so let's go see this tiny house."

———

"WELL, WHAT DO YOU THINK?" Celeste asked as I eyed the structure before me.

My mother had lived in all sorts of trailers and mobile homes. I thought I'd seen the worst.

"It's not a converted cargo container." One positive as I felt I had spent more than enough time inside those to last a lifetime. Celeste's current pick was buttercup yellow with dark blue shutters and a door. I eyed the front porch of the tiny house which was nothing more than a step that was wider than the two that led up to it. "It's on wheels."

She nodded. "So, I can move it from place to place. I sort of like the idea of being mobile. But Derek said there is plenty of room to keep it here in this community until I get a vehicle that can tow it."

"Hmmm," I said for lack of anything better to say.

"Wait until you see the inside."

"Will we all fit?" I looked from my mother's plus-sized backside to the builder, who wasn't at all slight. The three of us combined probably outweighed Celeste's perspective home.

"I'll wait out here," the builder, Derek, his name tag read, must have had the same thought.

Celeste headed up the steps and ducked so that her topknot didn't bonk into the door. After a reluctant moment, I followed.

The interior was all made of whitewashed wood with teal and turquoise accents. I could see right away why it appealed to Celeste. My mother loved beach themed anything.

"See, it's got everything I need," Celeste said as she took the two steps necessary to move from the living room, which was essentially a bench with a pretty teal cushion on top and into the galley kitchen which was a single sink, a mini-fridge that looked big enough for a single bottle of wine and a brick of cheese and maybe a cluster of grapes. If they were really small grapes. A butcher block countertop as long as my fore-arm. No dishwasher. No stovetop or oven. Although considering the kitchen curse, my mother wouldn't use either of those. The pantry was a single cabinet that also shared space with the dishes. A washer/dryer combo unit was hidden behind a section of white paneling. Celeste proudly showed me each little nook and cranny, which took about three and a half minutes. I opened my mouth and then closed it, unsure of what I ought to say.

"What more do I need?" Celeste asked.

"How about a table? Somewhere to set up your laptop and eat a sandwich?"

"I could get a folding card table and maybe a few chairs and store them in the utility cabinet outside." She moved over to the ladder that led to the sleeping loft.

I looked around. "Where's the bathroom?"

Celeste was already halfway up the ladder, her neon pink panties on full display beneath her short skirt. "Right over there."

She pointed to a door that headed into what I thought was a closet. I was partly right. The toilet sat in the middle of a tiled room and a detachable showerhead was hung above it. That was it, the whole bathroom.

"So you shower while sitting on the toilet?" I asked.

"It's for efficiency. Come on up, you need to see this, Jackie."

She was so giddy ever since I had mentioned a girl's vacation and I hated to burst her bubble but try as I might, I could not imagine her navigating that ladder in the middle of the night to go to the bathroom.

"Are you sure this is strong enough to support both of us?" I could see the bottom of Celeste's sandals hanging over the edge of the full-sized mattress.

"Plenty sure." The sandals waggled at me along with coral pink toenails.

I reached the top of the ladder and then tried to decide

how to get off it without hitting my head on the ceiling. Celeste reached out a hand and I took it. She yanked, I surged up, cracked my noggin, and then cursed.

"This will be fun if you bring a date home," I grumped as the stars receded.

Celeste winked at me. "There's always the couch."

Note to self: Never sit on my mother's sofa.

"So, what do you think?" She asked, sounding like a kindergartner showing off a prized finger painting.

"Where are you going to keep your clothes?" I asked.

She reached overhead and depressed a silver leaver, revealing a cabinet the size of a shoebox.

"Seriously?" I asked. "I have hats with more storage than that."

She huffed out a breath. "Jackie, would you just give it a chance? Not everyone wants or needs three bedrooms, two baths, and stone counters."

I opened my mouth to respond but couldn't think of anything to say.

She huffed out a breath. "The truth is I don't really enjoy things, not since John."

I reached out and squeezed her hand. "That's understandable."

She sniffled. "I just need a place to come back to that fits me, my life as it is. A place where I can be me and I don't need to do for anyone else."

And really what could I say to that? "If you really think this will make you happy, Mom, then I'm all for it."

She turned her head to look at me. "Really?"

I did an up and down gesture with my shoulders. "Who am I to tell you how to live?"

"Thank you, baby." Celeste rolled over and hugged me.

"Just one thing?" I asked when she pulled away.

"Anything."

"How the hell do I get down from here?"

I managed to get down by sliding my bottom half over the edge until my foot connected with the ladder rung. I stepped down and then down again. Celeste managed it much more easily. Still, I was worried about her doing so in the middle of the night.

"I'd still like it better if you found one with a bed on the ground floor."

"Maybe I could get one of those beds that folds up into the wall," Celeste suggested. "Then I'll just use the loft for a reading nook."

We exited the tiny house where Derek stood talking to a man wearing blue overalls.

"Something is clogged up in there, blocking the water flow." The man who wore a nametag that read Rick was saying. "Somebody, more like several somebodys must have been flushing them baby wipes down the toilet. A man shouted. More cries rang out as plumbers ran from the area where they had been working. "It's gonna blow!"

"Might want to back up, folks," Rick said in a flat tone.

Celeste and I beat a hasty retreat even as Celeste asked, "What's happening."

Rick shook his head. "Too much pressure built up the line. Stupid baby wipes, every time. I tell them not to flush them, but they keep doing it."

Two seconds later a geyser erupted from the worksite. A geyser of sewage.

It shot up twenty feet into the air. Arced out in several directions and then splat.

The tiny house we had just been inside was coated in raw sewage and a giant bezoar of crumpled baby wipes sat on the front porch.

I stared at the house. Derek stared at the house.

"Does this affect the price at all?" Celeste asked.

## 17

Luke whistled low under his breath. "Damn, Logan is going to be sorry he missed seeing you in that getup."

"Thanks," I took a wobbly step out of Bessie Mae. "Mom, these heels are frigging ludicrous."

"Yeah, but they accentuate the gams." Celeste waved and putt-putted off to make all her big dreams for tiny living come true in the little house of sewage.

"The gams? Do I even want to know?" Luke asked.

"Probably not." I tottered on the seafoam heels that matched the slinky strapless dress with a heart bodice that accentuated the girls perfectly. "My mother is much better at shopping for clothing than she is shopping for tiny homes.

Luke extended an elbow to me. "Do I want to know?"

"Definitely not."

We had agreed to meet up at the base of the monstrously long driveway, a fact that I was regretting. The sun had slipped beyond the horizon and the sky was busy turning an even deeper shade of blue. There were solar lights alongside the driveway, a warm and welcoming invitation to the mammoth stone house set overlooking a peaceful inlet to the sound. Other well-dressed patrons were following suit, exiting limos and town cars. A BMW passed us as we moseyed on up with the rest of the guests.

"So, who is this lady, anyway?" Luke asked.

"Her name Is Minerva Upton. Not sure if that's her real name or just the one she uses in her artist circles."

"And how does our owner of the cargo crates know her?"

"His wife runs one of the local art galleries."

"Remind me again what he looks like?"

"About five-ten, thinning sandy blonde hair and a massive overbite." I extracted my cell from the small beaded clutch Celeste had convinced me to swap for my trusty shoulder bag for the evening. I pulled up a photo from our owner's Linked-In profile.

Luke and I stood to the side as guests moved their way up the steps. I don't know if it was because I had just come from Celeste's tiny house but the place looked larger than your average shopping mall and appeared to be just as crowded.

"There you are." A woman in her mid-forties, eyes bright from sparkling wine that she held in her left hand moved over to Luke's side.

"Um…?" My ex glanced around.

Both his eyebrows shot up when she gave him a hug.

"Darling, I've been looking for you *everywhere*." She strongly emphasized the last word in case he didn't pick up on her desperation. "There is someone I simply *must* introduce you to."

The wine in her hand clearly wasn't her first of the evening.

"Go with it," I mouthed over her shoulder as she led Luke away. I plucked a random canapé off a passing server's silver tray and moved farther into the room, winding my way through the sea of bodies. The entire downstairs of the house seemed to be one long art gallery. Chaises were scattered throughout, directly in front of well-lit canvases. From what I could tell the art itself was abstract scenes, dark backgrounds slashed with lively blobs of brighter color. I stopped in front of one that looked like nothing more than a crime scene photo done in black and white. Decent place for a snack, especially because I couldn't remember the last thing I had eaten.

Odd that old poo faithful hadn't affected my appetite. Then again, I hadn't gotten covered in it so all in all, it was a good day.

Someone moved up alongside me. I ignored them, focusing all my interest on the fluffy little treat that looked like a work of art itself. I took a bite of the savory and closed my eyes in bliss. Damn, that was good.

"I know something else that can put that look on your face."

I turned to the female voice to my right. Her hair was wrapped up in a gold turban that matched the golden gown that swathed her angular figure. Her eyelashes were fake, and her eyebrows had been shaved off. She had the skin of a lifelong sun worshipper and her talons—they were too long to just be considered nails—were the same eerie red as the splotch on the artwork. Her eyes sparkled with mirth.

"And what is that?" I covered my mouth as I finished the savory.

"Darling, I would much rather *show* you than tell you." She winked at me. It was an intense fluttering of her lashes that looked like a weird sort of mating ritual.

Before I could decide what to say, she turned her attention to the crime scene photo. "Do you like it?" I couldn't place her accent. It was raspy and melodic, cultured and just a wee bit above it all. Something about her reminded me of a gypsy wise woman.

"I don't know enough about art to have an opinion."

"You don't need to know anything to have an opinion. I asked if you liked it."

Not really but it seemed rude to say so. "It feels familiar," I said. "Like something I've seen before."

She turned to me then, her gaze speculative. "Does it now? Tell me, have you seen gruesome death?"

I wrinkled my nose. "How did you guess?"

"Because I painted it for you."

"*You* painted?" Thank god I hadn't said it gave me the willies. "Then you must be...?"

"Your hostess, Minerva Upton." She lifted my hand and brought it to those eerie blood-red lips. "Come, you will be my special guest tonight."

"Oh, well, actually I was looking for someone..."

"And you've *found* someone. You know the expression, it's my party? Well, so it is. All of these other ass-kissers are here for the sake of my prestige. That and five dollars will get you a cup of coffee." She snorted. "But you...you have seen things. I want to know more about you...?" One nonexistent eyebrow went up in inquiry.

"Jackie," I said, intentionally not using my last name. Of all the rotten luck. How was I supposed to find and—ahem, *persuade*—our missing landlord when I had the hostess's personal attention?

A slight man with a pallid complexion moved over and whispered something in her ear.

"Excuse me, darling. I will be back in a few moments to ring the gong for dinner. Stephan, make sure Jackie is seated to my immediate right." That last was addressed to the whey-faced stranger. With that, Minerva sailed off leaving a trail of expensive perfume in her wake.

What was it with these people collecting Parkers like we were trading cards?

"Champagne?" A deep voice said from behind me.

"No thanks," I had half-turned away when the familiar timber registered. "Shit, Logan what are you doing here?"

The Dark Prince had indeed materialized by my side. He wore the same livery as the other servers, but the black and blue around his nose plus his height made him stand out instead of blend in.

"What does it look like, I'm serving."

"You were supposed to stay back and lay low for the night."

"Take a freaking glass already." Logan nodded to a dour-faced man also wearing livery. "No need to draw extra attention to us."

I reached for a champagne glass. "Have you seen Luke?"

He gestured off to the left. "He's been cornered by a half dozen society wives, waiting for you to rescue him."

A small group clustered around a nearby painting and Logan moved

dutifully toward them with the tray of champagne flutes. I moved to a secluded alcove and waited for him to catch up.

"And who is going to rescue you?" I had a brief flash, imagining some poor server passed out and folded up in the back of the catering van.

"Relax, it's a legit gig. They were scrambling for help and I was registered at the temp agency nearby. It was just a matter of a phone call."

"Still, you shouldn't be seen here, bullying someone." I hissed.

But Logan shook his head. "It's not just about that. I got a tip that Corrine is here, too."

My lips parted. "A tip from where?"

"Apparently, you aren't the only one who has been seeing her in Miami. A Navy buddy of mine called and said her name was on the guest list. I texted you about it but you never answered."

I frowned. "She's supposed to be on the run and now, all of a sudden she's showing up at swanky parties?"

"I don't know what's going on. But I thought it might be worth the risk if we can find her and get her to clear my name."

I had to agree. "Just don't get yourself into more trouble."

Logan gave me a smoldering once over. "You look delicious by the way. And I'm not the only one who thinks so. Do you know who that was you were talking to?"

"Minerva Upton?" I nodded. "She wants me to sit next to her at dinner."

Logan snorted. "More likely she wants you to pose naked for her next masterpiece. She's batting for the home team and my bet is she's sizing you up for her next home run."

I rolled my eyes. "Save me from sports metaphors."

Logan looked past my shoulder. "Shit, I need to get back to work before the caterer tosses me out on my ass. Good luck."

"You too."

A gong rang out. I looked over to an archway whose doors stood wide open to see Minerva gesturing toward the dining room. "Thank you all for joining me tonight. This is a first in the Miami art world, a dinner that not only accompanies art, but *is* art. Come join the revel." She waved her hand in the air in a grand flourish.

Like a flock of well-dressed sheep, the patrons lined up. I glanced around looking for Corrine or our stingy property manager but came up empty.

"There you are," Luke made his way to my side. "Did I see you talking to her?"

I nodded. "She wants me to sit next to her at dinner."

Luke shook his head. "She wants a hell of a lot more from you than that. Apparently, she just broke up with her former life partner and is looking for a revenge chippy. I guess you've been tapped."

"You're as bad as Logan. He's here, by the way, looking like the world's scariest waiter." I quickly brought him up to date on the latest Corrine sighting.

"Have you checked your phone? Vasquez might be trying to get in touch with you about an update."

I looked but didn't see anything on the screen. We made it through the bottleneck and into the dining room.

"Ms. Jackie?" The pallid assistant stepped in front of me. "If you will be so kind as to come with me."

I moved to follow him but Luke gripped my wrist.

"What?" I asked him.

"Don't leave me alone. The socialites will descend like buzzards on a fresh carcass."

"You have no one to blame but yourself for being so damn pretty." I turned to face the assistant. "Is there any way my ex-husband could be seated on my other side?"

His thin lips compressed until they were practically nonexistent but he nodded and gestured for us to follow.

I'd half expended one long dining table but instead, there were a multitude of smaller ones, all draped in expensive cream-colored linens. Crystal water goblets stood off to the side along with empty wine glasses that had been turned upside down.

I settled into the seat pale nervous guy pointed me to. It was a larger table reserved no doubt for the hostess and her special guests. It was on a raised platform in the center of the room. Luke sat beside me on the right. The chair to my left was still empty.

I scanned the crowd. "Anything?"

Luke, who had eyes like a hawk, swept a glance over the crowd. "That might be him over by the door. Pudgy, looks like a human version of a bulldog?"

I craned my neck to see where he was looking. "That's our guy."

"Okay, so should we go together or—?"

Before Luke could finish his statement another gong rang out. Our artist had appeared beside me, one nonexistent eyebrow arched. "I see you brought a chaperone."

"This is my ex-husband, Luke. Luke, our hostess, Minerva Upton."

Luke got to his feet but she waved him down. "Sit, sit. There's no need to stand on ceremony. Any friend of Jackie's is welcome at my table."

"That's very kind," Luke gave me a speaking glance.

Minerva lowered herself into the seat beside me. Almost as if it was a cue, the waitstaff began wheeling in long carts draped with snowy linens and dishes contained withing silver cloches.

Logan appeared, having stopped his cart at the table catty-corner to ours.

When the trays were laid out and the murmurs had subsided, Minerva raised her voice. "Now, everyone. Feel free to dig in." She tossed me a lascivious wink and gestured for me to lift the cloche.

I did, feeling like a bit of a spectacle. Beneath the lid sat a small, oblong bowl in a pink color filled with some sort of golden broth. It looked like a child's rendering of a flower done in ceramics. I looked over to the artist, wondering if I was missing something.

She removed her own cloche, that hint of amusement still on her face. "Please, eat your fill."

Not wanting to seem rude, I picked up the silver spoon nestled on a perfectly pressed gold napkin.

"Not that way," she shook her head. Then, wrapping her long fingers around the bowl, she picked it up and brought it to her lips.

"Oh, my bad." I copied the movements. The broth was warm, but not hot. Someone gasped.

"It's good," I said and made to set the bowl down.

"Don't stop," the pushy woman said.

Beside me, Luke made a strangled sound. I shot him a quelling look and then raised the bowl again.

Odd cries and murmurings filled the room. I had no idea what the hell was going on, but it was nothing after the geyser of shit. We had a mission to accomplish. If I could just make it through the soup course, maybe Luke could slip away and…

"Jackie, look at the bowl." Logan had snuck up behind me.

"What?" I scowled up at him. "What are you talking about?"

"Just look at the damn bowl."

I looked and then did a double-take.

The oddly shaped bowl full of golden broth was empty and had revealed the highly detailed design within. What I had thought was some sort of clunky flower petals was in fact a perfect rendering of an open labia. All the details carved inside were anatomically accurate. An image straight out of a filthy porno.

"Well, what do you think?" The pervy artist leaned in. "Do you like my pussy?"

And how the hell do you answer that question and not sound either flirty or repulsed?

When in doubt I go with honesty. "I have never seen anything quite like it."

She threw her head back and laughed. "That, my little party crasher, was the perfect answer."

I blinked at her. "You knew?"

"I spotted you right away and had my assistant look you up. So Jackie, now that you've had a sip of my nectar, tell me what you are doing here. And please, Jackie darling, don't disappoint me and make it boring."

## 18

The guys were still laughing about it an hour later when we had gotten back to the apartment.

"Pussy bowls. Jesus H Christ on a pogo stick." Luke wiped the tears from his eyes.

"Maybe we should just be grateful she didn't decide to serve clam chowder," Logan said.

"Which would have been worse, the red or the white?" Luke wheezed.

"Oh shut up, both of you. At least we got what we were after."

After fessing up about why we had crashed, my new friend Minerva had taken it in stride. She'd approached our reluctant landlord on our behalf and returned five minutes later, check in hand.

"She was well within her rights to boot us out on our party-crashing asses. Instead, she was a good sport about the whole thing."

Logan shook his head. "Jackie Parker makes friends wherever she goes." He leaned his head back against the couch.

Luke's phone rang.

"Ugh, if that's about the Sunnyvale complex, I'm not dealing with it tonight." I had a blister forming where Celeste's gam-enhancing shoes had rubbed my heel raw.

"It's Marcy. I'll catch you guys later." Luke headed out the door.

I smiled and propped my head on my fist. "He really likes her."

"I think so." Logan reached down and pulled my bare foot up onto his lap.

"What—?" I asked.

"I'm going to rub your feet. You were wincing every time you took a step by the end of the night."

His thumbs pressed into the fleshy part beneath my big toe and I groaned in ecstasy. "Oh, don't stop."

He chuckled. "You sound like your new pal, Minerva."

I cracked one eyelid. "How is it you can be so observant about something like that my feet hurt?"

Logan didn't answer right away, though he kept the massage going and as long as he continued with the orgasmic foot rub, I wasn't going to push.

"I pay more attention to you than anyone else," he said after a while. "I'm not sure when it started or if it was a conscious choice. There was a time when I resented you because of it. I didn't like it, that feeling like I was missing stuff because I was so fixated on you. That's why I kept leaving. It was easier not to be in Miami, not to see you because I could forget what an impact you had on me. It's like the rest of the world blurs and you're the only thing in focus."

Though it pained me, I pulled my foot out of his grip. "And do you still resent me?"

He shook his head. "No. You're just clearer to me, Jackie. Anytime you're hurt or in danger, I can't focus on anything else."

A sudden realization. "That's the real reason you don't want me to be part of Damaged Goods, isn't it? Not that you thought I was a liability, or even your feelings for me but because working with me made you less effective."

He blew out a sigh. "Yeah. That and it was weird, trying to hide my feelings for you and you being with Luke."

I slid across the musty sofa, slinky dress splitting until I could straddle him. "I'm not with Luke anymore. I'm with you."

"You were almost with that artist."

I shook my head. "She was just having fun. Unlike you, I'm not homophobic."

"When was I ever…?"

"Vasquez."

"That was because you were suggesting I whore myself out!"

I lowered my lips and kissed along the side of his jaw, then whispered in his ear, "Now why would I ever do a thing like that?"

His hands clamped on my hips. "Because you are an evil teasing temptress and you like to make me dance like your pet monkey."

I pulled back so I could stare into his eyes. "Do you really believe that?"

"At times."

A slow smile spread across my face. "Well, that's better than the truth."

"Which is…?"

I made a scoffing noise. "Yeah, right. Like I'm going to tell you."

Logan's strong fingers moved up over my hips in a slow caress. "I could make you tell me."

"You could try."

I didn't see it coming. One minute he was poised to caress and the next a shriek escaped as he tickled me senseless.

"Stop," I panted as I collapsed onto my back. "I can't breathe."

He didn't slow his assault and I squirmed until I could free myself and make a dash for the bedroom door.

Logan caught me before I could lock myself inside and scooped me back against his chest and breathed in my ear. "Do you submit?"

I tried to use a knee or an elbow but my heart wasn't in it. I wanted this. Wanted him.

The way I always did. But I was still me, whether I was with Logan or not. "Never."

I could feel his smile against the back of my neck. "That's what I was hoping you would say."

---

I AWOKE the next morning naked with a big grin on my face. I pulled on a pair of khaki-colored shorts and a blue button-down shirt and then headed into the other room. Luke was snoring on the couch and I bypassed him, retrieved my purse, wallet, and keys and made my way outside and then down the stairs to the Big Black Truck.

My aim was a quick doughnut and coffee run, but more than anything, I needed to breathe some humid Miami air that had nothing to do with work or the guys for a few minutes to catch my breath.

I'd just pulled in to the drive-thru and was studying the menu, trying to decide if three doughnuts would leave me unable to button my jeans when I saw two women wearing black leather jackets with broken hearts stenciled onto the backs heading for two motorcycles.

One had a big red rooster tail. The other a pronounced snaggletooth.

A jolt went through me as I recognized Snaggle Toothy Ruthie and Rooster Tail, the bitches who'd shoved me into the cesspool.

The guy in front of me appeared to be paying in pennies and was taking forever. The bikes rumbled to life. Helmet in place Rooster Tail backed out of her space and then headed for the exit.

My gaze went to the doughnuts on the sign, then back to where Snaggle Toothie Ruthie was backing out. She waited behind the first for the traffic to let up.

"Screw it," I turned the wheel sharply and pounded on the gas so that the truck hopped the concrete divider. If I had been driving Bessie Mae, I would have been stuck but the Big Black Truck took it like a champ. A pissed off puke green VW bug driver leaned on the horn and an old lady in a rust-bucket Pontiac gave me the finger. People sure were cranky when waiting for morning doughnuts.

I rolled over the barrier like I was in a monster truck rally and hit the exit just as the motorcycle pulled out into the steady flow of morning traffic. The highway was divided into two lanes and I followed several car lengths back in the opposite lane so the motorcycle babes wouldn't notice me.

"This is stupid," I said out loud. "What a jackass."

Though I was talking to myself, my virtual assistant mistook my intent.

"Dialing Logan." The impersonal female voice announced.

"No!" Shit, I really needed to reprogram that thing.

"Jackie?" The Dark Prince's voice was thick with sleep. "Where are you?"

This might be one of those moments. The kind where the fate of our entire relationship hinges on whether I chose to tell Logan what was up or lie out of my ass.

My gut said to fib. It wasn't a big deal, I had no intention of calling him after all. But Logan had promised to be honest with me. Could I offer him anything but the ugly truth?

"Early morning doughnut run gone sideways," I said. "I spotted a couple of those ladies from the motorcycle club that trashed our apartment complex and decided to follow them."

"Where are you?" The tone sharpened.

"Overton and heading South."

Logan swore and I heard a clang as he tripped over something. Then, "Damn it, you're in the truck?"

"What other option did I have?" Celeste had Bessie Mae and it's not like I could ride Logan's motorcycle solo.

"Okay, follow them but do not engage them until we get there." Then in the background. "Luke, wake up."

"We? You're bringing Luke? What, like on the back of your motorcycle?" I was so lost in the odd image that created that I almost missed it when my lady riders turned off the main road into a chain-linked parking area that was full of motorcycles. "We're heading into a warehouse district. I think this is their hangout."

"Don't stop. The windows are tinted so they shouldn't recognize you. We'll be there as soon as possible." Logan barked and disconnected.

I drove past the place where the motorcycles turned off and circled the block. Picking a spot across the street, I pulled up and watched the entrance. The two I had followed dismounted and then headed into the squat cinderblock building.

I frowned at the sign up above it. Fashionistas Inc. was written in gold filigree on a black sign that was carved into the shape of a slinky sleeveless dress. What the actual hell was going on here?

Quickly, I googled Fashionistas Inc. and my jaw dropped

when I recognized the two I had followed. Holy frigging crap, they were a clothing brand! All fair trade, all organic. And from the look of their website, a pretty lucrative one, too.

So what the hell were these successful businesswomen doing destroying an apartment complex on their off-hours? They must really have a grudge with the property owner.

I started scrolling through the about us section where individual bios were listed. The owner was a woman named Gretel Volk. I didn't recognize her face though the name sounded familiar.

"Volk, Volk, Volk. Where have I heard that before?"

A white truck with the same broken heart image from the back of the motorcycle jackets pulled in across the street, blocking my view. My knee bounced as I waited for the thing to load or unload and get the hell out of the way. The skin between my shoulder blades was itching like mad. I tried rubbing against the edge of the seat but the itch only grew worse.

The passenger door was flung open and I blinked when I spotted the same blonde beauty I had just googled climbing into my truck.

"Gretel Volk?" I asked unnecessarily.

"I know who you are, Ms. Parker." Her accent was distinctly German. "And I know why you are here."

"You're the one who asked the motorcycle club to trash the apartment complex," I said, feeling both proud of myself and a little bit ridiculous.

"Are you recording me?" One perfectly sculpted eyebrow arched. "You must tell me if you are."

I shook my head. "Nope, no wires or recording devices."

She nodded. "It was not a good idea. I know it wasn't. But he stole that property from my father."

That's where I knew the name from. In my cursory search

of the previous property owners, I had seen the name Volk listed. "What do you mean he stole it?"

Greta was all cool and composed. "My father was a good man but he wasn't a citizen. Your client called immigration on him and had him detained. He needed money to stay in the country and he was left with no choice but to sell the land at a discount and put up that tenement on it."

"So, you're destroying the apartment complex, hoping everyone will leave and run the bastard out of business so you can pick up the land that you think belongs to you?"

Greta nodded. "It was a foolish vendetta. I promised my father on his death bed that I would get his property back. He meant for it to be the start of a new life for us and it was very important to him. I never meant for anyone to get hurt. We do good work here." She gestured toward her building.

"I'm sure you do." From the reviews I'd been reading she had established a loyal base of very happy customers. She was employing a middle-aged motorcycle gang of women and she looked good doing it. She must have been desperate.

"Listen, the attacks on the complex have to stop. Your ladies are terrorizing the tenants and destroying private property."

"Are you going to call the police?" Greta didn't sound fearful, just resigned.

I thought about it for a minute. Two wrongs didn't make a right. But my job was to make sure no further damage was done to the property and I was getting Greta's word, which I had a feeling I could trust.

"You know something, Greta? I think your Dad would want me to give you a break here. I think your being successful would mean more to him than that piece of property ever could."

She licked her lips. "Thank you."

A motorcycle rumbled up with one person on board.

Alas, no sidecar. Luke followed a minute later in a beat-up Prius driven by another guy I didn't recognize. I saw him pass a few bills up to the Uber driver and climb out onto the street.

I rolled down the window and was instantly smacked in the face with the scent of hot road tar. "Day late and a dollar short, guys."

I introduced Greta to the Parker brothers, who looked a little taken aback. Greta for her part smiled and patted my arm. "Thank you, Jackie. I promise, my ladies won't cause any more trouble over there."

"What the hell was that?" Logan asked as Greta in her white business suit sauntered back across the street.

I peered at them over my sunglasses. "Hell hath no fury like a female entrepreneur scorned."

He smirked at me. "I'll keep that in mind. Want to go for a ride with me?"

I nodded and slithered out of the truck. "We can go grab a coffee. I've been up for over an hour and am completely java-less. Not sure how much longer I can make it. Luke, you want anything?"

Luke shook his head. "Between the scare and the smell of that Uber, I think I'll skip it. See you guys in a bit."

Logan handed me the extra helmet and had just secured his own when his cell chimed. He doffed the helmet and answered. "What? Where?"

More listening.

"Jackie and I will be right there," Logan said and hung up.

"What was that?" I flipped up the visor to ask.

Logan's face had drained of color. "My lawyer's dead."

"What?" I was having a hard time picturing such a hearty man gone. "Was it a heart attack? A stroke?"

"Murder." He blew out a breath. "He was murdered."

# 19

I stood on the sidewalk next to Logan as we waited for Vasquez to finish up inside Buck's McMansion. It was a newer build in a gated community. We'd ridden past a clubhouse, a pool and tennis courts on our way here. It looked like a happy place, where people had block parties and community events. Cripes, poor Buck.

"Do you think it has something to do with your case?" I asked Logan.

His jaw was set in stone. "I'm not going to rule it out."

Despite the heat, I shivered.

Vasquez appeared, his expression grim. "What would it take to convince the three of you to go into witness protection?"

"More than you've got in your piggy bank," I said. "We're down a house and if we aren't in Miami, we can't work."

"If you are in Miami you might wind up dead."

I swallowed and looked to Logan. "So this is about his case for sure?"

"When was the last time either of you talked to Buck?" Vasquez asked.

I thought it through. Was it yesterday or the day before? "I'm not sure. Two days ago, I think?"

"We're still waiting on the medical examiner so I don't know about the time of death, but according to his secretary, he went out to lunch yesterday and never came back. She got worried and called his house. The wife is out of town visiting family. His cleaning service arrived this morning and found the body."

I swallowed. Just like that, a man could disappear and wind up dead. I moved to stand a little closer to Logan.

"You need to tell me what he was working on for your case." Vasquez turned to the Dark Prince.

"Trafficking," I said before Logan could protest. I trusted Vasquez and I knew Logan did too. "The family that Corrine married into was involved in human trafficking."

Vasquez stared at me for a minute and then looked to Logan. "Is that true?"

Logan nodded. "Yeah. Buck was looking for Corrine to see if she would be willing to testify to what I helped her escape from."

Vasquez shook his head. "This is a nightmare scenario."

"What do you mean? It has to be Corrine's father-in-law pulling the strings, right? Can't you just have him arrested?"

"He's not in Miami. In fact, he's not even in the country." Vasquez scrubbed a hand over his face. "If he's calling the shots, it's from Ecuador."

"So?" I asked.

"So, that's a little bit out of my jurisdiction. You say he was involved with trafficking, that's a Homeland Security case. And once they get it, there's nothing we can do. Even if I found the person who committed this murder, the higher-ups would cut a deal for the bigger fish."

Vasquez turned his gaze to Logan. "What did you do to piss this guy off?"

"Helped his daughter-in-law escape his clutches," Logan said. "Maybe."

"Corrine has been spotted around Miami," I added. "If someone has her, it's probably under duress."

Logan stared as the medical examiner wheeled the gurney from the front door. "But if Emmanuel Gutiérrez Jr. is dead, why would *el jefe* bother? And why kill my lawyer?"

Vasquez shook his head. "Could be pride. He could be out to punish you for breaking apart his family. If you are unwilling to go into witness protection, I would advise you to find another lawyer you can trust to handle your case. Buck was a criminal defense attorney, I'm not even sure this is related to your situation yet, just betting on a hunch. Call me if you change your mind."

"Come on," Logan gestured toward the motorcycle.

But I was frowning up at the house. "Why here?"

Logan paused. "What do you mean?"

"Vasquez said the secretary said Buck was heading out for lunch. Whoever killed Buck lured him to his home. Why?"

Logan moved back to my side. "Does it matter?"

"Hang on a second." I jogged after Vasquez.

A uniformed officer blocked my path before I could enter the house. "You can't go in there, ma'am."

Ugh with the ma'am thing. "I need to speak with the Sargent."

"You'll have to wait outside." He got on his radio and called in. A moment later, Vasquez appeared.

"Where was Emmanuel Gutiérrez's body found?"

Vasquez frowned.

"I'm betting it was a private residence, right?"

"A rental where he was staying." The detective confirmed.

"So, no cameras like you would find downtown around Buck's office."

"Oh, there were cameras everywhere. But the footage

from Gutiérrez's time of death has vanished." Vasquez gave me a speaking look.

Because no one outside of *el jefe's* circle could know the identity of the killer. They were planning to take care of him themselves.

I returned to Logan my cell already pressed to my ear. "Luke? Meet us back at Gertie's ASAP."

"What's going on?" Logan asked.

"I think I know where Corrine might be."

Logan frowned. "How?"

"Let's meet up with Luke first I don't want to go over it more than once."

Logan obviously didn't like it, but he acquiesced. I climbed on the motorcycle behind him and we headed for our rendezvous with Luke.

About a mile in a Black Lexus pulled up behind us at a stoplight. Logan glanced over his shoulder and I followed suit. Two men wearing all black suits emerged from the vehicle. They moved forward with purpose.

Logan gunned the motorcycle and we sped through the intersection, narrowly missing a bakery truck.

A moment later there was a cacophony of horns as the Lexus surged after us. My hopes that Logan was just being paranoid, that those guys weren't really after us, faded.

I held on to the Dark Prince for dear life as we whipped around a corner. I'd never felt so vulnerable, the reality that there was nothing between my back and the Lexus full of thugs but whatever distance Logan managed to achieve had me short of breath.

Up ahead traffic was slowing to a standard midmorning standstill as we got closer to downtown. Logan cut through a side street and came out the wrong way on a one way, narrowly missing an oncoming car. He hopped the bike up on the sidewalk that was mostly free of pedestrians, cut across another intersection and then doubled back into a parking garage.

He rode up two levels and then backed the motorcycle behind a white conversion van.

I was off the bike in an instant, fighting with my helmet. Logan reached for it and help me free myself.

"Why the hell did you come downtown?" I snarled.

Two levels below us, tires screeched.

Logan flipped his visor up. "Take the elevator down to the ground floor and call Luke to come pick you up. Stay visible."

"What?" I asked.

"I love you." Down went the visor and then he was pulling out into the garage again, this time, heading for the exit.

My lips parted as the Lexus appeared around the corner. I dove and rolled beneath the van just as Logan zipped past them.

My heart pounded as I watched the Lexus back up and then cut the wheel hard so that the front tires maneuvered. They scraped some paint off the front bumper but they were once again in pursuit of my Dark Prince.

My heart was hammering so hard in my chest that I thought it would break free of my ribcage and make a run for it. What the hell had just happened?

Logan had risked coming downtown, not in hopes of losing the tail but because he wanted to drop me off safely. So he could lead our pursuers away from me. Damn his noble streak.

My hands shook and I felt as though I had just finished running a marathon. I took another full minute under the van to convince myself that no, I couldn't stay there all day, that I needed to call Vasquez, call Luke, call someone to get Logan. The guys in the Lexus had lost sight of us, yet they had still followed us into this parking garage. That meant they were tracking Logan somehow. He needed my help and I couldn't do diddly freaking squat on my belly beneath the van.

I took a deep breath and rolled out and then got to my feet and headed toward the elevator. My mind was churning over and over what had just happened. Once inside the elevator, I fished my phone out of my jeans pocket. Logan had told me to call Luke, but at the moment I was more worried about him than myself.

"Jackie, this isn't a good—"

"We were just followed into downtown," I told Vasquez. "Some men in a black Lexus. Logan dropped me off in a parking garage and led them away but they are still after him."

"Did you get the plate?"

By the time I'd thought to look, the car had been heading back down the ramp. "A partial only, L7V. I think they are tracking him somehow. It could be the bike or his cell."

"What direction was he heading when you last saw him?"

"Out of a parking garage." I bitched, not because it was an unreasonable question but because I didn't have anything better to give him to work with.

The elevator doors dinged open and I made my way out onto the street.

"Do you need a ride?" Vasquez asked.

"No, I'm going to call Luke. Just…find him for me, Enrique."

"I will." The Sargent promised and hung up.

---

THE BIG BLACK TRUCK pulled up at the curb eleven and a half minutes after I called Luke. I scrambled up into the passenger's side and fastened my seat belt. "Any word?" Luke asked me.

I shook my head. "No. We need to go to Fort Lauderdale, to the friend who you dropped Corrine off with, who said she disappeared."

"What?" Luke frowned. "Why?"

"Because," I said. "She can tell us what happened between the time you and Logan dropped Corrine off and Corrine's disappearance," And subsequent reappearance in and around Miami.

"You really want to leave while you don't know what's happening with Logan."

I turned my head slowly to face him. "Want? No. I'm scared to death. But short of combing the streets looking for his motorcycle or the Lexus, which Vasquez and company are much more capable of doing, there's nothing I can do here to help him. But I can locate her, for his sake."

Luke huffed out a breath. "All right. I'm pretty sure the map is still saved in my phone's GPS."

It took us an hour and fifteen minutes to reach the small Mediterranean style house a few blocks from the beach. Luke took the time to go over what he knew about Corrine's old college friend while I tried repeatedly not to hawk my phone for new messages.

"Her name is Becky Evans. She's thirty-four and works in personal finance. Not married, one kid who she sees every other weekend."

I raised my eyebrow at this last part. "How come?"

"Part of the custody arrangement with the ex, at least according to Logan. She got the house, and he got their daughter."

Priorities sounded a little shady to me. It was a nice-looking house though and maybe the daughter was a holy terror. Not my place to judge.

I hopped out of the truck and made my way up the brick pavers to the front door. It was unpainted but stained a beautiful red-brown and enhanced with wrought iron scrollwork. Luke knocked once and the door was pulled inwards.

Becky Evans had the same long blonde hair as Corrine and the same delicate features. She wore a sheer beach cover-up over a pink string bikini and bejeweled sandals. I could easily envision her and Corrine as sorority sisters wearing matching pink t-shirts washing cars for charities and what-not. Her brown eyes went from Luke, to me and she frowned. "I thought you said no one could know that she came here."

"Becky, this is my ex-wife, Jackie Parker," Luke said.

I patted him on the arm but didn't otherwise interrupt.

Becky held the door back, admitting us to her house. "Corrine hasn't come back. All her stuff is still here."

As was my habit, I took in what I could see of the house from our position by the front door. The living room sat off to the left behind an oversized arched doorway. The décor was light and bright with an L shaped cream-colored couch that faced a gas log fireplace with a television mounted above it. The kitchen was large with dark cabinets and thick slabs of granite. A round glass table stood in front of an open sliding glass door that led to a huge pool. As far as hideouts went, it was definitely a cut above Logan's bungalow.

Hell, who even installed gas logs in south Florida? It was considered cold if you didn't have to put the AC on for a twenty-four-hour cycle.

"Tell me what went on before Corrine left," I said when we were seated around the glass round table out on the patio.

Becky had elected to lie in the sun. She shed the cover-up the way a snake sheds its old skin and closed her eyes against the noon sun. "Not too much. She spent most of her time in her room. It was just like you said, Luke. No trips to the grocery store. The only time she left the house was to jog."

"And did she do that at the same time every day?" I asked.

Becky cast me an irritated glance. "Roughly yeah. She liked to jog at sunrise and sunset."

"Same as she did while living at Logan's," Luke muttered.

And I was willing to bet the same way she had when she was living on a compound in Ecuador. Habits are easily tracked and anyone who was paying attention, the way Logan did to me, would have known to wait for Corrine to leave on one of her ritual jogs.

"You mind if I look through her room?" I asked Becky.

"Third door down the hall on the left." She said.

Luke came with me. "She doesn't seem all that broken up over Corrine's having gone missing, even though her stuff is still here."

"What was their reunion like?" I asked. "Lots of girly squeals or big hugs?"

"None of that. It was more casual, like when you see Marcy."

I thought about that as I pushed my way into the guest room where Corrine had been staying. It wasn't a very large space but it had its own three-piece bathroom. The walls were a soothing spa green, the floors a honey oak color and all the furniture was bright. Other than the black duffel on the foot of the bed, it showed no obvious signs of being occupied.

I pawed through the bag. Corrine had run from her former life with nothing. I knew Logan had bought her a prepaid cell phone as well as clothes from a second-hand store. A few sundresses, denim shorts, and tanks, underwear still in the plastic packaging. A one-piece bathing suit, one pair of cheap flip flops, a Dolphin's ball cap. A toothbrush and small tube of toothpaste in a ziplock bag and travel-sized deodorant, shampoo, and body wash that you would get out of the .99 bin. Becky's whole outfit cost more than the contents of this bag.

I scanned the room again. There were no personal touches, like a book or cell phone charger. It looked like a room in a B&B.

"This is weird. She stayed here for days and there are no dirty clothes." I rolled open a drawer to the wicker dresser, just in case Corrine was an unpacker. Empty. Same for the other three drawers and the two in the nightstand.

Luke emerged from the bathroom. "Not so much as a damp towel."

I moved to the window where I could see Becky lounging by the pool. "Do you think she repacked everything in case Corrine came back?"

"Either that or she lied to us." Luke looked at the bed. "Think about how we've sprawled out all over Gertie's apartment. There ought to be something here."

"Why lie though? And why send us back here?"

Our eyes met as the thought occurred to both of us at the same time.

"To stall us here," Luke breathed.

I was already three steps out the door. "Come on, let's get the hell out of here."

We made it to the living room when the first goon walked through the door. Luke shoved me behind him. "Out the back, go!"

He ran for the other man, surprising him with the attack. I yelled his name as goon two entered through the room.

"Run, Jackie!" Luke was fighting for his life and I knew he wouldn't even try to escape unless he was sure I got away.

I ran for the sliding glass door and skidded to a halt when Becky sat up, a small revolver pointed directly at my chest.

She looked like she knew how to use it too.

"Going somewhere?" She asked. "We haven't even had gazpacho yet."

I t wasn't the black Lexus but a silver Audi that was
parked at the curb in front of Becky's house.

I recognized that car. I'd seen it on the street that
day at Curly Cues. "It was you I saw," I said to Becky. "You
were driving around town, pretending to be Corrine. Why?"

"Because you ruined my plans to frame Logan for
Emmanuel Gutiérrez's murder." She gestured and goon one
snagged me by the arm and shoved me down on the sofa
next to a battered and bloodied Luke.

I stared at her. "You killed him? Why?"

"That was our plan all along, mine and Corrine's. She's
not the innocent you think she is."

"I never thought she was." I didn't mention that the
Parker brothers had.

"She just wanted him gone from her life but I saw the
opportunity it presented. *El jefe* needs someone around the
Miami area to take charge of placement, the job Emmanuel
did. And I convinced Corrine that if we could off her abusive
spouse, we could take over."

"From what I've heard about *el jefe*, I seriously doubt he would be okay with your murdering his son."

"Which is why I needed Logan to take the fall. Corrine agreed it was the best way."

"And so you broke in and tranqed my dog. Why?"

"Insurance. Corrine was my backup scapegoat in case I couldn't pin the whole thing on Logan. I could have just shot the stupid animal, but I wanted you to believe that Corrine was behind it."

Which I had. "You really thought this through," I said to Becky.

"It's my time. Did you know that I met Emmanuel Gutiérrez first? Before Corrine came on the scene, I thought he was going to ask me to marry him. That could have been my mansion, my empire. But no, he had to fall for her fake damsel in distress act." She made a disgusted noise. "Men."

"But why would you want him?" I asked her. "He hit his wife!"

"And he was the sole heir to unbelievable wealth. You know what they say, no pain no gain."

"Imagine that. Someone preferring her helpless act to your sociopathic one," Luke grumbled.

Becky smiled at him and then nodded to goon two, who reared back and sucker-punched Luke in the stomach. He let out a woof of air, his face turning purple.

"Stop," I shouted. "What is it you want from us?"

"Leverage," Becky said. "I already have Corrine. If I can get Logan too and turn them both over to *el jefe*, I'll be set for life. Logan Parker is like mist. Just when I think he's in my grasp, he evaporates. He does have one weakness, though. The two of you."

So, we were to be held hostage, possibly tortured so that Becky could prove her worth to *el jefe*.

"Now, which one of you is more important to Logan? His brother? Or the woman he's been in love with for years?"

"Me," Luke gasped at the same time I snapped, "I am."

Becky looked between the two of us and then grinned. "Brotherly love is a beautiful thing," she grinned. "But he risked his relationship with you for her. So call me a hopeless romantic, but I think Jackie is the one we want."

She nodded toward goon one who grabbed me by the arm and hauled me to my feet. "Take her to the camera. I'll be there in a second."

"Luke," I called out, afraid they were just going to shoot him instead of risking him getting away.

Goon one backhanded me. I tasted blood and would have gone down if not for his vice-like grip on my upper arm.

He dragged me down the hall opposite the guest wing and down the steps to the garage. It was a two-car tandem sort of structure, long but only wide enough for one vehicle. The space nearest the bay door was filled by a silver Corvette. And the back part was draped in white cloth.

"Don't bother screaming," Goon one shoved me down onto a cane chair. "The garage is soundproof."

"Do this sort of thing a lot, do you?" I asked him.

He didn't answer. Instead, he used cable ties to bind first my wrists and then an ankle to each chair.

When he moved away, I saw Becky had arrived, still in her cover-up, still holding that revolver. In her other hand she held a phone.

"Be a dear and let's get this on the first take. You say exactly what I tell you to say. No secret messages, no names or hidden warnings."

I stared into her flat eyes and nodded once.

"Logan, I am being held against my will. At midnight tonight, I will be shipped to *el jefe* unless you take my place."

I repeated the message verbatim, though I bit back my fear as best I could.

Becky watched the recording once over. "I would have liked a little more genuine emotion. Maybe a tear."

I glared at her.

"Tell me, Jackie. You don't mind if I call you Jackie, do you? Woman to woman, are you sleeping with them both? Corrine didn't know but I bet you were smart enough to realize it's the best way to get two big strong men to do your bidding." She gestured to the mouth-breather.

"Go to hell, bitch," I spat.

Once again, I was backhanded for my efforts.

"Come on, I have what I need."

"What about her?" The goon asked.

"Leave her," Becky's sandals slapped against the wooden stairs as she ascended out of the garage. "You better hope your guy shows, Jackie. I doubt you will like meeting with Emmanuel Gutiérrez senior any more than Corrine will."

With that, I was shut in the dark.

---

I DIDN'T SCREAM, though I kind of wanted to. Nor did I picture Ms. Personal Finance bedding down with the goons because, ick. No, I thought back to all the YouTube videos I'd watched with Logan over the past several months. Being a rolling stone meant that Logan hadn't spent umpteen zillion hours watching cat videos, fainting goats or anything else, so since he was bedridden and otherwise at my mercy, I felt it was my job to show him what he'd been missing. We'd whiled away his early days flipping between funny videos, ranty videos and special interest videos. Logan's favorites though had been the DIY and informational ones. I'd learned how to patch holes in drywall, how to replace the carpeting and install doorstops.

One morning I'd come in carrying his breakfast tray—cereal of course since I don't cook—he'd been watching one on escaping being tied up.

"Kinky," I'd remarked.

"Come here," He'd held out an arm to me and swerved the laptop so I could see it, replaying the video from the beginning. "This is good stuff."

The video was three ways to break out of zip tie cuffs.

The first way involved finding something small enough to disengage the locking mechanism. Since I was ankle bound to the chair with nothing within easy access, that ruled out option one.

The second option was to clench your hands into fists while being bound. That way when your captor left you could release the fists and easily slip your hands out of the stranglehold on the cuffs.

Too bad I hadn't thought of that at the time.

It was the third way I had decided to attempt. I brought my bound wrists up to my face and snagged the loose end with my teeth the way the guy in the video had done. I pulled, tightening the cuffs to the point of pain. Then, after saying a prayer that this would actually work, I raised my bound wrists above my head, spread my arms out wide like a flapping chicken's wings and using gravity and momentum, I flung my arms down and pulled them apart in one sharp motion.

The tie snapped.

I stared, stunned for a minute. Son of a gun, it had actually worked.

While rubbing the circulation back into my wrists, I considered the problem of freeing myself from the chair. I couldn't use the same technique for my ankles, but with my hands free I could reach behind the drop cloths and explore. No razor blades or box cutters but I did find a set of Allen wrenches on a small keyring. I tried the smallest but it was too big to fit in the space for the securing strap on the zip ties.

So, I inserted the end of the keyring into the catch and used that to disrupt the lock. All the blood was rushing to my head as I fiddled with the thing but at last, it popped open.

I sat up for a moment, lightheaded but unwilling to stop at two-thirds of the way free. Becky's house was in a neighborhood. If I could get loose, I could open the garage door and run across to a neighbor's house and call Vasquez.

I didn't let myself think about where Luke was or what had been done to him. I couldn't worry about if Logan had been caught, if he had seen that video or what he was planning. One thing at a time, just like the instructor on the video had lectured.

I was so intent on the final lock that I didn't notice when someone rolled up the garage door.

"Impressive," Becky said as she held the revolver against my temple. "But I'm afraid it's too little, too late."

The Corvette was backed out of the garage and the Audi backed in to take its place. The trunk lid was opened.

I swallowed. If I had been Luke or Logan, I could have done a nifty quick snatch and grab maneuver to disarm her and maybe make a break for it. But then I saw Luke's inert form already in the trunk and knew it was no use.

I sagged back against the chair and she gestured for goon two to finish the job of freeing my ankle from the chair leg.

"Is he dead?" I asked.

"Not yet," Becky said. She had changed out of her cover-up and now wore a teal sheath dress that hit just above her knees.

I read between the lines though. She wasn't going to let us

go. Luke, Logan, Corrine and I knew who she was and what she planned. There was no way Becky would let us live to run to the authorities.

"How about we use bungee cords this time?" She suggested to her minion. "And make sure you disable the trunk release mechanism. Wouldn't want Ms. Parker here making a break for it before Logan shows up."

I flinched and she noticed. "Yes, that's right. He's agreed to trade himself for you. What a guy. Now, behave and get into the trunk with your ex-husband."

I swallowed and had no choice but to comply.

---

"LUKE," I whispered into the dark.

I could hear his heavy breaths, though I couldn't see his face. He was handcuffed and judging from the sore spots I'd seen on his wrists before the trunk had been shut, he had been for a while before they'd beaten him unconscious.

I wished he would wake up, so I'd know he wasn't about to slip into a coma and never wake up. I needed him to help me find a way out of this mess before Logan and Corrine ended up on a one-way trip to Ecuador and crazy Becky offed us so she could keep her trafficking ambitions a secret.

The bungee cords allowed even less flexibility than the zip ties. They were looped several times over my ankles, knees and wrists. Sadly, I hadn't watched any videos on how to escape bungee cords.

"Luke," I hissed in what I thought was his ear. "Wake up."

There was a soft groan and he shifted his weight as though trying to escape the pain.

"It's okay," I soothed him the same way I'd done when he was sick and plagued by vivid and restless dreams. "Everything will be okay."

Even if he woke up, he was bound too. Damn it, how could we get out of this situation?

The car hit a pothole and something made a metallic sound from under me. My eyes went wide. The jack. Of course. If I could get free and get to it, I could set it up and use it to lever the trunk open.

As soon as I had the idea, I dismissed it. Luke and I were lying on top of the jack, both of us bound. There was nowhere to go. We had to wait until we got to our destination and hope something shifted a little more in our favor.

The odds weren't too good.

Luke groaned again and I soothed him. "Hey, let me tell you something. Marcy is the greatest girl in the whole wide world. And if she makes you happy, you should go for it. Everyone has crazy family members that come with the mix. I have Celeste, you have Logan. So don't let Gertie's oddness or Marcy's devotion to her big sister get in your way. I mean it, Luke. Because if you want something in this life you need to go after it and grab on with both hands." A tear slid down my cheek. So much time just gone.

Would I ever see Logan again? To tell him I wanted the same things that he wanted? A stable home and him every night?

And maybe to set up a foster family for a kid like Harper Green, who had survived the unthinkable.

I didn't know if I could make it work, but damn it, if we got out of this, I was going to freaking try.

"Are you trying to convince me or yourself, Ace?"

I startled back and hit my head on the inside of the trunk. "You're awake?"

"Yeah. That was some speech. I didn't want to interrupt."

I blushed to the roots of my hair. Luckily, between the still healing burn and the darkness, Luke didn't know that. "Any ideas on how we get out of here?"

"The jack," he suggested.

"I'm tied with bungee cords and we're lying on top of it."

Luke inched his own cuffed hands up. "If you can roll over, I can try and unfasten them.

I inched and shifted and banged my head a few more times but finally, I did manage to wriggle around so that Luke's cuffed hands had access to my bungeed wrists. But he'd barely started working the ties when the car slowed.

We both froze.

"How long have we been on the road?"

"A little over an hour, I think. It was somewhat hard to tell."

"We're back in Miami. My guess is somewhere in the port."

"Why the port?"

"Because Becky plans to ship us and Corrine to Ecuador if Logan doesn't show up. And we won't be going via conventional means."

Car doors slammed. Voices, muffled by the trunk and then it popped open, I surged upright though I wasn't at all surprised to find the barrel of a gun in my face.

"Get her out of there," Becky ordered goon one. Or maybe it was goon two. I'd lost track of which was which. All the big hairy thugs looked the same.

I was hefted up by my armpits and dumped on the ground. My left hip sang as I landed on it.

"Easy," Luke barked and tried to wriggle out of the very back of the trunk. Becky slammed the lid in his face.

"What are you doing?" Bound as I was I couldn't do more than squirm on the ground.

"My mama told me never to keep all my eggs in one basket. Untie her feet so she can walk."

I swallowed and glanced around at our new surroundings. A parking area, not too far from the lot where we'd done the inventory. Luke's guess had been spot on, we were at the Port of Miami.

Was Logan here too?

"I'll handle her," Becky said when my feet were untied. "You two stand guard and wait for Parker to show up. He'll be on his motorcycle."

"What if he called the cops?" I asked as she led me towards a giant orange shipping container. "We have friends in the police force."

"He wouldn't do that, not with your life on the line." Becky moved to a long container. She produced a key and inserted it into the heavy-duty master lock that secured the heavy metal doors. It clicked open and she removed it and reached for the door.

The interior was pitch black but as the door swung open, I could see eyes peering out at me.

"Miss me, Corrine?" Becky asked with a smile.

Corrine was tied and gagged with duct tape. I wondered if Becky had watched YouTube videos on how to kidnap and contain people, as she seemed very versatile in the tying up thing. Or maybe some things were just instinctive to power-mad women.

"Oh, don't be like that, I brought you some company." Becky gestured for me to get into the container. "It gets easier from here on out, Jackie. Either this container will be plucked up and loaded on the ship bound for Ecuador, or Logan shows and the two of you will swap places and you can rejoin your ex-husband."

She probably meant at the bottom of Biscayne Bay.

"Corrine, I am afraid is going to be setting sail no matter what. What do you think your father-in-law will do when he receives you as my little partnership gift?"

Corrine's eyes were full of horror.

Becky backed out of the container, a triumphant smile on her face. "Good luck."

She slammed the door, shutting us away from the light. A moment later the snick of a padlock.

We were trapped.

There is something about being enclosed in total darkness that is scarier than facing down a person with a gun. The darkness of the trunk had been nothing compared to the container. When it's so dark you can't even see light through the cracks or tell if your eyes are open or closed. It's a primal thing, a level of instinctive fear that you can't reason with or think your way out of.

My eyes tried to adjust but they needed light to work. I slumped against the container wall, jelly-legged. Though I knew there was plenty of air in the container, I was struggling to catch my breath. Behind her gag, Corrine was trying to say something but there was a ringing in my ears as my blood pressure shot up and up and up.

I slumped to the ground and over onto my side. Oddly it was the soreness for the hip I'd been dropped on that kept me from passing out.

"Ow," I said and felt better for it.

Okay, so, my situation had changed and not for the better. Even if I could get free of the bungee cord, there was nothing I could do to escape. I'd seen Becky unlock the container, heard her slide those same latches into place. If we were going to get out of here, someone was going to need to let us out.

It would be one of three people. Becky, Logan or *el jefe*.

No sense dwelling on that now. "Corrine? Where are you?"

From over to the right I heard her make another muffled noise. I stood and rested my shoulder against the metal side of the container. Using the wall as a guide, I managed to make my way to the back corner, then turn to the back wall. I shuffled my feet so that I wouldn't kick her when I finally reached her.

My toe tapped against something soft at the same time my nose detected the scent of unwashed flesh and human waste. It was almost as bad as Tom the hoarder. Only Corrine hadn't done this to herself. Well, not directly anyway.

Since my hands were bound in front of me, I could still use my fingers. I bent over until I could feel the texture of her unwashed hair. Then, like a blind person looking for an identity, I slid my fingers over her face until I found the edge of the duct tape.

It had been wrapped around her face several times, was even stuck in her hair.

I dug down with my nails, trying to get a grip on the edge and she flinched back.

"Sorry," I said even as I traced the line to the edge. Finally, I was able to pinch the corner between my right thumb and forefinger. I yanked, she yelped, the muffled sound echoing through the container.

It was slow going and she winced and cried out when the sticky side ripped at her hair or skin. I didn't stop to apologize though, too intent on the work I was doing.

Finally, I heard her suck in a full breath and I stopped, not wanting to make her bald. If we got out of here, she could cut the tape loose.

"Water," she croaked, her voice dry and raspy.

"I don't have any." I slumped, exhausted to the ground a few feet back from her. "How long have you been here?"

"I don't know." Her voice was thin.

"You helped Becky kill your husband and frame Logan for it?"

"You don't understand."

"I do," I snapped. "Logan told me. He was trying to help you and you set him up to take the fall."

"It was the only way," she pleaded. "The only way *el jefe* wouldn't come after me."

"So instead of just hiding and waiting and trusting Logan to help you, you set him up for either jail or a death sentence." I'd never contemplated murder before, but it was a good damn thing my hands were still tied.

She fell silent for a time while I seethed. Let her stew in her own waste. She deserved it

Except, she was the only chance I had to get out of this mess. If we were both free, options opened up. I sighed. "Okay, let's start working on freeing your arms."

She held them out in front of her and I got down to work.

Even though there was more tape, the job on her wrists was easier because there wasn't long hair to keep getting snagged. She gasped when I made the final circle, taking off all the small hairs and possibly a layer of skin.

"Untie me," I ordered, shoving my wrists in her face.

She did, her hands shaking as she worked the bungee cord hook free. I winced as circulation returned to my wrists in a pins and needles style tingling. I shook them out repeatedly while Corrine set to work on her ankles, picking at the tape much more carefully than I had.

Untied and now armed with a bungee cord, I got up and

felt my way back along the container until I reached what I thought was the part where the large bifold doors met. Then I sank down and started to brood.

Sometime later, I'm not sure how much time, Corrine made her way up to the front to sit beside me.

"I didn't intend for Logan to be blamed," she said.

I glared at her, at least in her general direction.

"Not long term anyway. I was going to send in a recording once I got away. Tell the police that I had planned his murder, gave his gun to Becky and that she was the one who killed him. By then we were supposed to be long gone."

"Until Becky turned on you."

"She was my only friend," there was a wiggle in Corinne's voice. "The only person I could trust. Or thought I could trust. She came up with this whole plan, get rid of Emmanuel. I didn't want to do it but she convinced me he would never stop looking for me. He had so much money, knew so many people. And she said that when he got me back what he did to me in retaliation would make what happened before look like a picnic. It was the only way she said. And I told her that even if we killed him, *el jefe* would retaliate. She said that was right, unless we blamed someone else."

So, Becky had played up Corinne's fears to convince her to kill her husband and pin it on Logan. Still...

"What about Logan and Luke? They were trying to help you."

I couldn't see her at all but it sounded like she was shaking her head. "I don't trust my judgment when it comes to men anymore."

"I guess I can understand that. There are good men in this world. Luke and Logan and from what Logan told me your brother Chris was one." I took a deep breath—through my mouth because I wasn't a masochist—and pushed on.

"Look, I'm sorry if I didn't offer to be your friend or to help you out. Maybe if I had gained your trust, you wouldn't have felt so desperate and we could have avoided ending up here."

I leaned my head back against the door. "God, can you believe my mother considered living in one of these things?"

"Why?"

"She's got this odd fixation with tiny homes. I can't pretend to understand it."

Corrine was silent for a time. Then, "Well, you can tell her it's not all it's cracked up to be."

"Right? Might as well just buy a coffin to live in."

The words fell flat.

"Who are those guys that are doing Becky's bidding anyway?" I asked after a time.

"Investors in her personal finance business, I think."

"She pretty much told me that she was screwing them to get her way."

"That's always been Becky's way. She was the sorority's town bike—everyone got a ride."

I snorted.

Corrine let out a breath. "I know I fucked up. That I never should have trusted her or told her so much about you and Luke and Logan. That I shouldn't have agreed to her plan. I know it was wrong, but I just couldn't bear the thought of going back to Emmanuel. He thought of me like a possession, something he could keep locked away."

"Then why did you marry him?"

She blew out a breath. "I didn't see that side of him at first. My mom had just died and Chris was gone all the time. I had no one. And then I met him. He was charming, considerate, he paid for everything. I had no idea what he did for a living. I know, I should have asked more questions. But he made me feel wanted, special. And when you're with someone who has a will stronger than your own it seems easier to go along with it."

"When did you find out about the human trafficking?"

"A few months after we were married. Emmanuel was gone all the time. He wouldn't let me talk to anyone, other than his father. There were no other women on the compound, no one for me to talk to. Only guards. I was bored and lonely and he had become distant. I wanted to know why. Normally, he kept his office door locked but he'd been in a hurry when he left that day. So, I went in and started snooping through the files on his laptop."

"No password?"

"He was too arrogant to ever imagine I would dare go through his computer."

"I would have done the same thing," I admitted. "In case Luke or Logan never mentioned it, I have a reputation for being nosy."

I heard the smile in her voice. "Yeah. So I went through the files. At first, I thought he was traveling all the time because he was cheating. Maybe I'd find a few emails, maybe some naked pictures. I was ready to come back home and decided that all I needed was a little ammo to convince him to give me a divorce. I didn't want his money. I just wanted to be free.

"When I opened the first file, I didn't know what I was looking at. There was a picture of a woman, a pretty young woman, and a number written next to her name. It was a sum, in US dollars next to the word purchased. I went on to the next and it was the same, except this time it was a boy. The next was a middle-aged man. Beneath each photo was an address as well as a list of other names. It took a while but I figured that the address was the place they had been sent and the names were those of their loved ones. The dollar amount was what he had received for each of them."

"That's terrible," I breathed. "What did you do?"

"I copied it all to a flash drive." She said.

I jolted. "Do you still have it?"

"It's at Logan's."

A thought occurred. "Did you tell Becky about the flash drive?"

"Yes, though I never said where."

Which was why she had tossed our place. It had never been about Logan's passport, but Emmanuel Gutiérrez's files on human trafficking.

"Jackie, do you think Logan will come?" Corrine asked.

I closed my eyes, though it made no difference in the dark. "He will. I just hope he has a plan."

---

*Logan*

LOGAN LOWERED the binoculars and passed them back to Enrique Vasquez who sat next to him in the Sergeant's SUV. "Those aren't the guys who chased us earlier."

"You're sure?"

He was, because he'd gotten a good look at their faces. "I think those guys worked for *el jefe*. Someone else is pulling the strings here."

He'd memorized the video that had been sent from Corrine's burner phone, the one where Jackie was tethered to a chair with zip ties and saying that he needed to trade himself for her. Where had she gone after he'd left her in the parking garage? He'd driven directly to the police station after dropping her off. He'd been so freaked out about her exposure on the back of his motorcycle that he hadn't been thinking clearly. What if the thugs had shot at him and hit her? And where the hell was his brother in all this?

According to what she'd told Vasquez, Luke was going to pick her up. There had been no signal from either her cell-phone, or Luke's or the GPS he had on the truck. There was no way Luke would have abandoned her.

He refused to think that his brother was dead.

"You're telling me that we're dealing with countless villains as well as a human trafficking ring," Vasquez swore. "I'm going to need to call this into Homeland Security."

"Just wait."

Vasquez glared at him. "What for?"

Logan didn't know. His gut was screaming that they couldn't swarm the place with law enforcement, not without risking Jackie and Corrine.

"Let me go in, see if I can spot where they are stashed."

Vasquez clearly didn't like that option. "You're a civilian."

"I have training." He glanced at the dashboard clock. "Look, it's twenty-five to twelve. Give me fifteen minutes to get the lay of the land. They don't have enough security to cover the entire place. So wait until 11:50 and then call HS."

The Sargent blew out a breath. "11:50 on the nose and then we do things my way."

Vasquez looked away as Logan secured his sidearm in his ankle holster.

"I'm not seeing this."

"Seeing what?" Logan grinned at him and then exited the car.

Even with the bright lights from the port, there were plenty of shadows to slip in and out of. Logan picked a spot and scaled the chain-link fence. He landed in a crouch that made his still healing thigh muscle scream in protest. So stupid. He wasn't twenty-five and hale anymore. He needed to keep the abuse to his body to a minimum or Jackie would read him the riot act.

He inhaled and exhaled through the pain and then moved

toward where he had spotted the goon by the silver Audi. The guy definitely looked like he was guarding something. Or perhaps someone.

The Audi had been parked under a streetlight. The man looked to be about two-fifty and all muscle. He definitely didn't have any experience with guard duty though. He stood by the trunk, his gaze staring down at his cellphone.

A thump sounded from the trunk. Logan's lips parted. Was Jackie in there?

Another thump and a bang. The guard turned to face the noise just as the trunk lid popped open and Luke sprang out like a jack-in the box.

The guard reached for his shoulder holster even as Luke, his two hands cuffed sailed through the air.

Logan didn't hesitate he ran for them. Luke had landed on top of the man and was using his handcuffs to choke the life out of him. The man tossed Luke off and then reached again for his weapon.

"Hold it," Logan cocked the hammer on his own weapon and pointed it between the man's eyes. "Hands up. Luke, get his piece and make sure he doesn't have any more."

Luke, his face bloody, his wrists red from where the cuffs rubbed him raw, did as Logan instructed. He patted the bruiser down and extracted a small silver handcuff key. Then he reversed the Glock and bashed it into the man's temple.

"Was that necessary?" Logan asked as the guard slumped on the pavement.

"He hit Jackie." Luke's eyes blazed. "Get these frigging things off of me."

"Where is she?" Logan reengaged the safety, uncocked the hammer and tucked the weapon into his waistband before addressing the cuffs.

Luke shook his head. "I don't know. Becky took her somewhere."

"Becky?"

"She's the one pulling the strings," Luke told a tale of how Corrine's sorority sister had killed her husband, set Logan up to take the fall, and then turned on her for the chance to prove herself to *el jefe*.

He listened to it all impassively. Now wasn't the time to react. Instead, he handed the spare weapon back to his brother. "Vasquez is waiting around the corner just outside the fence."

"Logan," Luke warned.

"Listen to me, little brother. One of us needs to make it out of here. You're a witness and I'm not leaving without her."

Logan could see Luke struggling between the notion that he could save Jackie and his inner boy scout's urge to do what was right.

It was a dirty trick, but he leaned hard on Luke's hero complex. "I'm the one they're after. If I need to, I'll trade myself for her. Then you can swoop in and save the day. Maybe she'll even take you back."

"You are so not funny," Luke grumbled.

"Wasn't trying to be." Well, maybe a little.

Luke clapped him on the shoulder. "Just don't be stupid. If you die mom will never forgive me."

"Noted." He said and then watched him disappear into the shadows.

Logan checked his watch. Quarter 'til midnight. He was running out of time.

"Jackie Parker, where the hell are you?" He asked and then headed deeper into the storage facility.

He'd find her, no matter what it took. Logan was not going to lose Jackie now.

## 2 2

The scrape of the master lock being removed was my first clue that something was happening. I scrambled to my feet. My ass had gone numb from sitting on the cold metal floor.

"What is it?" Corrine asked. "What's going on."

"Just, get behind me." It was a stupid thing to say. She was the valuable hostage. But she was weakened from days of captivity and didn't have a weapon. If one considered a bungee cord a weapon. I wrapped it around one fist for easy access.

The door scraped and then was opened. I blinked like a bat at the harshness from the street lamps. Corrine threw an arm up over her face to block it out. And then Becky emerged holding her little revolver. "You're in luck, Jackie. My guy just spotted Logan."

I squinted like a mole to see if I could spot him. "Where is he?"

"I'll take you to him."

She gestured with the barrel of her tiny firearm for me to exit the cargo container.

I moved and Corrine took a step after me.

"Nope, not you." Becky trained the weapon on her former sorority sister.

"Please," Corrine begged. "Please, don't send me back there."

"Send? Oh, but you aren't being sent anywhere. *El jefe* is coming here personally for this delivery."

Corrine made a whimpering sound.

"Out, Jackie." Becky gestured again with the gun.

Corrine gripped my arm. "Please, don't leave me alone."

I pulled back and tried to pry her loose. "I'm sorry." It was the truth—I was sorry that I couldn't help her. She was terrified but I was as helpless as she was.

She clung, sobbing like a child and I half expected her to crumple to the ground.

She didn't. Instead, when we had closed the distance, she lunged for Becky, hair matted, eyes wild.

The sound of a gunshot echoed off the interior of the cargo container. Becky stumbled back and I didn't hesitate, my bungee cord already out. I moved up behind her and wrapped it around her neck. Her hands flew up, fingers digging into the cord. The gun clattered to the ground. I pulled and pulled and pulled.

"Jackie." Someone called my name but I was beyond hearing. The surge of adrenaline spiked through my bloodstream and tears streamed down my face.

Becky slumped but I kept right on pulling because what if she was faking it?

"Hey, hot stuff. You got her." A hand landed on my shoulder.

"Logan?" I turned and my grip on the cord slackened when I saw his face, broken nose and all.

Becky crumpled to the ground and I threw myself into his arms.

"It's okay," He murmured into my hair. "They can't hurt you anymore. Let me go and check on Corrine."

I wrapped my arms around myself as he moved over to where Corrine lay sprawled on the floor of the cargo container.

"Is she dead?" I asked.

In answer, Logan placed her wrist down and then reached up to shut her eyes. "She caught it at point-blank range in the chest. She was dead before she hit the ground."

My throat clogged and my lips parted.

Logan moved over to check on Becky. "She's alive."

"Here, tie her up with this." I nudged the bungee cord over to him. "Seems fitting.

"Good, I used the cuffs Luke gave me on the other bastard." He nodded out into the lot.

"Luke's okay?"

"He's on his way along with your pal Vasquez and by now several agents from Homeland Security."

As if on cue lights flashed out in the water and sirens blared as our section of the port filled with police, federal agents and all the other good guys.

Logan left Becky where she was and ushered me out of the cargo container and past the handcuffed form of goon one to wait for the police. Tremors shook my whole body.

"Jackie?"

"She rushed her," I said, not really seeing anything. "Becky told Corrine that *el jefe* was on his way to get her and she went at her, even though Becky had the gun pointed right at her."

Logan swallowed hard and lowered his head. "She took herself out of the picture before he could get to her. Before anyone could get to her."

"Not your fault," I told him.

He pulled me tight against him. "Yours either."

I thought about how I had set her free of the duct tape. How I had attacked her for her choices.

"I'm not so sure about that."

Logan held me close to him and rocked me back and forth.

At least it was over.

---

"WHAT DO you mean it's not over?" I stared across the interrogation table at the weary face of Enrique Vasquez. "You can't just let him loose?"

"Believe me, Jackie, it's not my call. With Corrine dead, there's no one to testify that *el jefe* is involved with human trafficking. Homeland Security is monitoring him, but without proof, they can't hold him on American soil."

"What about the flash drive?" I asked. I'd told Luke, Logan, and Vasquez everything that Corrine had told me, including about how she had made copies of the files from her husband's computer.

"We looked everywhere," Vasquez said. "So did HS. No sign of it."

"If you let us out of here, maybe we could help."

Vasquez shook his head. "The agent in charge wanted to speak with you."

"Well, tell him to hurry the hell up." I bitched. "It's been a long night and you're telling me that the asshat who firebombed my house is going to go home scot-free. I don't think I have much patience left for federal agents."

Vasquez eyed me warily. "Maybe you should go home. I'll have the agent follow up with you there."

I waited until the Sargent left the room before turning to Logan. "Was that as bad as I think it was?"

"Probably worse." Logan dropped a kiss on my forehead. "Come on, let's go home."

His motorcycle was parked in the police parking lot, as was the Big Black Truck, which still contained my helmet as well as my ex-husband.

Logan stared at his brother. "You made it all the way to Fort Lauderdale and back already? How come they let you out so fast?"

Luke shrugged. "Either because I was cooperating or because I didn't know anything about the trafficking, *el jefe* or any of it. One of those for sure. I heard you pitched a fit."

I opened my mouth to ask how when the aforementioned fit had only happened two minutes ago when Logan talked over the top of me.

"They wanted to question us separately. I wasn't about to let her out of my sight." His tone was dark and menacing.

Luke shook his head. "Sometimes it's hard to remember you are one of the good guys." He handed me the helmet. "See you guys later."

"Where's he going in such a hurry?"

Logan asked as Luke backed out, cut the wheel and headed out of the police lot.

"Probably to make a declaration of love to Marcy. Or to get drunk in a bar. One of those for sure," I quipped and Logan shook his head.

"Luke won't drink and drive. Do you want to head back to the apartment or see if they'll let us get into my place?"

I thought about it for a beat. "Your place."

After securing the helmet I climbed on the back of the motorcycle and held on.

Logan took it easy and didn't take any detours. For once the traffic cooperated and we made it home in under twenty minutes. I removed the helmet and stared at the fire burned wreck of my bungalow.

Logan propped the kickstand down on his motorcycle and then took my hand. He didn't say anything, just squeezed once and let me stare my fill.

It had mostly turned out okay. Sure my house was burnt, but I had a place to live. Sasquatch and Abu were fine, Becky was getting locked up as were her goons and the guys that had tried to chase me and Logan down. The ones who had firebombed my house and killed Buck on *el jefe's* orders.

Human trafficking, arson, murder, the bastard was going to get away with it all because Corrine had rushed Becky and we couldn't find the flash drive.

I turned away and focused on his house, tugging him up the steps behind me.

A cool rush of air conditioning greeted me and I looked around at all the beautiful craftsman style furniture that I had picked out for this home and felt a little bit better. At least the place hadn't been completely tossed in the hunt for the missing flash drive.

"So this is home now," I said as I looked around the space that was both familiar and a little bit off.

"For as long as you want it to be," Logan moved closer and wrapped his arms around me from behind.

"Are you sure about this?" I turned so that I could face him. "Are you sure we're ready for this?"

"Sure? No." He said, always honest.

I licked my lips. "I could always move into a tiny home with Celeste? Or maybe Garret Green's old job is available." I had options, I reminded myself. I wasn't going to be homeless if this didn't work out.

I would just be heartbroken.

Logan's eyes searched my face. "Is that what you want?"

Slowly, I shook my head. "I don't want to rush this, but I'm ready to be with you, fulltime."

He smiled then and pressed his forehead to mine. "I'm not

sure but I know what I want, Jackie Parker, uncensored and live coming at me 24/7."

I kissed him then and he scooped me up and carried me into the bathroom for a much-needed shower.

Watersports indeed.

---

"You want to adopt Harper Green?" Logan asked me.

I lay on my back and stared up as the ceiling fan swirled above our heads. "I want to try. I know it's nuts and that our lives are nuts. You're still technically out on bail, though Vasquez said he would take care of getting the DA to drop the charges. But even if it's not Harper, I want to help."

"Have you thought about having a baby of your own? That might be easier."

I swallowed. "Yeah, it probably would be."

Logan tucked a hand behind his arm. "But then you wouldn't be helping someone who really needs it."

I rolled over and propped my chin on his chest. "I love that you get me."

"You're the only woman I will ever understand." His gaze grew troubled. "I can't believe Corrine set me up like that."

"She was scared, Logan. Scared and desperate. I'm just sorry I didn't reach out to her when you first brought her here. It might have changed the outcome."

"Hey, none of that now." Logan held me tightly against him. "I set it up so you wouldn't like her. A stupid game because I was fucking insecure. So if you go off and wallow in guilt know that I'll be right there beside you."

I closed my eyes. "I know and I know that in the end, she made her choices, too and neither one of us is responsible for them."

"Look at us all mentally stable and shit," Logan smirked.

"I wouldn't go that far." I touched the side of his face. "Have I mentioned that I'm sorry about that?"

He waggled his eyebrows. "I can think of a few things you can do to make it up to me."

He reached for me, careful not to touch the huge ugly bruise on my hip and my stomach growled. Loudly.

I made a face. "Guess it's been a while since I ate anything."

"What do you want?" He was already out of bed and reaching for a pair of jeans which he pulled on commando. Be still my heart.

"What have you got?" I asked.

"Not sure. Eggs, maybe bread if it's not moldy. French toast?"

"Sounds delightful," I grinned up at him.

"Come on, you can help cook."

"Oh no, no way. Kitchen curse, remember? I have had more than enough fires in my life for one week."

He laughed and headed out to the kitchen.

I pulled on one of Logan's clean t-shirts—black, big shocker—and then made my way down the hall to the guest room where Corrine had been staying.

The bedspread was smooth, the sunny yellow walls bare. Much like the guest room at Becky's, there were no signs that anyone had been staying here. I pulled drawers all the way out and checked to see if there was anything taped beneath. Ran my fingers along the grooves of the bedframe. Then rummaged through the closet, pulling out extra pillows, shaking out blankets and towels, looking for anything odd. Defeated, I flopped down across the bed.

Did I really think that I would magically find the flash drive when both seasoned detectives and homeland security hadn't managed to do so?

I open my eyes and stared at a cable outlet across the wall. There was no t.v. in the room.

"Logan?" I called. "Did you install cable in here?"

He appeared in all his bare-chested glory in the doorway. "No, I have wifi and gave Corrine my Netflix password and a spare laptop, which the police took. Why?"

I pointed to the outlet. "That's why."

He frowned. "It could have been here from Mr. Murphy's time."

"It's too new looking. See how all the other plates are yellowing and cracking with age?" I was already up on my feet. "Get me a screwdriver. Flathead."

"You're sexy when you talk tools." He disappeared and a moment later returned with the screwdriver.

I used it to pry the plate loose. It popped off in my hand, having been stuck to the wall with what smelled like clear nail polish.

Secured to the back with more nail polish was a tiny flash drive.

The doorbell rang.

Logan and I exchanged a look. "That's probably the agent from homeland security. You might want to get some pants on."

"Screw that." I stomped out to the door and threw it open. A white guy in his mid-forties with a professional crew cut stood there. He raised an eyebrow at my uber casual ensemble. "Jackie Parker?"

I folded my arms over my chest. "That's me."

"I'm agent Towers. May I come in?"

"No. I have nothing to say to you. What you can do is take this and go find all the victims of *el jefe's* trafficking ring." I tossed him the flash drive, outlet cover and all.

He blinked in astonishment. "Is that...?"

"I don't know what else it could be, but do your job and leave me out of it, there's nothing more I can tell you."

I shut the door in his face.

Logan stared at me openmouthed. "I can't believe you just did that."

"I'm hangry," I told him. "Is breakfast almost ready?"

"For my sake, it had better be."

"You said you were ready for Jackie Parker, uncensored. Be careful what you wish for, Logan Parker."

The Dark Prince grinned. "I have nothing left to wish for, I've got what I've always wanted."


THERE'S MORE fun to be had with the Misadventures of the Laundry Hag series. Read chapter 1 of, Skeletons in the Closet for free on my website!

## IT'S NOT MY WORDS THAT COUNT.
## IT'S YOURS!

Please consider leaving an honest review for this book. Reviews help readers like you find books they enjoy, or warn them off from ones they won't. Reader reviews help the authors you love sell books and help them put money toward the next title. Even a sentence or two can mean the difference between a series that continues and one that flops. I found one of my favorite series from a two star review. So if you want more, tell the world.

ALSO BY JENNIFER L. HART

Stay-at-home-mom-turned-reluctant-cleaning-lady-turned-
amateur-sleuth. Hijinks ensue in this laugh-out-loud mystery series.

Misadventures of the Laundry Hag: Book 1 Skeletons in the Closet

Also available on audiobook narrated by Suzanne Cerreta

# ABOUT THE AUTHOR

*USA Today* bestselling author Jennifer L. Hart writes about characters that cuss, get naked and often make poor, but hilarious, life choices. Her works to date include the Misadventures of the Laundry Hag series, the Damaged Goods mysteries and the Magical Midlife Misadventures paranormal women's fiction series.